The
Light That Lures

PERCY BREBNER

1st WORLD
LIBRARY
Literary Society

The Light That Lures

Percy Brebner

© 1st World Library – Literary Society, 2004
PO Box 2211
Fairfield, IA 52556
www.1stworldlibrary.org
First Edition

LCCN: 2005901360

Softcover ISBN: 1-4218-1175-8
Hardcover ISBN: 1-4218-1075-1
eBook ISBN: 1-4218-1275-4

Purchase *"The Light That Lures"*
as a traditional bound book at:
www.1stWorldLibrary.org/purchase.asp?ISBN=1-4218-1175-8

1st World Library Literary Society is a nonprofit
organization dedicated to promoting literacy by:

- Creating a free internet library accessible from any
computer worldwide.
- Hosting writing competitions and offering book
publishing scholarships.

The Light That Lures
contributed by Tim, Ed & Rodney
in support of
1st World Library Literary Society

contributed by Tim, Ed & Rodney
in support of
1st World Library Literary Society

PROLOGUE

ACROSS THE WATERS OF THE BAY

Seated on a green hummock, his knees drawn up, his elbows resting on his knees and his head supported in his open hands, a boy sat very still and preoccupied, gazing straight into the world before him, yet conscious of little beyond the visions conjured up by his young mind. His were dim visions begot of the strenuous times in which he lived, and which were the staple subject of conversation of all those with whom he came in contact, yet his shadowy dreams had something of the past in them, and more, far more, of that future which to youth must ever be all important. But this young dreamer was not as dreamers often are, with muscle subservient to brain, the physical less highly developed than the mental powers; on the contrary, he was a lad well knit together, his limbs strong and supple, endurance and health unmistakable, a lad who must excel in every manly exercise and game. Perhaps it was this very superiority over his fellows which, for the time being, at any rate, had made him a dreamer. While other boys, reproducing in their games that which was happening about them, fought mimic battles, inflicted and suffered mimic death, experienced terrible siege in some small copse which to their imagination stood for a beleaguered city, or carried some hillock by desperate and impetuous assault, this boy, their master in running, in swimming, in wrestling, in sitting a horse as he galloped freely, was not content with mimicry, but dreamed of real deeds in a real future.

It was a fair scene of which this boy, for the moment, seemed to be the centre. Before him lay the great expanse of Chesapeake Bay scintillating in the light of the afternoon, a sail here and there catching the sunlight and standing out clearly from a background of distant haze. A wide creek ran sinuously into the land, the deep blue of its channel distinct from the shallow waters and the swamps from which a startled crane rose like an arrow shot across the vault of the sky. To the right, surrounded by its gardens and orchards, stood a house, long, low, large and rambling, the more solid successor to the rough wooden edifice which had been among the first to rise when this state of Virginia had become a colony for cavaliers from England. Flowers trailed over the wide porch and shone in patches of brilliant color about the garden, alternating with the long-cast shadows of cedar, cypress, and yellow pine; fruit turned to opulent red and purple ripeness in the orchards; and the song of birds, like subdued music, came from tree and flower-lined border. In close proximity to the house Indian corn was growing, and a wide area of wheat ripened to harvest, while beyond, like a vast green ocean, stretched the great tobacco plantation, with here and there the dark blot of a drying shed like a rude ark resting upon it. In the far distance, bounding the estate, a line of dark woods seemed to shut out the world and wrap it in impenetrable mystery. Over all this great estate the boy sitting on the hummock was known as the young master, but he was not dreaming of a future which should have wealth in it, pleasure, all that the heart of a man can wish for; but of toil and hardship bravely borne, of fighting days and camp fires, of honor such as heroes attain to.

He had been born in stirring times. For more than five years past war had been in the land, the struggle for freedom against a blind and tyrannical government. It had been one thing to make the Declaration of Independence, it had been quite another matter to carry it into effect. Early success had been followed by disasters. Washington had been defeated on Long Island; his heroic endeavor to save Philadelphia by the battle of Brandywine against an enemy far superior in numbers had failed; yet a month later a large British force had been compelled to surrender at Saratoga. These fighters for freedom seemed to know defeat only as a foundation upon which to build victory. England might send fresh armies and fresh fleets, but there were men on land and sea ready to oppose them, ready to die for the freedom they desired and the independence they had proclaimed; and it was only a few months ago that the war had been virtually ended by the surrender of Lord Cornwallis at Yorktown.

Colonel Barrington had taken an active and honorable part in the conflict, yet in the beginning of the trouble, like many another man of his class, he had been for peace, for arbitration, for arrangement if possible. His fathers had been among the earliest settlers in Virginia, representatives of an English family, whose roots stretched far back into history. They had come to rest on this very spot of earth, had raised their first rough wooden dwelling here, calling it Broadmead, after the name of their home in England. Love for the old country was still alive in Colonel Barrington, and it was only after grave deliberation that he had drawn the sword, convinced that he drew it for the right. Doubtless there were some in this great conflict who were self-seeking, but this was certainly not the case with Henry Barrington. He had much to lose, nothing personal to win which seemed to him of any consequence. Broadmead he loved. He had been born there. In due time he had brought home to it his beautiful young wife, daughter of a French family in Louisiana, and until this upheaval the years had passed happily, almost uneventfully, yet bringing with them increasing prosperity.

The boy, dreaming dreams and stretching out toward an ideal, might well have taken his father for model, but, while reverencing him and knowing him to be a great and good man, his young imagination had been fired by a different type of hero, the man whose restless and adventurous spirit had brought him four years ago to fight as a volunteer in the cause of freedom; who had come again only a year since and had done much to bring about the surrender of Lord Cornwallis; the man who, only the other day, had been publicly thanked by General Washington speaking for the nation he had helped to found; the man who was at this moment his father's guest - the Marquis de Lafayette. There was much of the French spirit in the boy, inherited from his mother, and to every word the Marquis had uttered he had listened eagerly, painting his hero in colors that were too bright and too many, perhaps. An hour ago he had stolen out of the house to this hummock, a favorite spot of his, to dream over all he had heard and of the future.

His eyes were fixed upon a distant white sail, sun touched, which lessened far out across the bay, which presently became a point of light and was then hidden in the haze of the horizon. That was the way of dreams surely, the road which led to the realization of hope. That ship might go on and on through sunlight and storm, through mist and clear weather, and some time, how long a time the boy did not know, it would reach another land, France perchance, surely the best of all lands, since it bred such men as the Marquis de Lafayette.

"Dreaming, Richard?"

The grass had deadened the sound of approaching footsteps and the boy rose hastily. His face flushed as he recognized his visitor.

He was a thin man, still young, with an earnest face which at once arrested attention. It was far more that of a visionary than was the boy's, a difficult countenance to read and understand. If, for a moment, the neatness and precision of his dress suggested a man of idle leisure, a

PERCY BREBNER

courtier and little more, there quickly followed a conviction that such an estimate of his character was a wrong one. Dreamer he might be, in a sense, but he was also a man of action. The spare frame was full of energy, there was determination in the face. This was a man who knew nothing of fear, whom danger would only bring stronger courage; a man who would press forward to his goal undaunted by whatever difficulties stood in the way. He was an idealist rather than a dreamer, one who had set up a standard in his life and, right or wrong, would live his life true to that standard. He was a man to trust, even though he might not inspire love, a leader for a forlorn hope, a personality which brought confidence to all who came in touch with it. His eyes, kindly but penetrating, were fixed upon the lad to whom he was a hero. He was the famous Marquis de Lafayette.

"Yes, sir, I was - I was thinking."

"Great thoughts, I warrant, for so young a mind. Let us sit down. This is a famous seat of yours, a good place to dream in with as fair a slice of the world's beauty to gaze upon as could well be found. Come, tell me your dreams."

The boy sat down beside him, but remained silent.

"Shall I help you?" said the Marquis. "Ah, my lad, I know that it is difficult to tell one's dreams, they are often such sacred things; but your good mother has been telling me something about you. We are of the same blood, she and I, so we talk easily and tell each other secrets, as two members of a large family will. She tells me, Richard, that you have thought a great deal about me."

"Indeed, sir, I have."

"And made something of a hero of me; is that it?"

"Would that anger you, sir?"

"Anger me! Why, my lad, the man who can become a child's hero should be proud of it. There must be something good mixed with his common clay for him to achieve so much. I am glad and proud, as proud as I am of General Washington's thanks the other day; you need not look at me with such disbelief in your eyes, for I only say what is true. So now tell me your dreams."

"They are only half dreams," said the boy slowly, but to-day they seem clearer. They have one end and aim, to be like you, to fight for the oppressed, to fight and to conquer."

"The dreams are worthy, Richard, but set yourself a higher standard. That you think so much of me almost brings a blush to my cheek, lad, for I am a poor hero. Yet, there is this in common between us, I too, have had such dreams - have them still. I am striving to make my dreams come true. So much every man can do. You have, or you will have presently, your duty set straight before you. Duty is like that; it never lies in ambush. Along that path of duty you must march and never turn aside. It is a strange path, for though it is distinct and clear that all may recognize it, yet for each individual it seems to have a different direction. It leads some to mighty deeds which must echo round the world; some it will bring to poverty, obscurity, disgrace perchance, but these are heroes, remember, as the others are, greater heroes I think, since no man knows them or cheers them on. You have not thought of such heroes, Richard?"

"No, sir."

"I thought not. That is why I came to talk to you. I cannot tell what your future is to be, I do not know in what way you are destined to travel, but duty may not call upon you to wear the sword or ride in the forefront of a charge. This country has just had a glorious birth, a rebirth to freedom. Your father has helped to fight for it; you may be called upon to work peaceably for it."

"I hope, sir, my duty will mean the sword and the charge."

"Your countrymen are probably glad to have peace," he answered.

"But this is not the only land where men are cruelly treated and would fight for freedom," the boy returned. "You came here to help us against the English. Some day may I not journey to help others?"

"Perhaps."

"My mother is French, therefore I am partly French. I love my father, but I am more French than English. I should love to fight for France," and the boy looked up eagerly into his companion's face.

"So that is the real secret out at last," said Lafayette, with a light laugh. "You would love to fight for France."

"Yes, sir; and it makes you laugh. I have not told it to any one else; I knew they would laugh."

"But you expected better things of me. Forgive me, lad, I was not laughing at you; yet you must learn not to mind the laughter of others. Whenever a man is in earnest there will always be some to ridicule what they term his folly. He is something of a hero who can stand being laughed at."

"Sir, did you not say to my father only to-day as you sat at dinner in the hall, that France was groaning under oppression, and there was no knowing what would be the end of it?"

"I did, Richard, I did."

"Then, Monsieur de Lafayette, it might be that some day I might cross the sea to help France."

The Marquis laughed softly and patted the boy's head.

"So that is your dream. I hope freedom may be bought without blood, but - "

"But you do not think so, sir."

"Why should you say that?"

"Partly because of the way you say it, partly because I have been told that you are farseeing. I have listened so eagerly to all the stories told about you."

"If such a fight for freedom came in France, it would be far more terrible than the war here," and the Marquis made the statement rather to himself than to the boy.

"Then it may be my duty to come and help you," said Richard.

"If the opportunity should come, see that your adventurous spirit does not make it your duty whether it be so or not. There are some years to pass before these young limbs of yours are fit for fighting, or this brain of yours has to make a decision. You have a good father and mother, they will guide you. Dream your dreams, and I doubt not, my friend Richard Barrington will become a hero to many. Are you coming back to the house with me? Within an hour I am leaving."

"You are going back to France?"

"Yes."

"It is a wonderful land, isn't it?"

"To a true man his own country is always a wonderful land."

"Yes, and I am mostly French," said the boy.

"No, lad. You are an American, a Virginian. Be proud of it."

"I am proud of it, sir; yet a Virginian gentleman might fight for France."

"And France might be glad to claim his sword. Yes, that is true. Well, lad, come in peace or in war, do not fail to make inquiry in Paris for Lafayette. He shall return you something of the courtesy which has been shown to him in this country and in your father's house."

"Thank you, oh, thank you a thousand times. I can talk about it to my mother now. She shall share my dreams."

As he went toward the house he looked back across the waters of the bay. Yet another sail, with the sun upon it, was fading slowly into the distant haze.

CHAPTER I

THE MAN BY THE ROADSIDE

A solemn twilight, heavy and oppressive, was closing a dull, slumberous day. It was late in the year for such weather. Not a breath stirred in the trees by the roadside, not a movement in hedge or ditch; some plague might have swept across the land, leaving it stricken and desolate, even the cottages here and there showed no lights and appeared to be deserted. The road ran straight between ill-conditioned and neglected fields, and for an hour or more no traveler had passed this way, yet it was a high road, and at a few miles distance was Paris. Yonder toward the northeast lay the city, the twilight heavy over it too, but it was not silent. The throb of human passion and anger beat in it with quick, hammering strokes, and men and women, looking into one another's eyes, either laughed while they sang and danced madly, or shrank away, afraid of being seen, fearing to ask questions.

The twilight had grown deeper, and the horizon was narrowing quickly with the coming of night, when the sound of horses' hoofs broke the silence and two riders came rapidly round a bend into the long stretch of straight road, traveling in the direction of Paris. They rode side by side as comrades and as men with a purpose, a definite destination which must be reached at all hazards, yet at a casual glance it would appear that they could have little in common. One was an elderly man with grizzled hair, face deeply lined, sharp eyes which were screwed up and half closed as if he were constantly trying to focus things at a distance. He was tall, chiefly accounted for by his length of leg, and as thin as a healthy man well could be. His horsemanship had no easy grace about it, and a casual observer might have thought that he was unused to the saddle. There would have been a similar opinion about anything this man did; he never seemed to be intended for the work he was doing, yet it was always well done. He was a silent man, too, and his thoughts were seldom expressed in his face.

His companion was a young man, twenty-five or twenty-six, although his face might suggest that he was somewhat older. His was a strong face, cleanly cut, intelligent, purposeful, yet there was also a certain reserve, as though he had secrets in his keeping which no man might know. Like his comrade, there was little that escaped his keen observation, but at times there was a far-off look in his eyes, as though the present had less interest for him than the future. He sat his horse as one born to the saddle; his hands were firm, his whole frame full of physical force, energy, and endurance - a man who would act promptly and with decision, probably a good man to have as a friend, most certainly an awkward one to have as an enemy.

"We delayed too long at our last halt, Seth. I doubt whether we shall see Paris to-night," he said presently, but made no effort to check the pace of his horse.

"I've been doubting that for an hour past, Master Richard," was the answer.

The grizzled man was Seth, or sometimes Mr. Seth, to all who knew him. So seldom had he heard himself called Seth Dingwall that he had almost forgotten the name. Born in Louisiana, he believed he had French blood in him, and spoke the language easily. He had gone with his mistress to Virginia when she married Colonel Barrington, and to him

Broadmead was home, and he had no relation in the wide world.

"Is it so necessary to reach the city to-night?" he asked after a pause.

"I had planned to do so."

The answer was characteristic of the man. As a boy, when he had made up his mind to do a thing, he did it, even though well-merited punishment might follow, and the boy was father to the man. Save in years and experience, this was the same Richard Barrington who had dreamed as he watched sunlit sails disappear in the haze over Chesapeake Bay.

"I was thinking of the horses," said Seth. "I reckon that we have a long way to travel yet."

"We may get others presently," Barrington answered, and then, after a moment's pause, he went on: "We have seen some strange sights since we landed - ruined homes, small and great, burned and desolated by the peasants; and in the last few hours we have heard queer tales. I do not know how matters stand, but it looks as if we might be useful in Paris. That is why we must push on."

"Master Richard," he said slowly.

"Yes."

"Have you ever considered how useless a man may be?"

"Ay, often, and known such men."

"You do not catch my meaning. I am talking of a man who is full of courage and determination, yet just because he is only one is powerless. A lion might be killed by rats if there were enough rats."

"True, Seth, but there would be fewer rats by the time the lion was dead, and a less number for the next lion to struggle with."

"A good answer," said Seth, "and I'm not saying it isn't a right one, but I'm thinking of that first lion which may be slain."

A smile, full of tenderness, came into Barrington's face which, in the gathering darkness, his companion could hardly have seen had he turned to look at him, which he did not do.

"I know, Seth, I know, but I am not one man alone. I have you. It seems to me that I have always had you, and Heaven knows I should have had far less heart for this journey had you not come with me. In the old days you have been nurse and physician to me. I should have drowned in the pond beyond the orchard had you not been at hand to pull me out; I should have broken my skull when the branch of that tree broke had you not caught me; and I warrant there's a scar on your leg somewhere to show that the bull's horn struck you as you whisked me into a place of safety."

"There was something before all those adventures, Master Richard."

"What was that, Seth?"

"It was a morning I'm not forgetting until I'm past remembering anything. We all knew you were coming, and we were looking every day to hear the news. When we did hear it, it was only part of the story, and the other part was most our concern for a while. The mistress was like to die, they said. I remember there was wailing among the plantation hands, and Gadman the overseer had to use his whip to keep 'em quiet. We others were just dumb and waited. Then came the morning I speak of. The mistress was out before the house again for the first time. I chanced to be by, and she called me. You were lying asleep in her lap. 'Seth,' she said, 'this is the young master; isn't he beautiful? You must do your best to see that he comes to no harm as he grows up.' Well, that's all I've done, and it's what I'm bound to go on doing just as long as ever I can. That was the first time I saw you, Master Richard."

Barrington did not answer. His companion's words had brought a picture to his mind of his home in Virginia, which he had never loved quite so well perhaps as at this moment when he was far away from it, and was conscious that he might never see it again. Only a few months ago, when he had sat on the hummock, falling into much the same position as he had so often done as a boy, he had even wondered whether he wanted to return to it. Broadmead could never be the same place to him again. His father had died five years since, and that had been a terrible and sincere grief to him, but he had his mother, and had to fill his father's place as well as he could. The work on the estate gave him much to do, and if the news from France which found its way to Broadmead set him dreaming afresh at times, he cast such visions away. He had no inclination to leave his mother now she was alone, and he settled down to peaceful, happy days, hardly desiring that anything should be different, perhaps forgetting that some day it must be different. Not a year had passed since the change had come. A few days' illness and his mother was suddenly dead.

He was alone in the world. How could Broadmead ever be the same to him again?

"Seth, did my mother ever say anything more to you about me?" he asked suddenly.

"She thanked me for saving you from the bull, though I

wanted no thanks."

"Nothing more?"

"Only once," Seth returned, "and then she said almost the same words as she did when I first saw you lying on her knee. 'See that he comes to no harm, Seth.' She sent for me the night before she died, Master Richard. That's why I'm here. I didn't want to leave Virginia particularly."

Barrington might have expressed some regret for bringing his companion to France had not his horse suddenly demanded his attention. They had traversed the long stretch of straight road, and were passing by a thin wood of young trees. Long grass bordered the road on either side, and Barrington's horse suddenly shied and became restive.

"There's something lying there," said Seth, whose eyes were suddenly focused on the ground, and then he dismounted quickly. "It's a man, Master Richard, and by the Lord! he's had rough treatment."

Barrington quieted his horse with soothing words, and dismounting, tethered him to a gate.

"He's not dead," Seth said, as Barrington bent over him; and as if to endorse his words, the man moved slightly and groaned.

"We can't leave him, but - "

"But we shall not reach Paris to-night," Seth returned. "Didn't they tell us we should pass by a village? I have forgotten the name."

"Tremont," said Richard.

"It can't be much farther. There's no seeing to find out his injuries here, but if you could help to get him over the saddle in front of me, Master Richard, I could take him along slowly."

A feeble light glimmered presently along the road, which proved to be the light from a tavern which stood at one end of the village, a rough and not attractive house of entertainment, a fact that the neighbors seemed to appreciate, for no sound came from it.

"Those who attacked him may be there, Master Richard, refreshing themselves after their dastardly work."

"They must be saying silent prayers of repentance, then. Stay in the shadows, Seth; I'll make inquiry."

Leading his horse, Barrington went to the door and called for the landlord. He had to call twice before an old man shuffled along a dark passage from the rear of the house and stood before him.

"Are there lodgings for travelers here?"

"Lodgings, but no travelers. Tremont's deserted except by children and invalids. All in Paris, monsieur. Ay, these be hard times for some of us."

"I'm for Paris, but must rest here to-night."

"You're welcome, monsieur, and we'll do our best, but it's poor fare you'll get and that not cheap."

"Are there no travelers in the house?"

"None; none for these two months."

"No visitor of any kind?"

"None. Only four to-day, and they cursed me and my wine."

"I have a friend with me, and a wounded man. We found him by the roadside."

"We'll do our best," said the landlord, and he turned away and called for his wife.

As Barrington and Seth carried the wounded man in, the landlord looked at him and started.

"You know him?" asked Barrington sharply.

"I saw him only to-day. I'll tell you when you've got him comfortable in his bed."

"Is there a doctor in Tremont?"

"No, monsieur. Over at Lesville there's one, unless he's gone to Paris with the rest, but he couldn't be got here until the morning.".

"I may make shift to patch him up to-night, Master Richard," said Seth. "I helped the doctors a bit before Yorktown, when I was with the Colonel."

Possibly no physician or surgeon would have been impressed with Seth's methods. He was never intended to dress wounds, and yet his touch was gentle.

"He'll do until the doctor comes to-morrow," said Seth, as he presently found Barrington at the frugal meal.

The landlord apologized for the frugality, but it was all he could do.

"May I never face less when I am hungry," said Barrington.

"You saw this man to-day, landlord, you say?"

"Yes. I told you that four men cursed me and my wine. They had been here an hour or more, talking of what was going forward in Paris, and of some business which they were engaged upon. I took little note of what they said, for every one is full of important business in these days, monsieur, but the man who lies upstairs presently rode past. I saw him from this window, and my four guests saw him, too. They laughed and settled their score, and five minutes later had brought their horses from the stable behind the inn and were riding in the direction he had taken."

"And attacked him a little later, no doubt."

"It would seem so," said the landlord.

"Should they return, keep it a secret that you have a wounded man in the house. Will that purchase your silence?"

The landlord looked at the coins Barrington dropped into his hand.

"Thank you, monsieur, you may depend upon it that no one shall know."

Seth presently went to see the patient again, and returned in a few moments to say he was conscious.

"I told him where we found him, and he wants to see you, Master Richard."

"Your doctoring must be wonderfully efficacious, Seth."

"Brandy is a good medicine," was the answer; "but the man's in a bad way. He may quiet down after he's seen you."

The man moved slightly as Barrington entered the room, and when he spoke his words came slowly and in a whisper, yet with some eagerness.

"They left me for dead, monsieur; they were disturbed, perhaps."

"Why did they attack you?"

"I was carrying a message."

"A letter - and they stole it?" asked Barrington.

"No, a message. It was not safe to write."

"To whom was the message?"

"To a woman, my mistress, from her lover. He is in the hands of the rabble, and only she can save him. For the love of Heaven, monsieur, take the message to her. I cannot go."

"What is her name?" Barrington asked.

"Mademoiselle St. Clair."

"Certainly, she shall have it. How shall I make her understand?"

"Say Lucien prays her to come to Paris. In my coat yonder, in the lining of the collar, is a little gold star, her gift to him. Say Rouzet gave it to you because he could travel no farther. She will understand. You must go warily, and by an indirect road, or they will follow you as they did me."

"And where shall I find Mademoiselle St. Clair?"

"At the Chateau of Beauvais, hard by Lausanne, across the frontier."

"Lausanne! Switzerland!"

Before the man could give a word of further explanation there was a loud knocking at the door of the inn which the landlord had closed for the night, and when it was not opened immediately, angry curses and a threat to break it down. The patient on the bed did not start, he was too grievously hurt to do that, but his white face grew gray with fear.

"It is nothing, only a late traveler," said Barrington. "And, my good fellow, I cannot go to - "

The man's eyes were closed. The sudden fear seemed to have robbed him of consciousness. It was quite evident to Barrington that he could not be made to understand just now that a journey to Beauvais was impossible. He waited a few minutes to see if the man would rouse again, but he did not, and seeing that an explanation must be put off until later, he went out of the room, closing the door gently behind him. As he descended the stairs the landlord tiptoed up to meet him.

"The men who were here to-day and cursed my wine," he whispered. "Two of them have returned!"

CHAPTER II

A BINDING OATH

The return of these men, if indeed they were responsible for the condition of the man upstairs, might augur further evil for him. They had perchance returned along the road to make certain that their work was complete, and, finding their victim gone, were now in search of him. Exactly what reliance was to be placed on the word of the wounded man, Barrington had not yet determined. He might be a contemptible spy, his message might contain hidden information to the enemies of his country; he was certainly carrying it to aristocrats who were safe across the frontier, and he might fully deserve all the punishment which had been meted out to him, but for the moment he was unable to raise a hand in his own defense and his helplessness appealed to Barrington. These men should not have their will of him if he could prevent it.

"Keep out of the way of being questioned," he whispered to the landlord, as they went down the stairs. It was characteristic of Richard Barrington that he had formed no plan when he entered the room. He believed that actions must always be controlled by the circumstances of the moment, that it was generally essential to see one's enemy before deciding how to outwit him, a false theory perhaps, but, given a strong personality, one which is often successful.

"Good evening, gentlemen! My friend and I are not the

PERCY BREBNER

only late travelers to-night."

The two men looked sharply at him. Their attention had been keenly, though furtively, concentrated upon Seth, who sat in a corner, apparently half asleep. In fact, having just noticed them, he had closed his eyes as though he were too weary and worn out to talk.

Both men curtly acknowledged Barrington's greeting, hardly conscious of the curtness maybe. They were of the people, their natural roughness turned to a sort of insolent swagger by reason of the authority which had been thrust upon them. They were armed, blatantly so, and displayed the tri-colored cockade. In some society, at any rate, they were of importance, and this stranger and the manner of his greeting puzzled them. He spoke like an aristocrat, yet there was something unfamiliar about him.

"Did you have to batter at the door before you could gain admittance?" asked one. Of the two, he seemed to have the greater authority.

"No, we arrived before the door was closed."

"Closed doors are suspicious," the man returned with an oath. "This is the day of open doors and freedom for all, citizen."

"Liberty, equality, and fraternity," Barrington answered. "It is a good motto. One that men may well fight for."

"Do you fight for it?" asked the man, truculently.

"Not yet," said Barrington, very quietly and perfectly unmoved, apparently seeing nothing unusual in the man's manner or his question, but quite conscious that Seth had sleepily let his hand slip into his pocket and kept it there.

"Late travelers on the road are also suspicious," said the man, stepping a little nearer to Barrington.

"Indeed! Tell me, of what are you afraid? My friend and I are armed, as I see you are. We may join forces against a common danger. Four resolute men are not easily to be played with."

"Aristocrats find it convenient to travel at night, and tricked out just as you are," he said. "I have taken part in stopping many of them."

"Doubtless an excellent and useful occupation," Barrington returned.

"And I have heard many of them talk like that," said the man, "an attempt to throw dust into eyes far too sharp to be blinded by it. You will tell me where you travel to and where from."

"Do you ask out of courteous curiosity, as meeting travelers may do, or for some other reason?"

"You may think whichever pleases you."

"I am not making for the frontier, if that is what you want to know," laughed Barrington.

"I asked a question which it will be well for you to answer," said the man, and it was evident that his companion was also on the alert.

"Have you authority to question me?" Barrington asked.

"Papers here," said the man, touching his coat, "and this." His hand fell upon a pistol in his belt.

"Leave it there. It is the safest place."

Seth's hands had come from his pocket with a pistol in it. Barrington still laughed.

"My friend seems as suspicious as you are. Let me end it, for truly I expected to be drinking with you before this, instead of trying to find a cause for quarrel. Your eyes must be sharp indeed if you can discover an aristocrat in me. I was for freedom and the people before you had struck a blow for the cause here in France. We are from the coast, before that from America, and we journey to Paris to offer our services to the Marquis de Lafayette."

Perhaps the man believed him, perhaps he did not, but the result of an appeal to force was doubtful, and wine was an attraction. He held out his hand with an air that the welcome of France was in the action. For the present they could pose as friends, whatever might chance in the future.

"Sieur Motier the Marquis is now called, but in America that name would not appeal. We may drown our mistake in wine, the first but maybe not the last time we shall drink together."

The landlord brought in the wine and departed without being questioned.

"Sieur Motier," said Barrington, reflectively. "News has traveled slowly to us in Virginia, and things here have moved quickly. You can tell me much. This meeting is a fortunate one for me."

Into weeks and months had been crowded the ordinary work of a long period of time. After nearly three years of strenuous effort, the Constituent Assembly had come to an end. With Mirabeau as its master spirit, it had done much, some evil, but a great deal that was good. It had suppressed torture, done away with secret letters, and lightened the burden of many grievous taxes. Now, the one man who was able to deal with the crisis if any man was, the aristocrat who had become the darling of the rabble, the "little mother" of the fisher-wives, the hope of even the King himself, was silent. Mirabeau was dead. In fear the King had fled from Paris only to be stopped at Varennes and brought back ignominiously to the capital. The Legislative Assembly took the place of the Constituent Assembly, three parties in it struggling fiercely for the mastery, one party, that high-seated crowd called the Mountain, red republicans whose cry was ever "No King," growing stronger day by day. Nations in arms were gathering on the frontiers of France, and the savagery of the populace was let loose. The Tuileries had been stormed, the Swiss Guard butchered, the royal family imprisoned in the Temple. Quickly the Legislative Assembly had given way to a National Convention, and the country was ripe for any and every atrocity the mind of man could conceive.

The patriot, sitting opposite to Barrington and drinking wine at intervals, told his tale with enthusiasm and with many comments of his own. He was full of the tenets of the Jacobin and Cordelian Clubs. For him the world, set spinning on a mad career when the Bastille fell, was moving too slowly again. There had been a good beginning, truly something had been done since, but why not make a good end of it? Mirabeau, yes, he had done something, but the work had grown too large for him. He had died in good time before the people had become tired of him. France was for the people, and there must be death for all who stood in the people's way, and a quick death, too.

"Blood must run more freely, there will be no good end without that," he said; "the blood of all aristocrats, no matter what they promise, what they pretend. From the beginning they were liars. France has no use for them save to make carrion of."

"And whose power is sufficient for all this?"

Barrington asked.

"To-day, no one's. To-morrow; - who shall say? Things go forward quickly at times. A sudden wave might even raise me to power."

"Then the good ending," said Barrington.

The man caught no irony, he only heard the flattery.

"Then the blood flowing," he laughed; "so, as full in color and as freely spilt," and he jerked the remains of the wine in his glass across the room, staining the opposite wall.

"And if not at your word, perhaps at that of Monsieur de Lafayette, Sieur Motier," Barrington suggested. He wanted the man to talk about the Marquis.

"He is an aristocrat with sympathies which make no appeal to me. The people have grown tired of him, too. I am honest, and fear no man, and I say that Motier has long been at the crossroads. He is, or was, an honest man, I hardly know which he is now, and even honest men must suffer for the cause. You say you are his friend, whisper that warning in his ear, if you see him; say you had it from Jacques Sabatier, he will have heard of me."

"Certainly, I will tell him," said Barrington, wondering if such a man as Lafayette could have heard of such a truculent scoundrel as this. "Is he in Paris?"

"I know nothing of him. He was with the army in the North, but he may have been recalled. He must obey like the rest of us. Do you ride with us to Paris to-night?"

"No. Our horses need rest, but we shall meet there, I hope."

"A true patriot must needs meet Sabatier in Paris," and the man swaggered out of the room, followed by his companion.

Barrington and Seth stood at the tavern door to watch their departure. It was not advisable that they should be alone with the landlord and have an opportunity of asking him questions.

The two men rode sharply through the village, but on the outskirts drew rein.

"Had you sharp enough eyes to discover anything?" Sabatier asked, turning to his companion.

"Nothing, except that one of them was too much like an aristocrat to please me."

"He comes to Paris, and may be dealt with there. What of Bruslart's messenger?"

"I saw no sign of him."

"Yet they journey from the coast and must have passed him on the road. He was beyond moving of his own accord."

"Do you mean they helped him?"

"Some one has. We were fools to allow ourselves to be disturbed before completing our work."

"Why did you not question the landlord or the men themselves?"

"Time enough for that," Sabatier answered. "Two men against two gives no odds to depend upon. Ride on toward Paris and send me back a dozen patriots, no matter where you find them. There are some in the neighborhood who have tasted blood in burning a chateau, whisper that there are aristocrats in Tremont. They shall find me by that farm yonder, snatching an hour's sleep in the straw maybe. Then get you to Villefort, where Mercier and Dubois are waiting. Bid them watch that road. Possibly the messenger was not so helpless as we imagined."

Jacques Sabatier did not move until the sound of his comrade's horse had died into silence, then he went toward the farm, tethered his horse, and threw himself down on the straw in a dilapidated barn. Sleep must be taken when it could be got. The days and nights were too full for settled times of rest. In his little sphere he was a man of consequence, not of such importance as he imagined, but, nevertheless, before his fellows. He had been at the storming of the Bastille, that gave him prestige; he had a truculent swagger which counted in these days, especially if there had been no opportunity of being proved a coward. Perchance Sabatier had never been put to the test. In a rabble it is easy to shout loudly, yet be where the danger is least, and this wide-mouthed patriot had much to say about himself.

His sleep was sound enough for the proverbial just man, sound and dreamless, aided perhaps by a liberal allowance of wine. At daybreak he was still slumbering, and the little crowd of men who presently found him in the barn had some trouble in rousing him. He struggled to his feet, his mind a blank for a moment.

"What is it? What do you want?" and for an instant there was a look in his eyes strangely like fear.

"You sent for us," said one.

"Ah! I remember." Sabatier was himself again. "There's work for us in the village yonder. Rats in a hole, comrades. We go to smoke them out."

A fierce undertone of approval was the answer.

So in the early morning there was once more a heavy battering at the closed door of the tavern, and shouting to the landlord to open quickly. He came shuffling down the stairs.

"It's over early for guests," he said sleepily, "but you're good men, I see. Come in."

Then he caught sight of Sabatier and trembled a little. He was an old man, and had been oppressed so long that he had become used to it. He understood very little of what was going forward in the country.

"Where are the aristocrats?" hissed a dozen raucous voices.

"Those guests of yours," said Sabatier.

"They have gone - went soon after you left last night. It was a surprise, but I had no power to stop them."

There was an angry movement toward the landlord.

"Wait," said Sabatier. "He is probably a liar. We shall see."

The men searched the house, some watching the doors lest the aristocrats should make a dash for freedom. Certainly there was a guest here still, but he made no effort to escape. At the top of the stairs was a door - locked.

"The key," Sabatier demanded.

"I will fetch it," was the timid answer.

The locked door was suspicious. Two men ran hastily to watch the window and prevent escape that way. And why delay for the key? Not a very strong lock this, a blow from a man's heel could break it, did break it, and the door crashed open, splitting itself from one of its hinges.

On the bed lay a man, half-dressed, his eyes wide open, fixed upon the ceiling, his head bound with a cloth, blood-stained. Very sunken was the head in the pillows, very thin looked the form stretched under the coarse blanket. Sabatier touched him and then looked swiftly round the room. A coat was thrown across a chair. He took this up, and there was a cut in the lining of it, high up near the collar.

"Who did this?" he asked.

The landlord did not know.

"Who did it, I say!" and he struck him in the face with the back of his hand, a heavy enough blow to send the old man to the wall.

"I do not know, sir, it's true I do not know," whined the landlord. "They brought him here half dead; had found him on the road, they said. He seemed to get better when one of them bound him up. When they came to look at him after you had gone he was dead. I left them alone with him, and in a few minutes they called me and said they must leave for Paris at once."

Sabatier flung the coat aside with an oath.

"This is Citizen Latour's business," he said to his companions.

"And he's been helping aristocrats," said one man, pointing to the landlord still leaning by the wall.

"What else?" said Sabatier, shortly, as he strode out of the room and down the stairs.

A cry followed him, but he did not stop.

"Mercy! I know nothing."

A wilder cry, half drowned by savage curses and the sound of blows. Still Sabatier paid no heed. He went into the room below, knocked the neck off a wine bottle and poured the contents into a mug and drank, smacking his lips.

A woman, half dressed, rushed down the stairs and into the street.

"Let her go," Sabatier cried, as a man was starting after her. "Maybe she's not too old to find another husband."

Laughing, and cursing, the men came tumbling down the stairs, ripe for deviltry; but for the moment here was wine to be had for the taking, everything else could wait.

When later they left, a woman came rushing toward them.

"Let me in! Let me in!" she cried. "He's not dead."

"Out of it," said one, pushing her roughly aside so that she stumbled and fell upon the road. "He's dead, or will be soon enough. Our work is thorough, and this might be a chateau instead of a wine shop by the way we've treated it. You watch a while. You'll understand," and he laughed as he closed the door.

The poor soul may have understood his meaning, or she may not, as she rocked herself to and fro in the roadway. The ribald songs of these patriots, these apostles of freedom, had not died as they marched and danced out of Tremont when there was a smell of burning in the air, and first smoke, then flame burst from the tavern, quickly reducing it to a heap of ashes. It was a strange grave for the charred remains of two men who yesterday had been full of life. This was a time when things moved apace and there was no prophesying from day to day.

Long since out of range of the smoke cloud rising in the morning sky, Richard Barrington and Seth urged their horses along the road.

"Is this a wise journey?" Seth asked suddenly.

"I cannot tell."

"Paris might be safer."

"I promised to carry a message to a woman," Barrington answered. "The man is dead; there remains my oath. Somewhere before us lies the Chateau of Beauvais, and that is the way we go."

CHAPTER III

BEAUVAIS

There are few fairer spots in this world than Beauvais. He who has dreamed of an earthly paradise and sought it out, might well rest here contented, satisfied. It lies at the top of a long, ascending valley which twists its way upward from the Swiss frontier into the hills, a rough and weary road to travel, yet with a new vista of beauty at every turn. Here are wooded slopes where a dryad might have her dwelling; yonder some ragged giant towers toward heaven, his scarred rocky shoulders capped with snow. Below, deep down from the road cut in the hillside, undulate green pastures, the cattle so small at this distance that they might be toys set there after a child's fancy; while a torrent leaping joyously from ledge to ledge might be a babbling brook but for the sound of its full music which comes upward on the still air, telling of impetuous force and power. Here eternity seems to have an habitation, and time to be a thing of naught. The changing seasons may come and go, storm and tempest may spend their rage, and summer heat and winter frost work their will, yet that rocky height shall still climb into cloudland, and those green pastures shall flourish. Centuries ago, eyes long blinded by the dust of death looked upon this fair scene and understood something of its everlasting nature; centuries hence, other eyes shall behold its beauty and still dream of a distant future. We are but children of a day, brilliant ephemera flashing in a noontide sun; these silent, watching hills have known generations of others like us, as brilliant and as short-lived; shall know generations more, unborn as yet, unthought of.

At the head of this valley, rising suddenly from a stretch of level land, is a long hill lying like a wedge, its thin edge resting on the plain. The sides, as they get higher, become more precipitous, but from the thin edge there ascends a road about which houses cluster, irregular and pointed roofs rising one above the other in strange confusion until they are crowned at the summit by the chateau standing like their protector to face and defy the world. To the right, dominating the whole of this region, is the great double peak, snow-clad and often cloud-bound, which seems to stand sentinel for the surrounding mountains as the castle does to the valley; God's work and the work of man. He who first built his castle there knew well that in might lay right, and chose his place accordingly. Now houses stretch down to the level of the plain, but it was not always so. Halfway through the village the road passes through a gateway of solid stone, flanked by towers pierced for defense, and the wall through which this gate gives entrance remains, broken in places, lichen-covered, yet still eloquent of its former strength and purpose. Within the gate the village widens into an open square rising toward the chateau, and this square is surrounded by old houses picturesque and with histories. Many a time Beauvais has stood siege, its lord holding it against some neighbor stirred by pride or love tragedy to deadly feud. In these ancient houses his retainers lived, his only so long as he was strong enough to make himself feared, fierce men gathered from all points of the compass, soldiers of fortune holding their own lives and the lives of others cheaply. From such men, brilliant in arms, have sprung descendants who have made their mark in a politer epoch, men and women who have become courtiers, companions of kings, leaders of men, pioneers of learning. Carved into these ancient houses in Beauvais are crests and mottoes which are the pride of these descendants now scattered over Europe. Such is the village of Beauvais, asleep for many years, the home of peasants chiefly, mountaineers and tenders of cattle, still with the fighting spirit in them, but dormant, lacking the necessity. A fair place, but to the exile, only through a veil does the fairest land reveal its beauty. Its sunlit hills, its green pastures, the silver sheen of its streams, the blue of its sky, he will see through a mist of regret, through tears perchance. No beauty can do away with the fact that it is only a land of exile, to be endured and made the best of for a while, never to be really loved. There is coming an hour in which he may return home, and he is forever looking forward, counting the days. The present must be lived, but reality lies in the future.

The Marquise de Rovere, brilliant, witty, proud as any woman in France, daughter of ancestors famous during the time of the fourteenth and fifteenth Louis, had in the long past a forbear who was lord of this chateau of Beauvais. Since then there had been other lords with whom she had nothing to do, but her grandfather having grown rich, unscrupulously, it was said, bought Beauvais, restored it, added to it and tried to forget that it had ever passed out of the hands of his ancestors. In due time his granddaughter inherited it, and after that terrible day at Versailles when the mob had stormed the palace, when many of the nobility foresaw disaster and made haste to flee from it into voluntary exile, what better place could the Marquise choose than this chateau of Beauvais? Hither she had come with her niece Jeanne St. Clair, and others had followed. In Paris the Marquise had been the center of a brilliant coterie, she would still be a center in Beauvais and the chateau should be open to every emigre of distinction.

So it came to pass that sleepy Beauvais had suddenly stretched itself and aroused from slumber. The Marquise was rich, her niece a wealthy heiress, much of both their fortunes not dependent upon French finance, and a golden harvest fell upon the simple mountaineers and cattle tenders. Every available room was at the disposal of master or lackey, and the sleepy square was alive with men and women who had intrigued and danced at Versailles, who had played pastoral games with Marie Antoinette at the Trianon, whose names were famous. Idlers were many in Beauvais, exiles awaiting the hour for return, for revenge upon the rabble, yet doing nothing to forward the hour; but there were many others, men who came and went full of news and endeavor. Beauvais was a meeting place. There one might hear the latest rumors from Paris, learn what help might be expected from Austria, from Prussia; and while news was gathered and given there was brilliant entertainment at the chateau.

"We may make even exile bearable," the Marquise had said, and she did her utmost to do so.

It was into this wideawake village of Beauvais that Richard Barrington and Seth, weary and travel-stained, rode late one afternoon, and came to a halt before the inn. They passed almost unnoticed, for strangers were a common sight, often quaintly disguised to escape their enemies.

There was no room in the inn, nor did the good landlady, who still seemed flurried with so much business to attend to, know where they would get a lodging.

"Every house is a hotel these days, and I think every house is full," she said. "All the world has come to Beauvais for the masked ball at the chateau."

"There are still holes to be found," said a man lounging by the door. "My friend and I were in the same predicament, but we have found a corner. I believe there is room of sorts still to be had in the house, and if Monsieur permits, I shall have pleasure in taking him there."

"You are very good," said Barrington.

The stranger led the way across the square to an old house set back between its neighbors, as though it were modest and shrinking from observation, or desirous of keeping a secret. Its door was narrow and down a step from the roadway; its windows small, like half-closed eyes.

"Monsieur must expect little and even then get less than he expects, and pay dearly for it; but it is such a hole as this or a night in the open."

"I am weary enough not to mind much where I sleep," said Barrington.

"Add it all to the account which the *canaille* must some day pay," answered the man.

A stuffy little loft of a room, adjoining another loft occupied by their guide and his friend, was all the space available, but it was better than nothing, and Barrington quickly came to terms with the owner of the house.

Monsieur le Comte, for so the proprietor addressed the man who had guided them to the house, departed, hoping for their further acquaintance presently, and offering them any help which it might be in his power to afford.

"We find ourselves in a strange place, Master Richard," said Seth, surveying the room.

"We may come to stranger ones before we see Virginia again," was the answer.

"Ay, that's true; and there's not a certainty that we shall ever see Virginia again," said Seth. "I took the precaution to say farewell to all the old corners of Broadmead before I left."

"It's a fool's game to step too far into the future. A wise

man never buys his own coffin," laughed Barrington. "We are in luck."

"I'm glad you think so, Master Richard. I see plenty of danger, but little luck. It was to help the people we came, and here we are at Beauvais to serve an aristocrat. Our friends the people are not likely to forgive us easily."

"There is a woman to help, Seth."

"I wonder how many excellent schemes a woman has brought to nothing."

"And that is why I say we are in luck," said Barrington, taking no notice of the comment. "How are we to get audience with this woman? The question has puzzled me upon the journey. We are met with the news that there is to be a masked ball at the chateau. Could we have arrived at a more opportune time?"

"You will go to the chateau?"

"Of course. I shall find some excuse and get a disguise that best fits it. Every one in Beauvais must be able to give me some description by which I may know Mademoiselle St. Clair. The rest will be easy."

"This faith of youth is very wonderful," said Seth.

"Not more remarkable than your forebodings," Barrington returned. "You have not always been so quick to talk of danger."

"Maybe it's the different air. I prefer the breeze that comes off Chesapeake Bay to that of these hills, and there's a devil of depression in this cockloft, it seems to me."

"Come out of it, then. Hunger and thirst are at the bottom

of your croaking. We will go eat and drink and gather news."

"And at this ball, Master Richard, see that you think more of the readiness of your arms than your grace in a dance."

Barrington laughed as he descended the narrow stairs, but he was not heedless of his companion's warnings. He was fully alive to the danger he was in, and if the truth must be told, was not particularly pleased to find himself in Beauvais. He would far rather have been in Paris. The romantic element in this unexpected adventure did not greatly appeal to him. He had crossed the ocean to help an oppressed people; he was full of enthusiasm for a cause, so much an enthusiast that the two braggart representatives of the people with whom he had come in contact at Tremont had in no way disillusioned him. Refuse must needs be cast on the wave crests of a revolution; but there was also Lafayette. He was the people's true representative, and Barrington longed to be at his side to help him. He had promised to deliver a message, believing that he was undertaking a comparatively small matter, and just when he learned that a journey into Switzerland was involved, interruption had come and the man had lost consciousness. Barrington had fully intended to explain to the wounded man that such a journey was impossible. After Sabatier and his companion had left the inn, he had gone upstairs for this purpose, only to find the man dead. He had made a promise to a dying man, and at all hazards that promise must be fulfilled. The sooner it was done, the sooner he could journey to Paris; and their arrival in Beauvais at the time of this masked ball was fortunate: there need be little delay.

A little later Monsieur le Comte found them.

"We must needs celebrate your escape," he said. "This is my friend, like myself an exile from Paris. You are also from Paris?"

"From outside Paris," Barrington answered. For the nonce he must pose as an aristocrat, and wondered by what name he might best deceive them. Seth, too, was a grave difficulty. He could show few marks of an aristocrat.

The Frenchman's next words saved him all trouble, however.

"We do not ask too many questions in Beauvais, Monsieur. That we are here proves that we do not uphold the people, and we need not too closely inquire who our neighbor may be. We shall not all wish to maintain the friendships made in exile when we return to France. Here's to your safe arrival, Monsieur, and to our speedy return. The sentiment is of the best vintage, though the wine may be inferior. I warrant the cellars of the chateau will do better for us to-morrow night. You go to the ball, Monsieur?"

"I am ill-provided for such an entertainment."

"As are many others," was the laughing answer, "since they were obliged to leave so hurriedly that there was short time for packing. That need not deter you, Monsieur, and if you have no opportunity of apprising the Marquise of your arrival, I believe there are some so poor in their exile that they would sell their invitation. We do things in Beauvais that would shame us elsewhere."

"I must confess to not being personally acquainted with the Marquise," said Barrington.

"Say no more, Monsieur; you shall have an invitation in the morning. A few louis will purchase it."

"You overwhelm me with courtesy," said Barrington.

"No, no; it is nothing. To-morrow evening I may have the opportunity of presenting you to the Marquise."

"And to her niece?"

"Mademoiselle St. Clair? That is as Monsieur wills," he laughed.

"I do not understand your merriment."

"Pardon, Monsieur, but there are not many who crave presentation to Mademoiselle. You have not heard of her?"

"Nothing but her name."

"Think, Monsieur, of a large woman with black hair and complexion more swart than beautiful, with large hands that could clasp mine and hide them, and feet flat and heavy; a figure that is no figure, all its lines pressed from within out of place and which shakes as she walks; a voice whose whisper is raucous. Then, Monsieur, conceive this woman unaware of her defects, who simpers and attempts to use her dull eyes in fascination. That is Mademoiselle St. Clair."

"Surely you exaggerate?"

"No, it is a fair picture," said the friend, "and yet she has admirers. Her fortune is as large as her person."

Barrington laughed. There could be small romance in the love story which fate had called him to assist, and certainly he would have small difficulty in finding Mademoiselle St. Clair.

"I will not trespass on your courtesy for an introduction to her, Monsieur," he said, "and since the wine is finished, you will pardon us if we retire. We have traveled far and are weary."

Monsieur le Comte looked at his companion when they had gone, and smiled.

"A new experience for Beauvais," he said; "a man who has not the honor of knowing Madame la Marquise and has not heard of the charms of Mademoiselle her niece."

"The picture you drew was a little too repulsive, I think."

"She will be masked," was the laughing answer. "He must have his invitation as promised. It will cost a few louis, and we are none too rich. We are dealers in this matter, and must have some profit for our labor."

"Monsieur le Comte, you are a genius," laughed his companion.

An hour later, Monsieur le Comte knocked softly at the door of Barrington's room.

There was no answer.

He knocked louder.

"Monsieur, I have the invitation."

Still there was no answer.

"Parbleu, they sleep like the dead," he murmured, and went back to his companion.

Seth lay like a log - in deep, dreamless sleep. It would take far more than a mere knocking at the door to wake him. Barrington, deaf to the knocking, deeply asleep too, was restless, turning and tossing with dreams - nightmares. He was falling over one of the precipices which they had passed on their way to Beauvais. He was imprisoned, almost suffocated, in a little room; the walls seemed to gradually close in upon him and then suddenly to open; he was ill, surely, for men were about him, looking into his face and muttering together. Again, he was in a crowd, a dancing, noisy crowd, searching for a great woman who shook as she walked. It was madness to seek her here, they were all pigmies, and he turned away; another moment they were all big, all the women had raven hair, large hands and feet; he would never be able to find the woman he sought. Then this scene faded and there came others, some horrible, all fantastic; and always there came, sooner or later, a woman, ugly, repulsive, masterful. She fascinated him. He was conscious of struggling to free himself. He could not. Something, some irresistible power, forced him to speak to her, to love her, to love while he tried to hate, and her great dull eyes looked at him, rewarding him. He knew her, forever hereafter must be possessed by her. This horrible woman, this Jeanne St. Clair, was his fate. Nightmare was his long after the day had broken and men and women were abroad in Beauvais.

CHAPTER IV

MADEMOISELLE ST. CLAIR

Sharp hammering at the door, long continued, finally brought an end to Barrington's nightmare hours and Seth's deep slumbers. The sun was streaming in through the little window, revealing the dust and the dilapidation of this lodging. Seth went to the door.

"Ma foi, I thought you had started on your last long journey," said the proprietor of the house. "My knuckles are sore with knocking. Monsieur le Comte bid me give you this card. You would understand and pay, he said."

"How much?"

"Six louis. It was arranged, he said, and I gave him the money before he went this morning."

"He has gone?" called Barrington from his bed.

"Madame la Marquise heard of his arrival, Monsieur, and sent to fetch him to lodgings in the castle. You will doubtless meet him in Beauvais during the day."

"Six louis for this card?" questioned Seth. "It is a long price."

"If you were not a stranger in Beauvais you would know that it was very cheap," answered the proprietor.

"Pay it," said Barrington.

Seth did so with a grumble, and wondered how much the proprietor was making out of the deal.

"We have fallen among thieves, Master Richard," he said as he shut the door. "I shouldn't wonder if any one could slip into this ball without payment of any sort. We've made a long night of it."

"Weariness and wine," answered Barrington. "The wine was strong, or this mountain air added to the potency of its effects upon us."

"Maybe. I never slept so soundly since I was a youngster."

"And I never had such horrible dreams," said Barrington.

"I've been thinking, Master Richard, that there may be worse than thieves in Beauvais," said Seth, after a pause. "We're rather like men at sea without the knowledge of how to handle ropes and set sail - an extra puff of wind, and we risk being overturned. There's something to learn about the methods of these Frenchmen, especially when every man sees a possible enemy in his neighbor. The gentlemen at Tremont did not much please me, nor was I greatly taken with Monsieur le Comte."

"We shall have plenty of time to learn their methods, Seth."

"But in the meanwhile the puff of wind may come, Master Richard. I don't like this masked ball."

"You may trust me to be careful."

"Your idea of precaution and mine may differ a little," Seth answered. "You don't see danger so far ahead as I do."

"That may be in my favor," laughed Richard. "Be at ease, Seth; I shall do nothing rash. Neither our blatant friend Sabatier, nor our courteous acquaintance of last night, shall catch me sleeping. I do not trust men very easily, nor women either, for that matter."

"Ay, Master Richard, it's a weight off my mind to know that this Mademoiselle St. Clair has so little attraction about her. I've been young myself and know the power of women. You've not been through that fire yet."

"A strange thing at my age, Seth. I have thought that no woman is likely to plague me much."

"Get well into your grave before you think that," was the answer. "I'm no hater of women, far from it, and I know a man's never safe. Why, a chit of twenty may make a fool of a veteran, and set his tired old heart trying to beat like that of a lad just out of his school days. Only last year there was a girl in Virginia sent me panting along this road of folly, and I'm not sure it wasn't Providence which sent me with you to France."

Beauvais presented a lively scene that day, but it was in vain that Barrington kept a sharp lookout for Monsieur le Comte and his friend. Many people came and went from the chateau, but they were not among them. Barrington did not particularly want to meet them, but he realized that circumstances might arise which would make them useful, and he would have liked to find out what position they held among the other exiles in Beauvais. A prominent one, surely, since the Marquise had fetched them to lodgings in the chateau, and therefore it was possible that Barrington's arrival had puzzled them. They might reasonably doubt whether he had any right to pose as an aristocrat and an exile, suspicion would certainly follow, and sharp eyes might be upon him at the ball to-night. Even as a go-between in a love affair there might be some danger for him, but was his mission only that?

When he left his lodgings that evening he had disguised himself as much as possible. He wore a cloak which his acquaintances of last night had not seen, he had procured a mask which hid as much of his face as possible. He went armed, and fastened in the lining of his coat was the little gold star he had taken from the dead man's coat. He fingered it through the cloth to make sure that it was safe as he crossed the, square and went toward the chateau. Seth may have been right, and the six louis thrown away, for no one took any notice of Barrington as he passed into the castle. Although he gave up his card of invitation, he was convinced that with a little diplomacy and a bold front he could have got in without one.

Exteriorly the castle retained much of its mediaeval appearance, and within the new had been cleverly and lovingly grafted onto the old. There were still dungeons enclosed in these massive walls, chambers wherein misery and pain had cried aloud to no effect. There were narrow passages down which tortured men must once have been carried, or at the end of which some oubliette opened to sudden destruction. Many horrible things must be in the knowledge of this massive masonry. The great hall, where men at arms, after a foray or raid upon some neighboring stronghold, must have caroused times without number, making the roof ring with their rude rejoicing, was alive to-night with men and women, exiles forgetting their exile for a while or exchanging news which might mean a speedy return to their homeland. All were masked, although it was apparent that many had no difficulty in recognizing their neighbors under the disguise, but although there were a few brilliant costumes and occasional flashes of jewels, the general impression of dress was sombre and makeshift. How could it be otherwise when the flight from Paris, or from the provinces, had been so sudden, no preparation possible?

At one side of the hall, the center of a little group, stood a white-haired woman of commanding presence. Jewels flashed in her dress, and there was laughter about her. Evidently this was the Marquise de Rovere, and she was busy welcoming her guests. With some it was more than a passing word of greeting, there was news to be imparted by one lately in communication with Austria or Prussia, or perchance with England; there was the latest news from Paris to be had from one who had just escaped from his enemies; there was news, too, of friends who had not been so fortunate, or who had willingly stayed to face the storm; there were rumors which had been gathered from all sources to be whispered. This chateau of Beauvais was a meeting place, a center for much scheming; and for a while the hours must be made to pass as pleasantly as possible.

These men and women were different from those he had come in contact with, of a different world altogether; yet his youth responded to the music and verve of it all. Because it was different, new and unfamiliar to him, that was no proof that what he had known was right, and this was wrong. His blood was pulsating, the atmosphere was exhilarating. Pleasure flung him her gauge, why should he not pick it up? A woman was beside him, dark eyes flashing through her mask, red lips wreathed into a smile. The next moment reserve had broken down and he was dancing with her, acquitting himself with sufficient grace to pass muster, and almost as ready with his compliment as she was to receive it.

"We shall dance again, monsieur," she said presently, when another partner carried her away.

"Until then I shall count the moments," Barrington answered, and it was perhaps this suggestion of the future which brought to his mind the real reason for his presence there.

A large woman, with raven hair, and of such a figure that it shook when she walked; among the dancers there were many who might pass for large women, the hair of one or two might be considered raven, but there was not one who completed the full description he had had of Mademoiselle St. Clair. Certainly she was not among those who stood near the Marquise, and Barrington went from vantage point to vantage point in search of her. Neither could he discover Monsieur le Comte or his friend. Lodged in the chateau, they had possibly obtained richer garments, and would be difficult to identify. The fulfillment of his mission was not to be so easy as he had imagined.

He had been watching from a corner near the entrance to the ballroom, partially concealed by a little knot of people who were standing before him. He could have overheard their conversation, but he was not listening. He was wondering how he could find mademoiselle. There was surely some other apartment where guests were, for his eyes were keen, and he had certainly not seen her yet.

"Monsieur does not dance?"

Barrington turned quickly. The little crowd which had stood in front of him had gone, and near him was a woman. It was difficult to know whether her words were a statement of fact, question or invitation.

"I have danced, mademoiselle."

"And are now waiting for some one?"

"No. If mademoiselle will honor me I - "

"I also have danced many times, monsieur, and am inclined to rest a little."

Barrington looked at her, and a pair of violet eyes met his

glance through her mask, deep, almost unfathomable eyes, difficult to read and filled with the light that lures men on to strange and wonderful things. Her auburn hair had brown and darker shadows in it, the color one may see in a distant wood in late autumn when the sun touches it; her transparent skin was delicately tinted, such a tint as may be seen in rare china. Her small, well-shaped mouth seemed made for smiles, yet there was a line of firmness in it suggestive of determination. There was a cadence in her voice, a musical rise and fall which held an appeal. The lines of her figure were graceful, there was youth and vigor in every movement, and without being above the medium height, the pose of her head on her shapely shoulders gave her a certain air of stateliness, natural and becoming to her it seemed. She was a woman designed for happiness and laughter, Barrington thought, and he felt she was not happy. He wondered if there were not tears in those violet eyes, and he had a sudden longing to behold her without a mask. It would have been easy for her to make him again forget his mission, and why he was in the chateau of Beauvais. Youth recognized youth, and that indefinite longing which is a part of youth seemed to enfold them for an instant. Perhaps the woman felt it as much as he did, for she broke the silence rather abruptly.

"I have noticed that monsieur has not entered much into the gayety."

Barrington was on his guard in a moment. He could not afford to be questioned too closely.

"I am greatly honored by mademoiselle's notice."

"That is nothing," she returned as though the implied compliment displeased her. "It seemed to me you were a stranger in Beauvais, and strangers here may have sad memories behind them."

"They do their best to forget, mademoiselle," he answered. The laughter of a woman as she passed, dancing, gave point to the assertion. "It is wonderful. I cannot understand it."

"Better laugh and live than die weeping," she said. "Those who live shall live to repay."

"And perchance some good shall come out of the evil."

She looked at him quickly.

"In Beauvais it is somewhat dangerous to be a philosopher, monsieur. We cling to one idea which by brutal force has been driven into our souls - revenge. It is not safe to preach anything short of that, we have suffered too much."

"There was not such a deep meaning in my words," he said.

"Still, the warning may not be out of place," and she turned to leave him.

"Before I go, mademoiselle, you may help me. Can you tell me where I shall find Mademoiselle St. Clair?"

"You know her?"

"Only by the description I have had of her."

"I wonder almost it was not sufficient to help you," and a smile played at the corners of her mouth.

"Indeed, mademoiselle, I marvel at it, too, for I assure you the description was most complete," laughed Barrington.

"From whom did you have it?"

"Pardon me if I am reticent on that point. It was given in confidence."

"You pique my curiosity."

"But you know her, mademoiselle?"

"Oh, yes."

"Cannot you guess how a man might describe her, with a desire perhaps to be a little witty at her expense, and inclined to exaggerate?"

"Indeed, I cannot. Have you some message for her which I may deliver?"

"Again pardon, but I must speak to the lady myself."

"So far I can help you. If you will follow me, not too closely lest we cause comment, I will bring you to her. I am supposing that you wish to see her alone, that what you have to tell her is a secret."

"It is a secret, mademoiselle."

"Follow me, then. And monsieur will do well to note if any one shows interest in our movements. We did not leave all intrigue and scandal behind us."

It was easy to follow her. She was a woman apart from all the other women about him, Barrington thought. Although he had only seen her masked he would know her again, he believed, no matter in how crowded a world of women he might meet her, no matter how long a time should pass before such a meeting. Obeying her, he glanced swiftly to right and left as he went. Eyes certainly turned to look after the woman, once or twice indeed she stopped to speak a few words to some friend, but Barrington could not discover that any one took the slightest notice of him.

A few paces separating them they crossed the great hall, and she leisurely passed into the corridor without. When Barrington stepped slowly into the corridor, he found that she had quickened her pace, and at the end of it she had paused a moment that he might see which way she turned. He followed more quickly, and found her in a small vestibule, part of the old chateau. A lamp was hanging from the corner of a wall, and on an oak settle were two or three lanterns with candles in them, such as a servant carries to guide his master or mistress on a dark night.

"Will monsieur light one from the lamp," she said hurriedly.

"I am to wait here while you fetch mademoiselle?" he asked. "Truly this is a secret place for delivering a message."

"Not too secret," she answered. "I am Mademoiselle St. Clair."

"You!"

The exclamation was a whispered one. A confusion of thoughts was in his brain. Already almost unconsciously he had laid the foundations of a dream fabric, and these were destroyed suddenly, burying him for a moment in the collapse.

"May I see monsieur unmasked?" she said.

Mechanically he removed the mask, and she looked into his face earnestly. She gave no sign whether she expected to recognize him, but it would seem that his face satisfied her, for she undid her mask and stood before him. She was a woman, and beauty must ever be the keenest weapon in woman's armory; there was a little glad triumph in her heart as she realized that this man bowed before her beauty. Barrington was startled that a mask could hide so much.

"Monsieur has been somewhat misled, it would seem, by his friend who was witty at my expense and inclined to exaggerate."

"I have been deceived, and I shall punish him for the lie," Barrington answered.

"I am at a loss to understand the deceit," she answered. "You have a message for me. I may find some explanation in it."

"Upon the roadside as I - " Barrington began, and then stopped. "Mademoiselle , forgive me, but such deceit makes a man suspicious. I was told to seek Mademoiselle St. Clair in a fat, ugly, simpering woman, and I find her in - in you. How can I be certain that you are Mademoiselle St. Clair?"

"I see your difficulty. Your doubt does not anger me. Let me think. Will it help you if I speak the name Lucien?"

"It seems convincing. Heaven grant, mademoiselle, that you are as honorable as you are beautiful. I must needs believe so and trust you. To you I can prove that I am an honest messenger," and Barrington tore from the lining of his coat a tiny packet of tissue paper. "I have to give you this little golden star, your gift to Lucien."

She took the packet with quick, trembling fingers, turned to the table, and by the light of the lantern unfolded the paper. With a little clink the star fell upon the table.

"This? This?" she said, starting back and pointing at it.

Barrington made a step forward at her sudden question, and then stood still, staring at the token.

It was no star of gold which lay in the circle of the lantern

light, but a common thing of iron, roughly made, rusted
and worthless.

CHAPTER V

THE WOOD END

Richard Barrington knew that he had fallen into some trap, the exact nature of it and the danger he could not know. After a pause, a long pause it seemed to Jeanne St. Clair, long enough for a villain to fashion a lying tale, he turned to her.

"It seems, mademoiselle, that I have been robbed as well as deceived."

"In spite of that," she said, pointing to the iron token, "I am inclined to listen to the message."

"Mademoiselle, I regret that I ever undertook to carry it. I had other business in hand, but an oath to a dead man was binding."

"A dead man? Lucien?"

"I know nothing of Lucien. For all I know he may already be making merry at my discomfiture. The dead man was one Rouzet, or so he told me, and he called himself your servant."

"He was Lucien's servant, a faithful one," she answered.

"At least he was faithful in some one's service since he died in it, and I can honor him for that even though he deceived me."

"You have told me so much you must tell me more," she said, a persuasive tone in her voice.

She must hear the story. Whether this man were honest or not she must make him speak. Whatever plot was on foot she must know it. To some one surely Lucien had given the gold star. Much must depend on her receiving the message he had sent with it.

"You must tell me," she repeated.

"And knowing far more than I do you may laugh at me for a simple gentleman easily fooled. Still, he is something of a hero who can stand being laughed at. Many years ago I had that from a countryman of yours, the Marquis de Lafayette. I was on my way to visit him in Paris, when this mission was thrust upon me."

Concisely but in every detail Barrington told her what had happened at Tremont, and explained how he had become acquainted with Monsieur le Comte at Beauvais. He made no attempt to conceal the fact that he had come to France to place himself at the disposal of Monsieur de Lafayette. If there were any risk in telling this woman so, he was rather relieved to have real danger to face instead of lying and intrigue; the one he might meet successfully, but he was no adept in battling with the other.

"You took the star from Rouzet's coat after he was dead you say, are you sure it was a gold star you took?"

"I made certain by looking at it."

"And you can thoroughly trust your servant?"

"As myself, mademoiselle."

"You have not told me your name," she said.

"Richard Barrington," he answered, and then he laughed a little. "Why I trust you, I do not know. I may be putting it into your power to do me a great deal of harm."

"If I have the power, I shall not use it," she answered.

There was a moment coming when she would have to decide whether these words constituted a promise given without reservation, or whether the promise were contingent on his being honest, as now she believed him to be.

"For that I thank you," he returned.

"And you have my thanks for coming to Beauvais. That you have been robbed only makes it clearer how bitter Lucien's enemies are. Have you any plan, Monsieur Barrington, by which I could reach Paris in safety?"

The question set his thoughts rushing into a new channel. He felt suddenly responsible for her, knew that to prevent her going even into the shadow of harm he was prepared to face any danger. It was not her beauty which influenced him, a moment ago he had been ready to despise it if she were a deceitful woman; something more subtle than her beauty appealed to him, herself, the revelation of herself which was in her question.

"It is impossible for you to go to Paris, mademoiselle. The crowd of refugees in this chateau is proof enough that the danger is too great. How any man, no matter what his need may be, could ask you to put yourself in such jeopardy, I cannot understand."

"Yet you undertook to bring the message to Beauvais. Was it in your mind to advise that no notice should be taken of it?"

"Indeed, mademoiselle, I thought of little beyond fulfilling the oath I had taken, and to go my way again as quickly as possible."

"The answer to the message must rest with me, Monsieur Barrington," she said, quietly. "It was not by my own will that I left Paris. I am not afraid to return. Will you help me?"

"Mademoiselle, I - "

"Please, Monsieur Barrington. It means life or death, perchance, to the man I love."

"Curse him for asking you to face such a danger."

"Hush, you cannot understand," she said, putting her hand upon his arm. "I know Lucien. From Beauvais you will journey to Paris. Will you let me go with you?"

"No. I will not help you to your destruction. I will carry whatever message you will to this man, but I will not do more."

"Then take this message: Jeanne St. Clair is on her way to Paris; she asked my escort, but since I would not give it she has found another. Tell him that, Monsieur Barrington."

"Have you no fear, mademoiselle?"

"For myself - none."

"Very well, I will try and see you safely into Paris. You will go most easily as a woman of the people, one who has some aristocrat enemy on whom she wishes to be avenged. Do you think you can play such a part?"

"I will do as you bid me."

"Hide your hair, mademoiselle; wear some hideous cloak which may do something to spoil your beauty. If you will go, I may be a safer escort than any other. I claim friendship with Monsieur de Lafayette, so I am for the people. Even if we cause suspicion they will hardly prevent our going to Paris. Your return - "

"We need not arrange for that now, monsieur. When will you start?"

"As soon as possible."

"To-morrow at dawn," she answered. "At the foot of the road leading up to Beauvais, you will see to your left a wood which ends abruptly as it approaches the valley down which we must go to the frontier. I have papers that shall help me to pass. I have always known that I should have to return to Paris. Amongst the trees at the end of the wood I will come to you to-morrow - at dawn."

"I and my servant will await you there, mademoiselle. At least two men shall do their utmost to protect you."

He picked up her mask which had fallen to the floor.

"Will you fasten it for me?" she said.

It was rather clumsily done. His fingers trembled a little as they touched her hair. He was very close to her; her personality, the faint perfume about her, took fast hold of him. What manner of man could this Lucien be who had won the love of such a woman as this?

He put on his own mask, and then taking up the lantern followed her back along the narrow stone passage. As she came to the corridor she stopped.

"Let me go alone," she said. "To-night we will not meet

again. To-morrow at dawn."

Barrington did not return to the ballroom, but after lingering in the great hall for a few minutes with a view of deceiving any one who might be watching his movements, he left the chateau. So far he had fulfilled his oath, but he had discharged it only to accept a much greater responsibility. To-morrow he would be riding towards Paris, the cavalier of a beautiful aristocrat. The position must be full of danger for him; truly it was thrust upon him against his will, yet there was an elasticity in his step as he went back to his lodgings which suggested compensations in the position. By a strange chain of circumstances, Jeanne St. Clair had come into his life; there was something added to the mere fact of living, whether of joy or pain he could not determine, but he was very sure that his outlook upon life could never be quite the same again. For good or ill this woman must influence him to some extent, she could never pass out of his life again, leaving him as he was before. There was a fresh wind blowing across the square of Beauvais, yet it was powerless to disperse the subtle perfume which lingered about him, which was an enfolding atmosphere, which must remain with him always. He told his tale to Seth in a short, direct manner, emphasizing no single point in it. The star had been stolen, when or how he did not attempt to guess. Monsieur le Comte had grossly deceived them, his purpose time would show. The woman was as far removed from his description as pole is from pole. He had delivered his message, but circumstances decreed that they could not return alone.

Seth listened to his young master, and made no comment until the tale was ended.

"She is a beautiful woman, then."

"Yes, I think that would be the world's opinion. It is not her beauty which has influenced me."

"Still, the future might have had less difficulty in it if a man had quarrelled with you to-night instead of a woman pleaded," Seth answered.

"True enough, but one cannot choose the difficulties he will face. We must take them as they come, and console ourselves with the reflection that there is a good purpose somewhere behind them."

"For all that, Master Richard, there are some who over-burden themselves with difficulties which do not concern them. It will be pleasant traveling with a pretty woman, but I fancy trouble is likely to ride in our company, too. They mostly go together, women and trouble; and the prettier the women are, the greater the trouble, that's my experience. There's just one question in my mind: on which side are we ranged - with the people or with the aristocrats?"

"With the people. Once this woman is in Paris, I - "

Seth looked at him, waiting for the completion of the sentence. It remained unfinished.

"A wise pause, Master Richard. Who can tell what may happen in Paris? Indeed, we may never reach Paris. At dawn, you said. That gives little time for rest. In these hills the sun gets up early."

Dim twilight was on all the plain, darkness in the wood, when Richard Barrington and Seth tied their horses to a tree and awaited the coming of Jeanne St. Clair at the wood end. Ever the first to catch the fire from the upcoming day, the summits of the great double mountain which domi-nated the country blushed a faint rose color which each instant glowed brighter and clearer, and then peak after peak was caught by the same rose flush, and light, like a gracious benediction, fell slowly into valley and gorge, while myriad shades of color pulsated into new life in earth and sky. The two men watched this magic beauty of the dawn in silence. So wondrous was it, so majestic, so far beyond the schemes and thoughts of insignificant man, that it was almost impossible not to see in it some portent, something of promise or warning. Even Seth, practical and farseeing as he was, forgot the actualities of life for a little space, while Richard's dreams took flight into that upper world of rosy flame and forgot the deep valleys, dark with difficulty and danger. This new day which was being born was perfect, with a beauty his eyes had never seen before; the woman he waited for was perfect, too, a revelation. She and the dawn filled his soul. They were more real than anything past, present, or to come, and his being sang a Te Deum of thanksgiving.

"She should be here," he said, turning to Seth and speaking in a hushed voice without knowing that he did so.

Seth laid his hand sharply upon his arm, and pointed through the trees to the road which came down to the plain from Beauvais. Four men were approaching, walking quickly and talking together. They came straight towards the end of the wood as men having a purpose.

"Quick! The horses!" said Barrington. "Draw back farther into the wood and let them pass."

Holding their horses, and hidden among the trees, they watched the men come to the spot where they had been a moment or two before. Here they stopped, looked round on every side and listened.

"They are looking for us," Seth whispered. "It may be the lady cannot come and has sent them to tell us so."

"Four of them!" Barrington said.

He did not move. These men were not lackeys, they were

gentlemen. Barrington wondered whether they had chosen this secluded spot to settle some private quarrel of last night's making.

"Scented danger and gone," said one.

Another shook his head and stared into the depths of the wood before him with such a keen pair of eyes that Barrington believed he must be seen.

"Not a man to run from danger," he said, "unless mademoiselle were strangely deceived."

The remark decided Barrington's course of action. He stepped forward followed by Seth, who tied up the horses again and then took up a position behind his master.

"Are you seeking me, gentlemen?"

"If your name be Monsieur Barrington," the man with the keen eyes answered.

"It is."

The four men bowed low and Barrington did the same.

"My companion thought we were too late," said the spokesman, "but I had a different opinion. We are four gentlemen devoted to Mademoiselle St. Clair, and she has charged us with a commission."

"You are very welcome unless you bring bad news," said Barrington.

"For you it may be," was the answer with a smile. "Mademoiselle will not need you to escort her to Paris."

Barrington had not sought such an honor. Until the

moment he had fastened her mask, touching her hair and touched by her personality, he would rather have been without the honor; now he was disappointed, angry. She had found another escort and despised him. She was as other women, unreliable, changeable, inconstant.

"You bring some proof that mademoiselle has entrusted you with this message."

"This," was the answer, and the man held up the little iron star.

"I am not greatly grieved to be relieved of such a responsibility, gentlemen," said Barrington, with a short laugh. "Perhaps you will tell mademoiselle so."

"Pardon, but monsieur hardly understands. For some purpose monsieur came to Beauvais with an attempt to deceive mademoiselle with this little iron trinket. It is not possible to let such a thing pass, and it is most undesirable that monsieur should be allowed to have the opportunity of again practicing such deceit. Mademoiselle listened to him, feigned to be satisfied with his explanation, in fact, met deceit with deceit. My opinion was that half a dozen lackeys should be sent to chastise monsieur, but mademoiselle decided otherwise. You were too good to die by a lackey's hand, she declared, therefore, monsieur, we are here."

"Four gentlemen for six lackeys!" laughed Barrington. "It is a strange computation of values."

"The methods are different," was the answer. "I think we do you too much honor, but mademoiselle has willed it. We have already arranged our order of precedence, and monsieur has the pleasure of first crossing swords with me. If his skill is greater than mine, then he will have the pleasure of meeting these other gentlemen. You have my word for honorable treatment, but it is necessary that the fight is to the death."

"And my servant here?"

The man shrugged his shoulders. Seth was beneath his consideration.

"There would have been fewer words with the lackeys' method, I presume," said Barrington. "I am not inclined to fight a duel."

"Monsieur is a little afraid."

"As you will."

"Afraid as well as being a liar and deceiver of women?"

"As much one as the other," Barrington answered carelessly.

"Then, monsieur, I am afraid we shall have to employ lackeys' methods."

"Now we come to level ground and understand each other," said Barrington. "There is no quarrel between us which a duel may settle. You are four men bound together to take my life if you can, but you shall not have the chance of taking it with a semblance of honesty by calling it a duel. You attack two travellers; if you can, rob them of what you will."

"That's better, Master Richard, I'm a poor hand at under-standing jargon of this kind, but I have an idea of how to deal with thieves and murderers."

"Be careful, Seth," Barrington whispered.

The attack was immediate and sharp, without ceremony,

and determined. Misunderstanding Barrington's attitude they were perhaps a little careless, believing him a coward at heart. Their methods, too, were rather those of the duelist than the fighter, and this gave Barrington and Seth some advantage. The keen-eyed man was as ready with his sword as with his tongue. He had been confident of saving his companions from soiling their blades had Richard consented to cross swords with him, and he advanced upon his enemy to bring the battle to a speedy conclusion. He even waved his companions aside, and it was with him Barrington had first to deal. Their blades were the first to speak, and in a moment the Frenchman knew that he had no mean swordsman to do with.

"This would have been keen pleasure had you been a gentleman," he said.

Barrington did not answer. He was armed for real warfare, his weapon was heavier than his opponent's and he took advantage of the fact. This was fighting, not dueling; and he beat the weapon down, snapping the blade near the hilt. The next moment the other Frenchman had engaged him fiercely.

With Seth there was even greater advantage. He was a servant and a lackey, and the punctilious gentlemen opposed to him were not inclined to cross swords with him. They looked to see him show fear, the very last thing in the world he was likely to do. Seth's arm was long and his method of fighting more or less his own, the most unceremonious, possibly, that these gentlemen had ever had to do with. Deeply cut in the wrist one man dropped his sword. In a moment Seth's foot was upon it, and as he turned to meet his other adversary he had taken a pistol from his pocket.

The Frenchman uttered an exclamation of surprise, and Seth laughed.

"If not the sword point, a bullet; either will serve," he said.

Then Seth was conscious of two things, one a certainty, the other imagination perhaps. Across his enemy's shoulder he caught sight of the road which led up to Beauvais, and down it came two men running towards the wood. After all, their opponents were to be six instead of four. This was certain. His master was separated from him by a few paces, and it seemed to Seth that he was being hard pressed. At any rate, if it were not so, the two men running towards them must turn the scale. Feigning a vigorous onslaught upon his opponent, who was already somewhat disconcerted, Seth deliberately fired at the man fighting his master, who fell backwards with a cry.

"Seth!" Richard exclaimed.

"Look! there are two more running to the attack. This is a time to waive ceremony and be gone. To horse, Master Richard!"

The keen-eyed man, who had been powerless being without a sword, now caught up the weapon which the fallen man had dropped.

"There's another pistol shot if you move," cried Seth, with one foot in the stirrup.

It is doubtful whether the threat would have stopped him, but the two men suddenly running towards him through the trees did. He knew them and they were not expected.

Barrington and Seth seized the opportunity, and putting spurs to their horses were riding towards the head of the valley which led down to the frontier. They broke into a gallop as soon as they reached the road, and for some time neither of them spoke.

"Had we waited the whole of Beauvais would have been upon us. All's fair in war."

"And in love, they say," Barrington added.

A low growl expressed Seth's opinion on this point.

"Right, Seth, right," was the bitter answer. "I have had my lesson, and enough of women for a lifetime. You have your wish. We ride alone to Paris."

The two men who entered the wood as Barrington and Seth rode out of it were lackeys, and ran to their master.

"Monsieur! Monsieur!"

"What is it?" he asked with an angry oath.

"Monsieur, there is some mistake. Mademoiselle St. Clair left Beauvais last night before the dance was over at the chateau."

CHAPTER VI

TWO PRODUCTS OF THE REVOLUTION

In the Rue Valette, a street of long memory, down which many students had passed dreaming, Calvin not least among them, there was a baker's shop at the corner of an alley. Students still walked the streets, and others, dreaming too, after a fashion, but not much of books. In these days there were other things to dream of. Life moved quickly, crowdedly, down the Rue Valette, and this baker's shop had gathered more than one crowd about it in recent days. Life and such a shop Were linked together, linked, too, with government. Give us bread, was one of the earliest cries in the Revolution. Is not bread, the baker's shop, the real center of all revolutions?

Behind this shop, entered by the alley, was a narrow courtyard, not too clean a depository for rubbish and broken articles, for refuse as well, which on hot days sent contamination into the air. A doorway, narrow and seldom closed, gave directly on to a stairway, and on the first landing, straight in front of the stairs, was a door always closed, usually locked, yet at a knock it would be immediately opened. Behind it two rooms adjoined, their windows looking into the court. The furniture was sparse and common, the walls were bare, no more than a worn rug was upon the floor, but on a hanging shelf there were books, and paper and pens were on a table pushed against the wall near the window. The lodging of a poor student, a descendant, and little altered, of generations of students' lodgings known in this city of Paris since it had first been recognized as the chief seat of learning in Europe.

The student himself sat at the table, a book opened before him. He was leaning back in his chair, thoughtfully, his mind partly fixed on what he had been reading, partly on other matters. He was not only a student, but a man of affairs besides. For most men the affairs would have closed the books permanently, they were sufficient, full enough of ambition and prospect, to do so, but Raymond Latour was not as other men. Life was a long business, not limited by the fiery upheaval which was shaking the foundations of social order. There was the afterwards, when the excitement would be burned out, when the loud orators and mad enthusiasts should find no occupation because none wished to hear them talk. The sudden tide sweeping them into prominence for a moment would assuredly destroy many and leave others stranded and useless, but for a few there was the realization of ambition. Those few must have power to grapple with their surroundings, brains to hold fast to the high position upon which the tide wave must fling them. Of these Raymond Latour would be. The determination was expressed in every feature, in the steel gray eyes, in the firm set mouth, in the square and powerful build of the man. Nature had given him inches above his fellows, muscles which made them courteous to him; and study had given him the power to use men. His ability was recognized and appreciated, his companions had thrust him into prominence, at the first somewhat against his will, but carried on the crest of the wave of popularity one easily becomes ambitious. He was of the Jacobins Club, almost as constant an attendant there as Robespierre himself, holding opinions that were not to be shaken. He was not of those who had thought the Jacobins slow and had massed themselves, with Danton and the Club of the Cordeliers, nor was he with the milder Lafayette and the Feuillants Club; he was no blind follower of any party, yet he was trusted without being thoroughly understood. It was difficult to decide which held the higher place with him, his country or his own interests. He could not have answered the question himself as he leaned back in his chair, a flood of thoughts rushing through his brain, one thought more prominent than the rest, destined perchance to absorb all others.

There were footsteps on the stairs without, and a knocking at the door. The visitor had swaggered up the Rue Valette, conscious that some turned to look at him as a man to be feared and respected, yet his manner changed as he passed through the alley, the swagger lessened with each step he mounted, and when Latour opened the door to him, the visitor was full of respect, almost cringing respect. Here was a strange caricature of equality!

"Welcome, Sabatier, I was thinking of you. What news?"

"The best. She has come. To-night she is a league from Paris at the tavern of the Lion d'Or on the Soisy road."

"Good news, indeed," Latour answered, and a flush came into his face as he turned away from his visitor as though to hide some weakness in his character. "How was it accomplished?"

"By Mercier turning first thief, then aristocrat, and playing each part so well that it seems to me he is now doubtful which he is. I have only just returned from the Lion d'Or."

"You saw her?"

"No, citizen. She is still in ignorance of her destination in Paris."

"She comes here to-morrow," said Latour, sharply, and his steel gray eyes were suddenly fixed on Sabatier as though they went straight to his soul with the penetration of a shoemaker's awl. "She is to be delivered to me, and you and the others had best forget that you have been engaged on any private mission."

"It is easy to serve Citizen Latour," Sabatier said.

"Spoken as a brother," was the answer. "It is advantageous to serve him as it would be dangerous to play him false, eh? Sabatier, my friend, most of us have some private revenge locked away in our hearts, the lack of opportunity alone prevents our satisfying it. In these times there is much opportunity, it is that alone which makes us seem more vindictive than men in more peaceable circumstances. Forget that you have helped me to mine, do not ask what form that revenge is to take. I may some day help you to yours and be as secret and reticent."

"I shall not forget the promise," Sabatier returned, and it was easy to see that he was pleased with the confidence placed in him.

"First thing in the morning get to the inn and tell Mercier and Dubois to bring her here. She must be made to understand that her safety depends upon it. They need tell her nothing more."

Sabatier had his hand upon the door to depart when Latour stopped him.

"What about the man who was robbed, this aristocrat you found at Tremont?"

"Safe in Beauvais, citizen, where he is likely to remain. I put fear into him at Tremont and he ran."

"He may come to Paris."

"Then he is easily dealt with," Sabatier answered, and

went out.

He was a friend of Citizen Latour, a trusted friend; his swagger was greater than ever as he went down the Rue Valette.

Half an hour later Raymond Latour passed along the street, avoiding publicity rather than courting it. He walked quickly until he came to the Rue St. Honore, when his pace slackened a little and he grew more thoughtful. His whole scheme was complete, and he reviewed every point of it to make certain there was no flaw in it. He became suddenly conscious of a man walking in front of him, one of many in the street yet distinct from them all. He was slight, so slight that he seemed tall, walked delicately, something feminine about him, a weak man, perhaps, whom strong men would despise; yet heads were turned to look after him, and a second glance found something definite and determined in the delicate walk, something feline. He went forward noticing none, straight forward, men of bigger bulk stepping out of his path. Latour, whose thoughts were of self just now, not of country, went more slowly still. He had no desire to overtake this man although he knew him well, and dawdled until he saw him enter a cabinet-maker's shop. All Paris knew that here Maximilian Robespierre had his lodging.

Latour quickened his pace and entered a house at the corner of a side street. Yes, his master, the Citizen Bruslart was in, was the answer to his inquiry, and the suspicion of a smile touched Latour's face at the man's hesitation. After waiting a few moments he was announced, and smiled again a little as he entered a room on the first floor, it was so unlike his own, even as the occupant was unlike him.

"You favor me by this visit," said Bruslart, rising to welcome his guest.

"You have not yet heard the reason of it."

If Latour expected his host to show any sign of anxiety he was disappointed, and it was the man's nature to respect courage even in an enemy. He hardly counted Bruslart as such, outwardly indeed they were friends. Had Lucien Bruslart been a coward he would hardly have occupied such an apartment as this and surrounded himself with so much luxury. There was danger in luxury, yet it was a part of the man, fitted him, was essential to him. He called himself citizen, sought the society of patriots, talked as loudly as any. He had talked to such purpose that, arrested and imprisoned as a dangerous aristocrat, he had been released and welcomed as a true son of Paris. For all this, he was an aristocrat to his finger tips, hated the very atmosphere of a true patriot, and washed their touch from his hands with disgust. His own interests were his paramount concern, he was clever enough to deceive friends and foes as it suited him; even Latour was doubtful how to place him. He was a handsome man, and had found that count for something even in Revolutionary Paris; he was a determined man, with wit, and that art of appearing to hide nothing. An aristocrat! By the misfortune of birth that was all. A patriot! It was a safe profession. Luxury! Why not?

"Is my country in need of my services?"

"Always; but this happens to be a private matter," Latour answered. "You have been in the Conciergerie, citizen."

"It is not very long since I was released," was the answer.

"Fear touched you in the Conciergerie."

"Narrow walls and uncertainty are unpleasant. You will know what I mean if you should ever be as unfortunate as I was."

"And a servant, fearful for your safety, fled to your friends for help. Is that so?"

"I have heard it since my release. He is a faithful fellow, and acted on his own initiative."

"Entirely?" asked Latour.

"Entirely. Let me be fair to him. I do not fear danger, citizen, but I have eyes to see its existence. It exists for honest men as well as others, and I have said to Rouzet, that was his name, 'If harm should come to me try and carry news to those who still love me in spite of the fact that I have turned patriot,' I even gave him a little gold trinket that it might be known his news was true."

"Since your release have you sent another messenger to prevent Mademoiselle St. Clair from coming to Paris?"

"She is coming to Paris!" Bruslart exclaimed, half rising.

"Have you taken any steps to prevent her doing so?" asked Latour.

"Do you suppose I would have called her here on my account? She is not a patriot. She would come to her death."

"That might be a way in which you could serve your country; a decoy to attract lovers and friends."

"Are you serious? Is this the meaning of your visit?"

"What is your answer to it?"

"Rather the guillotine, citizen. Is the answer short and definite enough?"

"Short enough and well spoken," said Latour, with a smile. "You will rejoice to hear that your messenger never reached mademoiselle."

For an instant Bruslart seemed surprised, but it was impossible to tell whether it was at the failure or at the fact that his visitor knew so much.

"If you can assure me this is true, I shall rejoice," he said. "I have been imprudent. It did not occur to me that she might come to Paris."

"A woman who loves will do much."

"If she loves. Women sometimes deceive themselves and us. But tell me how you are able to bring me this news."

"You were an aristocrat, citizen, therefore suspected and watched. Your servants were watched, too, and this man's movements were noted. He was followed out of Paris. He was caught upon the road and questioned. Some patriots have rough manners, as you know, and your servant was faithful, perchance showed fight. All I know for certain is that he is dead."

"Poor Rouzet," said Bruslart, covering his face with his hands for a moment. "Poor Rouzet, I believe his family has been attached to ours for some generations."

"And were more faithful than their masters, doubtless. No, citizen, the words do not refer to you, you are no longer an aristocrat," Latour went on quickly. "Still, a word of friendly advice, you talk too much like one. I understand, but the people are ignorant."

"Thank you for your advice. I must be myself whatever else I am."

"As a patriot it would be well to think no more of made-moiselle," Latour went on. "Such love is unnatural the people will affirm. Are there not women in Paris as beautiful? Find one to love and there will be proof of your patriotism."

"You take much interest in me," said Bruslart.

"Is there not a kind of friendship between us?" was the reply. "Were I Lucien Bruslart, I should leave Paris. I know a man who would do something to help him."

Bruslart looked at him steadily for a moment. "Again I thank you," he said quietly, "but, my friend, you are not the only man who is competent to prophesy in what direction things may turn. You have set yourself a goal to win, so have I. It would almost seem that you expect our aims to clash."

"Diable! Is that all you can see in good advice," said Latour. "I thought your wit went deeper."

"Need we quarrel?" said Bruslart.

"No; let us laugh at each other. In our different ways, doubtless, we shall both be satisfied."

Latour did not often laugh, but he laughed now as he turned to the door. The curtains over the archway leading to an inner room swayed outwards with the draught as he opened the door, and then seemed to draw back suddenly, as Latour said good-by, still laughing. The door was closed, the footsteps went quickly down the stairs, the curtains hung straight for a little space. Then they parted sharply, and a woman, holding them on either side of her, stood between them.

CHAPTER VII

A JEALOUS WOMAN

The archway archway into the inner room was behind Bruslart, but he did not turn as the curtains parted. He knew the woman was hidden in that room, she had gone there when Latour was announced; he knew that she must have overheard the conversation, that she would ask questions, but for the moment he was absorbed in Latour's news. That Rouzet had failed to reach Beauvais was a disaster he had not reckoned upon.

"Lucien!"

"My direct and opinionated friend has gone, Pauline, you may come out of hiding."

Still for a moment the woman stood there grasping the curtains, as though she would will the man to turn and look at her. She was angry, the flash in her eyes Was evidence of the fact, yet she was not unconscious of the picture she made at that moment. A woman is seldom angry enough to forget her beauty. Beautiful she certainly was, or Lucien Bruslart would have taken little interest in her. Beauty was as necessary to him as luxury, and in this case was even more dangerous. Here was another proof that he was no coward, or he would surely not have placed himself in the hands of Pauline Vaison. She was dark, her figure rather full, voluptuous yet perfect in contour. Her movements were quick, virile, full of life, seductive yet passionate. She was a beautiful young animal, her graces all unstudied, nature's gifts, a dangerous animal if roused, love concealing sharp claws ready to tear in pieces if love were spurned. Her personality might have raised her to power in the dissolute Court of the fifteenth Louis, even in this Paris of revolution she might play a part.

Letting the curtains fall together she came and faced Lucien, who looked at her and smiled.

"I heard all he said. I listened."

"Interesting, wasn't it?" Lucien answered. "It is a marvel to me how fast news travels, and how important unimportant things become. I shouldn't Wonder if he knows exactly what I have eaten to-day."

"Paris knows something of Latour," she answered. "He is not a man to waste his time over trifles."

"It certainly appears that he considers me of some consequence since he troubled to visit me."

"And you lied to him."

"My dear Pauline, you are imaginative. Kiss me. You are a delightful creature. I never spend an hour in your company but I discover some new grace in you."

Her kisses were not to be had when she was angry.

"You lied to him and you have deceived me," she said, still standing before him, her body erect, her hands clinched.

"It is not always advisable to speak the exact truth, you know that well enough, Pauline; but I have not deceived you. Does a man deceive the woman he really loves?"

"The lie and the deceit are one," she returned. "You sent for this other woman, this Mademoiselle St. Clair. It was not your servant's plan. Latour was a fool to believe you."

"Was he? My dear, wise Pauline, his point of view and yours are not the same. You are jealous, whereas he - "

"I stop at nothing when I am jealous," she said. "The sooner you discover that phase in my character the better for you, Lucien."

"I discovered that after I had known you ten minutes," laughed Lucien, "and I am not afraid. Shall I tell you why? I have not deceived you, nor have I any intention of doing so. This Latour is too inquisitive, and inquisitiveness is always asking for a lie. Latour got it and is quite satisfied. Mademoiselle Pauline Vaison is a woman, a woman in love, and just because she is so, is suspicious. All women in love are. So I have not told her all my plans. To complete them it was necessary to get Mademoiselle St. Clair to Paris, so I sent for her."

"You are in love with her. You - "

"She is rich," Bruslart answered. "Her fortune is in her own hands. Wait, Pauline. Had I wanted to marry her, what was to prevent my crossing the frontier when so many of my friends and acquaintances did? But I am in love with her fortune. If I am to make myself felt in Paris, if I am to do what I have set my heart to accomplish, money I must have. True, I am not penniless like some of our ragged patriotic comrades, but, believe me, power will eventually rest with the man who can scatter the most gold to the people. That man I am scheming to be."

"Therefore you would marry this woman," said Pauline.

"Therefore I would obtain part of her fortune."

"That is what I say; you would marry her."

"No, I had not thought of that," said Bruslart, carelessly.

"How, then, can you obtain it?"

"Once she is in Paris, there are many plans to choose from. I have not yet decided which one to take; but certainly it will not be marriage. She, too, is a woman in love, and such a woman will do much for a man. A few marks of a pen and I am rich, free to work towards my end, free to help Mademoiselle St. Clair to return to Beauvais. You say you heard all that Latour told me?"

"Everything."

"Then you heard his advice concerning marriage. Find a woman in Paris, as beautiful, more beautiful than this emigre aristocrat, a woman who is a patriot, a true daughter of France, marry her, prove yourself and see how the shouting crowds will welcome you. Latour might have known this part of my scheme, so aptly did he describe it. I have found the woman," and he stretched out his hand to her.

"Lucien!"

She let him draw her down beside him, his caress was returned with interest.

"Together, you and I are going to climb, Pauline. For me a high place in the government of France, not the short authority of a day; brains and money shall tell their tale. Citizen Bruslart shall be listened to and obeyed. Citizeness Bruslart shall become the rage of all Paris. Listen, Pauline. I have cast in my lot with the people, but I have something which the people have not, a line of ancestors who have ruled over those about them. Revolution always ends in a strong individual, who often proves a harder master than the one the revolution has torn from his place. I would be that man. Two things are necessary, money and you."

"And your messenger has failed to reach mademoiselle," she whispered.

"Another messenger may be found," he said, quietly. "Besides, it is just possible that Latour was lying, too."

"Perhaps you are right;" and then she jumped up excitedly, "I believe you are right. What then? Other men may be scheming for her wealth as well as you."

"And others besides Latour have spies in the city," Bruslart answered.

"You are wonderful, Lucien, wonderful, and I love you."

She threw herself into his arms with an abandon which, like all her other actions, was natural to her; and while he held her, proud of his conquest, not all Lucien's thoughts were of love. Could Pauline Vaison have looked into his soul, could she have seen the network of scheming which was in his mind, the chaotic character of many of these plans, crossing and contradicting one another, a caricature, as it were, of a man's whole existence in which good and evil join issue and rage and struggle for the mastery, even then she would not have understood. She might have found that one end was aimed at more constantly than any other - self, yet in the schemes of most men self plays the most prominent part, and is not always sordid and altogether despicable. She would not have understood her lover; he did not understand himself. He was a product of the Revolution, as were thousands of others walking the Paris streets, or busy with villainies in country places; character was complex by force of circumstances, which, under other conditions, might have been simple and straightforward.

With some a certain straightforwardness remained, not always directed to wrong ends. It was so in Lucien Bruslart. It was not easy for him to be a scoundrel, and self was not always master. Even with Pauline Vaison in his arms he thought of Jeanne St. Clair, and shuddered at the way he had spoken of her to this woman. What would happen if Jeanne came to Paris? For a moment the horrible possibilities seemed to paralyze every nerve and thought. He spoke no word, he did not cease his caressing, yet the woman suddenly released herself as though his train of thought exerted a subtle influence over her, and stood before him again, not angrily, yet with a look in her eyes which was a warning. So an animal looks when danger may be at hand.

"If you were to deceive me," she said, in a low voice, almost in a whisper, the sound of a hiss in it.

"Deceive you?"

It was not easily said, but a question only half comprehended, as when one is recalled from a reverie suddenly, or awakes from a dream at a touch.

"To deceive me would be hell for both of us, for all of us," said the woman.

He tried to laugh at her, but he could not even bring a smile to his lips at that moment.

Pauline caught his hand and pulled him to the window, opened it, and pointed.

"There. You know what I mean," she said.

The roar of Paris floated up to them, the daily toil, the noise of it, its bartering, its going and coming. Men and women must live, even in a revolution, and to live, work.

Underneath it all there was something unnatural, a murmur, a growl, the sound of an undertone, secret, cruel, deadly; yet the woman's pointing finger was all Lucien was conscious of just now.

"You know what I mean," she repeated.

He shook his head slightly, dubiously, for he partly guessed. In that direction was the Place de la Revolution.

"If this other woman should take my place, if you lied to me, I would have my revenge. It would be easy. She is an aristocrat. One word from me, and do you think you could save her? Yonder stands the guillotine," and she made a downward sweep of the arm. "It falls like that. You couldn't save her."

Lucien stood looking straight before him out of the window. Pauline still held his hand. She waited for him to speak, and when he did not, she shook his hand.

"Do you hear what I say?"

"Yes" and then?"

"Then, Lucien, I should have no rival. You would be mine. If not, if you turned from me for what I had done - God! That would be awful, but I would never forgive, never. I would speak again. I would tell them many things. Nothing should stop me. You should die too. That is how I love. Lucien, Lucien, never make me jealous like that."

She kissed his hand passionately, then held it close to her breast. He could feel her heart beat quickly with her excitement.

"That would put an end to all my scheming, wouldn't it?" he said , drawing her back and closing the window.

"Perhaps Latour would thank you."

"I wasn't thinking of Latour," and she clung to him and kissed him on the lips.

Into Lucien's complex thought Latour had come, not unnaturally, since this conversation. This exhibition of latent jealousy was the outcome of his visit. Without formulating any definite idea, he felt in a vague way that Latour's career was in some way bound up with his own. There was something in common between them, each had an interest for the other and in his concerns. Lucien did not understand why, but Latour might have found an answer to the question as he went back to the Rue Valette.

He was not sure whether Bruslart had spoken the truth, he did not much care, yet he felt a twinge of conscience. It troubled him because he had not much difficulty in salving his conscience as a rule. It was generally easy to make the ends justify the means. He had taken no notice of the swaying curtains as he left Bruslart. He never guessed that a woman stood behind them. There might have been no prick of conscience had he known of Pauline Vaison.

He entered the baker's shop in the Rue Valette. Behind the little counter, on which were a few loaves and pieces of bread, an old woman sat knitting.

"Will you give me the key of those rooms? I want to see that everything is prepared."

The old woman fumbled in her pocket and gave him the key without a word.

"She comes to-morrow," said Latour. "You will not fail to do as I have asked and look after her well."

"Never fear; she shall be a pretty bird in a pretty cage."

Latour paused as he reached the door. "She is a dear friend, no more nor less than that, and this is a nest, not a cage. Do you understand?"

The old woman nodded quickly, and when he had gone, chuckled. She had lived long in the world, knew men well, and the ways of them with women. There might be some things about Citizen Latour which set him apart from his fellows, but all men were the same concerning women.

Latour crossed the courtyard and went quickly up the stairs to the second floor. The rooms here corresponded with his own below, yet how different they were. Everything was fresh and dainty. Cheap, but pretty, curtains hung before the windows and about the alcove where the bed was. The furnishing was sufficient, not rich, yet showing taste in the choice; two or three inexpensive prints adorned the walls, and on the toilet table were candlesticks, a china tray, and some cut-glass bottles. The boards were polished, and here and there was a rug or strip of carpet; the paint was fresh and white - white was the color note throughout. Here was the greatest luxury possible to a shallow pocket, very different from Bruslart's room, yet with a character of its own. Latour had chosen everything in it with much thought and care. He had spent hours arranging and rearranging until his sense of the beautiful was satisfied. Now he altered the position of a rug, and touched a curtain by the bed to make it fall in more graceful folds. Then he sat down to survey his work as a whole.

Still there was the prick of conscience, not very sharp, indeed, and becoming less persistent as he argued with himself. The Raymond Latour of to-day was a different man from the old Raymond Latour, the poor student, the nobody. Was he not mounting the ladder rung by rung, higher and higher every day? He had been listened to in the Legislative Assembly, applauded; he was a man of mark in the Convention. He was still poor, and his ambition was not towards wealth. The road lay straight before him; it led to fame, he meant it also to lead to love. Give him love, and these little white rooms were all the kingdom he asked to reign in. Love, the only love that had ever touched him. He remembered its first coming. A restive horse, a young girl in a carriage and in danger. It was nothing to seize the horse, hold it, and quiet it; he had flushed and stammered when the girl had thanked him, all unconsciously casting the spell of her great beauty over him. Never again had he spoken to her. He was only a poor student, the child of simple folk in the country dead long ago; she was of noble birth, her home a palace, her beauty toasted at Versailles He saw her often, waiting to see her pass, and each day he thought of her, setting her on the high altar of his devotion. He knew that his must always be a silent worship, that she could never know it. Then suddenly had come the change, the tide of revolution. The people were the masters. He was of the people, of growing importance among them. The impossible became the possible. He had education, power he would have. Strong men have made their appeal to women, the world over, in every age. Why should not this woman love him? The very stars seemed to have fought for him. She would be here to-morrow, here in Paris, in danger; here, in these rooms, with no man so able to protect her as himself. He had spoken among his fellows and won applause, could he not speak to just one woman in the world and win love?

"This is a nest, not a cage," he murmured. "To-morrow, I shall speak with her to-morrow."

It must have been almost at this same moment that Pauline Vaison flung open the window and Lucien Bruslart looked in the direction of her pointing finger toward the Place de la Revolution.

CHAPTER VIII

ON THE SOISY ROAD

The Lion d'Or on the Soisy Road was well known to travelers. Here the last change of horses on the journey to Paris was usually made, or, as was often the case, a halt for the night and arrangement made for an early departure next morning. In these days it was no place of call for those who would leave the capital secretly. Patriots were inclined to congregate about the Lion d'Or and to ask awkward questions. Even in fustian garments nobility hides with difficulty from keen and suspicious eyes. For those traveling towards Paris, however, there was not such close scrutiny. If they were enemies of the state, Paris would deal with them. There were lynx-eyed men at the city barriers, and a multitude of spies in every street.

To-day three travelers had halted at the Lion d'Or, travel-stained, horses weary, going no farther until to-morrow. One of the three was a woman, a peasant woman wearing the tri-color cockade, who was needed in Paris to give evidence against an aristocrat. That was good news, and better still, her fellow-travelers were undoubtedly true patriots and had the will and the wherewithal to pay for wine. There was no need to trouble the woman with questions. She might be left alone to gloat over her revenge, while patriots made merry over their drinking.

She was alone, in a poor room for a guest, one of the poorest in the inn, but good enough for a peasant woman.

Her companions had shown her the advisability of choosing this room rather than another. She would be undisturbed here after her frugal meal, except by her companions perchance, and she had thrown back her rough cloak, showing fustian garments beneath, yet she was a strange peasant woman surely. Hands and face were stained a little, as though from exposure to sun and weather, but underneath the skin was smooth. Exposure had cut no lines in the face, labor had not hardened the hands. At the inn door her form had seemed a little bent, but alone in this room she stood straight as an arrow.

One of her companions entered presently. Citizen Mercier he called himself; a hateful name handle, he explained, but necessary for their safety. He wore the tri-color, too, and plumed himself that he passed for as good a patriot as any. He closed the door carefully.

"So far we have managed well, mademoiselle. I have found a friend here who will ride into Paris and bring us word in the morning how we can most safely enter the city. We must be a little patient."

"Did he know anything of Lucien Bruslart?"

"I did not ask. It was difficult to get a moment to whisper to each other. And I will not stay with you. It would not be wise to take too much interest in a peasant woman," and he smiled and shrugged his shoulders.

Jeanne St. Clair continued to stare at the door after he had gone. Her thoughts followed him as he went down the stairs to join his companions and take his share of the wine. Lucien had chosen a strange messenger, a friend Monsieur Mercier had called himself, yet Jeanne had never known him nor heard of him before. He puzzled her. Loneliness, and the circumstances in which she was placed, naturally made her thoughtful, and it was easy to be suspicious.

Truly, Monsieur Mercier had proved himself a friend, full of ideas, full of resource, for danger had threatened them more than once upon the long and tedious journey from Beauvais. They had been obliged to halt at strange taverns, and there had been many delays. Now they were within a few miles of Paris - of Lucien. Yes, Monsieur Mercier had proved himself a friend, and yet, had it been possible, she would sooner have called another man friend, a man who was her enemy. How, easily she had believed him! Richard Barrington. She spoke the name aloud, but not easily, trying to say it exactly as he had done, and the deliberation which she gave to each syllable made the name sound pleasant. She had not thought him a scoundrel when he fastened her mask for her. She had been most easily deceived, taken in by an absurd story.

The truth had come quickly. Richard Barrington could hardly have left the chateau when a man whispered Lucien's name in Jeanne's ear. She did not trouble to take this man into the chamber in the round tower, but she led him aside where he could talk without fear of being overheard. This was some trick, but she must hear what he had to say, her safety to-morrow might depend upon it.

Monsieur Mercier introduced himself as a friend of Lucien's, and quickly told his story. Lucien was in danger, grave danger, and mademoiselle ought to know. For her Paris did not hold such danger as it did for most aristocrats; it was well known that she had been good to the poor; she would certainly be able to help Lucien. Mademoiselle knew Rouzet, Lucien's servant; he had started for Beauvais taking with him a little gold star which mademoiselle had given to Lucien. Not an hour afterwards it was discovered that there were others, enemies, anxious to get mademoiselle to Paris. Rouzet had been followed. Mercier, with a friend, had immediately ridden after him, only, alas! to find him dead upon the roadside and the star gone. They continued their journey toward Beauvais, with only one clew to the

scoundrel who had murdered and robbed the faithful
Rouzet. He was not a Frenchman. Even now Mercier did
not know his name, but he and his friend had distanced the
foreigner and his companion on the road and arrived first
in Beauvais. Lodgings were scarce owing to the ball, and
Mercier had waited for the villains, had taken them to a
lodging next his own, nothing more than adjoining cock-
lofts, but with this advantage, that part of the woodwork
dividing them could be easily removed. An invitation to
wine (carefully drugged) had followed, and during the
night the golden star was retrieved from the lining of the
thief's coat; and lest he should discover the loss too soon,
and so hamper any plan which it was advisable to make, a
rough-cut iron star was left in its place. Here was the gold
trinket, and glancing round to make certain no one was
watching, Mercier had put it into her open hand.

This tale must be the truth. She had made no mention of
Barrington, how could this man know of the iron cross
unless his tale were true? Richard Barrington had declared
he knew nothing of Lucien, but Mercier knew everything
about him and much about her, too. She would not believe
him until she had questioned him closely. As Mercier
frankly answered her, she understood with how improbable
a tale Barrington had deceived her. Mercier was quick with
advice. He knew that Madame la Marquise had no great
affection for his friend Lucien. This other man might
discover the trick played upon him and frustrate them. A
hundred things might prevent mademoiselle from leaving
the chateau if she delayed. To-night Beauvais was crowded,
it would be easy for her to go, and Jeanne had consented to
start in an hour.

She was proud, a daughter of a proud race. The nobility
were suffering many things at the hands of the people. This
fellow Barrington should be punished. Retaliation was
justifiable. There was not a man in the chateau of Beauvais
who would not stand her champion. She sought out the

Vicomte de Montbard, told him that this foreigner had come to her with a lying message from friends of hers in Paris. She had met deceit with deceit, and at dawn he was to wait for her at the wood end.

"Mademoiselle, lackeys shall beat the life out of him," was the answer.

"No, not that way. Go to him yourself, challenge him. If underneath his villainy there are concealed the instincts of a gentleman, let him have the chance of dying like one. But go with one or two others, prepared for treachery. He may be a scoundrel to the very core of his heart."

"Believe me, mademoiselle, you treat him far too courteously."

"Monsieur le Vicomte, he has touched me as an equal. I believed him to be a man of honor. Let him so far profit by my mistake, and be punished as I suggest."

"You shall be obeyed, mademoiselle. To-morrow I will do myself the honor of visiting you to tell you how he met his punishment - his death."

It was not boastfully said. The Vicomte was one of the most accomplished swordsmen in France.

Within an hour Jeanne St. Clair had left Beauvais.

All this came back to her most vividly as she sat alone in that upper room of the Lion d'Or. In what manner had Richard Barrington taken his punishment? She despised him for his mean deceit; by her direction he had been punished; yet with the knowledge that he was a scoundrel came the conviction that he was a brave man. The scene in that round chamber took shape again. It was curious how completely she remembered his attitude, his words, his manner, his looks; and not these only, but also the something new in her life, the awakening of an interest that she had never before experienced. It was not his mission which aroused it, it was not the man himself; it was only that, coincident with his coming, some secret chamber of her soul had been unlocked, and in it were stored new, dreams, new thoughts, new ambitions. They were added to the old, not given in exchange for them, but they had helped her to appreciate the man's position when he found the star was iron instead of gold, they had helped her to believe his tale. Her short interview with this man had suddenly widened her view of life, the horizon of her existence had expanded into a wider circle; this expansion remained, although the man had deceived her. In spite of that deceit there was something in this Richard Barrington to admire, and she was glad she had demanded that his punishment should be administered by gentlemen, not by lackeys. Certainly he was not a coward, and no doubt he had met his death as a brave man should. This train of thought was repeated over and over again, and always there came a moment when out of vacancy the man's face seemed to turn to her and their eyes met. She had not the power to look away. There was something he would compel her to understand, yet for a long while she could not. Then suddenly she knew. This surely was a vision. The spirit of the dead man had come to her. Why? Jeanne muttered a prayer, and with the prayer came a question: had she been justified in sending this man to his death?

When the vision finally passed from her she could not tell; whether she had fallen asleep in her chair she could not tell; but coming to full consciousness that she was alone in a mean room of a tavern on the Soisy road, the question still hammered in her brain as though it would force an answer from her. Was it only her loneliness and the shadows creeping into the room which brought doubts crowding into her mind? This friend of Lucien's, this Monsieur Mercier, what real guarantee had she of his honesty? He had brought her the gold star. It seemed a sufficient answer, but doubts are subtle and have many arguments. Why should she believe his story rather than Barrington's? Might not Mercier have been the thief? They were within a few miles of Paris. They had arrived at the Lion d'Or early in the day, why had they not pressed on to Paris? Their safety demanded patience, Mercier had said. Was this true? Was this the real reason for the delay?

The shadows increased, even the corners of this narrow room grew dim and dark. There was the sound of distant laughter, loud, coarse, raucous, many voices talking together, a shouted oath the only word distinguishable. Was this place, crowded with so-called patriots, safer for her than Paris? She started to her feet, suddenly urged to action. What was Monsieur Mercier doing?

She crossed the room and opened her door quietly. The passage without was dark save for a blur of light at the end where the top of the staircase was. Walking on tiptoe, she went toward this light. She would at least make an effort to discover how her companions were engaged.

From the top of the stairs she could see nothing, nor was it a safe place, for the light fell on her there. She crept down the stairs which were in darkness until she could see into the room from which the noise came. Even when bending down and looking through the banisters she could only see a part of the room. There were more visitors than chairs and benches, some sat on casks standing on end, and by way of applause at some witty sally or coarse joke, pounded the casks with their heels until the din was almost deafening. At a table upon which were many bottles, one or two of them broken, sat Monsieur Mercier and his comrade Dubois, both in the first stages of intoxication when men are pleased to have secrets and grow boastful.

"There's going to be good news for you, citizens," Mercier

hiccoughed. "I've done great things, and this good fellow has helped me."

Dubois smiled stupidly.

"Tell me, is there any more room in the prisons, or are they filled up with cursed aristocrats?"

Jeanne held her breath. Was Mercier playing a part for her greater security? How well he played it!

"There'll be room for you and your friends," laughed a man, "or they'll make room by cutting off a few heads. It's very easy."

"There's more demand for heads than supply," growled another. "There's some calling themselves patriots that might be spared, I say."

Drumming heels greeted this opinion.

"Very like," Mercier answered. "Shouldn't wonder if I could throw this bottle and hit one or two at this moment, but I'm thinking of emigres."

A savage growl was the answer.

"They're safe over the frontier, aren't they?" laughed Mercier. "They won't bring their heads to Paris to pleasure Madame Guillotine, will they? No," cried Mercier, clasping a bottle by the neck and striking the table with it so that it smashed and the red wine ran like blood. "No, they think they're safer where they are. The only way is to fetch them back. Lie to them, cheat them until we get them in France. Then - "

He slapped his hands onto the table, into the spilled wine, then held them up and laughed as the drops fell from his finger ends. His meaning was clear.

"Bring them back, Citizen Mercier, and you'll be the first man in Paris," said one.

"That's what I am doing. I've been to Beauvais, playing the aristocrat, and doing it so well that one cursed head is already being carried to Paris by its owner, and others will follow."

Jeanne crouched on the stairs, holding her breath.

"Long live Mercier!" came the cry.

There was an instant's silence, then a thud as a man jumped from a cask, overturning it as he did so.

"The woman upstairs! The peasant woman! There are plenty of heads in Paris. Why not to-night, here, outside the Lion d'Or? Madame Guillotine is not the only method for aristocrats."

There was a shout of acclamation, a sudden rush to the room door. A man staggering with the drink in him, fell upon the threshold, bringing two or three companions down with him.

"Stop!" Mercier cried, suddenly sober, it seemed. "She's a peasant, my witness against an aristocrat. I'll shoot the first man who goes to her."

This was dangerous acting surely.

Jeanne had started back as the rush was made. Should she make an attempt to reach the inn door and flee into the night, or rush to her room and lock herself in? Her room, it was safer. They would fight among themselves, whether she was to be disturbed or not. Locked in her room she would at least have a moment for thought. The decision came too late. She had not seen any one reach the stairs, but even as she turned a man was beside her - touching her.

CHAPTER IX

THE MAN ON THE STAIRS

For those wishing to leave Paris in a hurry, the Lion d'Or was a dangerous place of call. The inn and its vigilant frequenters had achieved a name in these days. An orator, waxing enthusiastic on patriotism, had made mention of its doings in the Convention, and in villages remote from the capital they were talked of. The King and Queen would never have got as far as Varennes, it was said, had they been obliged to travel by the Soisy road.

For travelers going toward Paris there was less danger, aristocrats did not often make that journey. Monsieur Mercier appeared to have thought there was no danger at all, and halted for the night, but there were travelers on the road behind him who were more cautious. They made a wide detour by devious bypaths, and came at length to a lane which joined the Soisy road between the Lion d'Or and Paris. They had taken care to avoid other travelers as far as possible, and even now the sound of a horse upon the main road made them draw into the shelter of some trees and wait. Through the trees, only a few paces up the lane, they had a good view of the horseman as he came.

"Look, Seth!"

"Our swaggering friend of Tremont," was the answer. "There has been devil's work along this road perchance."

"Sabatier," murmured Barrington.

There was no doubt of it. He passed them at no greater distance than a stone's throw, and he was a man too marked in features to be mistaken. He went his way, unconscious of their presence, to carry his good news to the Rue Valette in Paris.

"There's something in that man's face which tells me that I shall quarrel with him some day," said Seth. "I can't help feeling that I shall live to see him a corpse."

"We must wait a little," said Barrington. "We must not run the risk of overtaking him."

It was in no way a reply to or a comment on Seth's remark, but rather the outcome of the recollection that Sabatier had said that all true patriots must needs meet with him in Paris. Naturally, Sabatier was closely associated in Barrington's mind with his self-imposed mission to Beauvais, and his unexpected presence here on the Soisy road set him speculating once more on the whole circumstances of his adventure. He had had enough of women to last him a lifetime, he had declared to Seth, and he meant it. Seth had smiled. His companion was not the first man who had said the same thing, and yet before half the year was out had been sighing for another woman's favor. Richard Barrington might hold to his conviction longer than that, but there are many half years in a lifetime, and the indefinite variety of women gave few men the chance of escape. For the present, Seth never doubted that his master had had his lesson, and was glad. There were periods in a man's life into which a woman should not enter, either in reality or in thought; they were but drags on the turning wheels of circumstance. This was such a period, and Seth let a great load of anxiety slip from him as the distance between them and Beauvais increased. Barrington's silence as they rode did not undeceive him; his master was not a man who talked for the sake of talking, yet from the moment they had driven spurs into their horses and dashed from the wood end, Barrington had hardly ceased to speculate on his adventure. A man does not easily forget a woman who has come to him as a revelation even though she deceive him. The sight of Sabatier, therefore, did not recall Jeanne St. Clair to his mind, she had hardly been absent from his thoughts for a moment, but set him speculating in another direction.

"How far do you suppose this inn, the Lion d'Or, is along the road yonder?" he asked suddenly.

"Not a mile," was the answer.

Barrington nodded thoughtfully. Seth's opinion agreed with his own.

"Sabatier, no doubt, came from there," he said after a pause.

"Probably. We were wise to miss it. It would not have been convenient to enter Paris in his company."

There was another pause of some duration.

"Has he been out hunting, stopping aristocrats?"

It was hardly a question, rather a speculation unconsciously put into words.

Seth shrugged his shoulders.

"It does not concern us. They may fully merit the hunting and deserve whatever fate they meet with. I am not in love with the patriots I have encountered, nor do I like the aristocrats I have seen any better. For my part I would as lief sail back to Virginia and let them fight out their own quarrel. A dog of breed has no cause to interfere in a fight between curs."

"I wonder whether we have passed mademoiselle and her escort upon the road," said Barrington.

"What's in your mind, Master Richard?" asked Seth, sharply.

"I have thought it strange that we did not overtake them."

"Better horses, or better knowledge of the country would account for that."

"Yes, but she may be at the Lion d'Or at this moment, and in the hands of men like Sabatier."

There was no need for Seth to ask questions. The burden of anxiety which had slipped from him was suddenly at his feet again and he took it up reluctantly. Barrington understood.

"I cannot go on leaving her in such hands," he said. "Think what it may mean. We know something of Sabatier."

Seth nodded, but with no encouragement. Had he known more of Jacques Sabatier, could he have seen the heap of ashes which had once been the inn at Tremont and known what was hidden beneath them, his attitude would have been different.

"There may be much to excuse her for not believing in me," Barrington went on. "We know only a little of the story. We may have been the bearers of a lying message. With her knowledge of facts, every word I uttered may only have convicted me of greater villainy. We have hardly been just, Seth."

"I can find no excuse for her sending us to the wood."

"I can, Seth. Such a scoundrel as she may have thought me was not fit to live. More than her own safety was at stake."

"Well, Master Richard?"

"I am going to the Lion d'Or."

Seth moved his shoulders, it was not a shrug, but as though he would get the burden he carried into as easy a position as possible.

"We are hardly likely to meet with such good luck a second time. We escaped from the wood end, but"

"There is no trap set for us this time," Barrington said. "She may be in no need of help, in that case we ride on to Paris, and she will be none the wiser. The plan is simple. We stay here till dark. I shall go back on foot, you will wait for me here with the horses. An hour should suffice. If she is in danger I must do what I can to help her. It is impossible to say what action I shall take, but wait here for me, Seth, all night. If I do not return by the morning, ride into Paris, inquire for Monsieur de Lafayette, and tell him what has happened."

"Let me come with you, Master Richard. We could tether the horses here. It is most unlikely they would be found."

"One man may go unnoticed where two could not," Barrington returned. "You must remain here, Seth."

There was a point beyond which Seth never ventured to argue, not quickly reached, as a rule, for Richard valued his companion's opinion and was ready to listen, but on this occasion it came almost at once. Seth looked into his face, saw the fixed purpose in his eyes and the sudden set of the determined mouth, and said no more. They talked presently of other things, but not a word of the business in hand until it was dark, and Barrington suddenly rose from the Stump of a tree on which he was seated.

"You quite understand, Seth."

"Yes. I shall let the sun get well up before I start for Paris."

"I hope we shall start together," said Richard, holding out his hand.

"Good fortune," said Seth, as their hands were grasped for a moment. Then Richard passed into the lane and turned along the Soisy road in the direction of the Lion d'Or.

The inn and its outbuildings stood back from the road, and isolated. The village was beyond it, hidden by a turn in the road. Two or three wooden tables stood on the space before the door, used no doubt on balmy summer evenings, but deserted to-night. The sound of laughter and much talking came to Richard as he approached, and he stood for a moment under a tree by the roadside to look at the front of the building, at the windows through which the sound of merrymaking came, and at the windows above which showed no light. Crossing the road, he found a gap in the hedge and went round to look at the back of the house. There was a garden, mostly of vegetables and not ill kept, a low, wooden fence, broken down in one place, enclosing it from the field in which he stood. A dim light came from two windows on the ground floor, but above every window was dark. If Mademoiselle St. Clair were there she must be without lamp or candle, or the windows must be closely shuttered. He took careful note of the back of the house and how the road lay in regard to it, for there was no knowing what difficulties the next few minutes might bring. Then he went back to the front of the house, and approaching quietly, looked in at the window across which the curtains were only partially drawn. He was prepared for any eventuality, and his hand in the pocket of his coat held his pistol, but he was startled at what he saw. Facing him sat Monsieur le Comte and his friend. These men had probably robbed him of the gold star, Seth was of the same opinion; certainly they had done their utmost to prevent his finding mademoiselle at the ball. Were they aristocrats? If so, they were playing with fire among this crowd of savage-looking patriots.

Monsieur le Comte was drunk, or feigning to be, and Barrington saw him take up the wine bottle and smash it on the table, and heard him declare that the only way to get the emigres into their power was to lie to them and cheat them. He stayed to hear no more. Surely this man's presence there, and his words, meant that he had lied to some purpose, meant that Mademoiselle St. Clair was in the inn. Her danger was great, for there was no doubt about the savage temper of the crowd in that room.

The door stood open, there was no one in the entrance, and Barrington slipped in.

"The woman upstairs! The peasant woman!" These were the words that greeted him. Horrible in their suggestion, they were a guide to him. He was upon the dark staircase when the rush from the room came, and the man fell upon the threshold. He drew back to the wall lest he should be seen, and touched some one. In a moment, for his own safety, he had grasped the arm beside him and then, as he realized that it was a woman he held, put his hand quickly over her mouth to prevent her crying out. He could not see her clearly, close as she was to him, but touch brought conviction.

"For your life, silence!" he whispered.

Mercier's threat to shoot the first man who attempted to go

to the woman upstairs had its effect, no one was inclined to run the risk, yet several remained about the doorway instead of going back to their wine. Barrington quickly calculated all the chances. To leave by the inn door without being seen was impossible; another way must be found, and there was not a moment to lose. Directly the wine fumes overpowered the man who, for an instant, dominated the situation, these bloodthirsty wretches would certainly rush upon their prey. The intention was visible in their sullen faces.

"You know me, will you trust me?" he whispered. He still held her arm, his hand was still over her mouth.

She nodded her head.

"Go up, quietly," he said, releasing her.

Jeanne knew him. Few moments had passed since her arm had been gripped in the darkness, but she had lived a long time in them, and exactly when she realized who it was who touched her she did not know. It never occurred to her to think it strange that he should be alive. She did not ask herself whether she really trusted him. At least, he was different from those men below, and she obeyed him.

"Is there another staircase?" he asked when they were in the passage above.

"I do not know."

"There must be," he said, as though their dire necessity would compel one. "Walk close behind me and tread lightly."

Comparative silence had reigned, only the uneasy shuffling of feet and the chink of a glass, now the noise of voices broke out again, angry voices, raised in argument and quarrel. Each moment Barrington expected a rush up the stairs. If it came, what could he do?

He remembered the position of the windows through which a dim light had shown in the rear of the house. The kitchen was probably there. If another staircase existed it would be in the direction of the kitchen. He turned along a passage to the left, his hand stretched out before him, lest he should stumble in the darkness. The noise below was deadened here.

"Might we not climb from a window?" Jeanne whispered.

He had thought of it. He tried to remember whether a tree or roof of an outbuilding against any of the windows made this means of escape possible. He felt sure such a way did not exist. He might have dropped from one of the windows in safety, but the woman could not do so. He had not answered her question when there was a new sound close beside them, a heavy tread.

"Stand close to the wall," he said. "Keep near, and whatever happens do not speak."

Some one was coming up stairs which were close to them, and in the dark. Barrington strained his ears to locate the position. If they were not seen escape was possible.

A thin, straight line of light was suddenly drawn perpendicularly, just in front of him, and then a door was opened. A man, one of the inn servants, carrying a candle, stepped into the passage. The light fell directly on the figures standing by the wall. The man was startled. So sudden an encounter was unusual, and in these days the unusual was dangerous. Only a fraction of time was necessary to bring him to this conclusion, but in it, Barrington had also reached a conclusion equally definite. As the man opened his mouth to call out, his throat was seized in a viselike grip and only the ghost of a sound gurgled and was lost. The candle fell to the floor. The noise of its fall seemed horribly loud.

"Stamp out the light," Barrington said in a low tone.

Jeanne did so, obeying him promptly.

The man was a child in Barrington's hands. His efforts to unloose the gripping fingers at his throat were feeble and futile. He was borne backward and downward to the floor, a knee was upon his chest, bending and cracking his bones, and then came oblivion.

"Come," said Barrington.

She was close behind him and they went down the narrow stairs which had a bend in them. There was a door at the bottom which was open, a light beyond.

Pistol in hand, Barrington stepped quickly into the kitchen. It was empty. There was a door between the windows, and the next moment they were in the garden. He took the woman's hand, guiding her to the broken place in the wooden fence. There he paused, looking back and listening. There was no sound of an alarm yet, no cries to suggest that the fiends had rushed up the stairs to wreak their savagery on a defenseless woman. For a moment Barrington contemplated taking a horse from the stable, but he dared not run the risk of the delay. Chance must bring them the means of entering Paris in safety.

"We must run, mademoiselle. My servant is waiting for me."

She gathered her skirts about her.

"Give me your hand again - it will help you."

So they ran across the fields, making for the road and the clump of trees in the lane where Seth waited.

CHAPTER X

THE SAFETY OF MADEMOISELLE

The two men had sat for a long while facing each other, one doing all the talking, the other listening eagerly.

"Early this morning we turned the horses loose in a field and reached the barrier on foot," said Barrington. "We came in with the crowd, two abusive men quarreling with a market woman over some petty transaction regarding vegetables. I assure you, Monsieur de Lafayette, I never used such coarse language to a woman before in all my life. She played her part excellently. They laughed at us at the barrier, and we entered still quarreling. The rest was easy."

So he finished his long story, which had begun with his personal affairs in Virginia, and ended with the account of mademoiselle's flight from the Lion d'Or on the Soisy road.

Lafayette had listened without interrupting the narrative, now he rose slowly, and, crossing the room, looked down into the street.

"Is it possible that, in spite of your protestations, you are not pleased to see me?" Barrington asked, after a pause.

"Yes and no, an enigmatical answer, but the only true one I can give," said Lafayette, turning to his companion and putting both hands upon his shoulders. "The face is still the face of the boy I knew, and of whom I have thought often;

there is exactly that courage and daring in you which I then perceived would one day assert themselves. Richard Barrington has grown into just the kind of man I expected, and on that account I am delighted to see him. But there is no place for him in France, there is no work for an honorable volunteer; besides which, he has already managed to slip into a very maelstrom of danger, and for that reason I am sorry he has come."

"I find the Marquis de Lafayette much altered when I hear him speak in such a tone of despair."

Lafayette smiled, and gently pushed Richard into a chair.

"That I do not despair easily, as a rule, may convince you that I am not troubled without reason. The country is in the hands of fanatics, there is no foreseeing what the end may be. On every side of us are enemies, but we are our own worse foes. We are split into factions, fighting and disputing with one another; the very worst of us are gaining the predominant power, and those who have honestly striven to bring good out of evil have been driven to the wall and are struggling for their lives."

"Yet you say my sword is useless."

"As useless as the wooden toy weapon of a boy," was the answer. "To-day I am of no account. At any moment I am likely to be seized by some of the very men who have been my supporters, some trumped up charge preferred against me, and then - then forty-eight hours or less may suffice to close the account."

"You are in immediate danger?" asked Barrington.

"A condition I share with nearly every honest man in France. It is not known that I am in Paris. I am supposed to be with the army. I came secretly, having affairs to settle in

PERCY BREBNER

case of the worst happening. I may find it necessary to cross the frontier, as so many others have done, and after the part I have played am not likely to find much welcome."

"You know, monsieur, that I would do anything to help you."

"My dear Richard, I know that; but you must not overburden yourself. By bringing mademoiselle here you have not brought her into a place of safety. You should have persuaded her to stay in Beauvais."

"I did my best."

"And for the moment you have saved her. That is something. Now set your fertile brain to work, Richard, and scheme how to get her back to Beauvais again."

"But Bruslart - "

Lafayette silenced him with a look, as the door opened and Jeanne entered. She had washed the stains from her face, and changed her attire. Both men rose, and Lafayette placed a chair for her.

"You have braved so much, mademoiselle, that one does not fear to speak the truth to you," said the Marquis. "I have been explaining to Monsieur Barrington that this house is no safe refuge for you. Things have changed rapidly since you left Paris."

"I know. We have not been without news at Beauvais," said Jeanne.

"I would to God you had never been persuaded to leave so safe a retreat. I am aware, mademoiselle, that you dislike me. You would call me a renegade from my order. It is true. I had dreams of a reformed, a regenerated France; my strivings toward these dreams have ended in failure."

"I think I can refrain from disliking a man who has the courage of his opinions," said Jeanne, quietly. "Had I had my own way I should not have fled from Paris. We were too easily alarmed, and our fear placed a weapon in the hands of our enemies."

"At least, mademoiselle, accept the position now. The weapon is in the hands of the people, and they are using it. Those who would have held them in check are powerless. Be advised. Let me, with the help of my friend here, do my best to get you safely back to Beauvais. After last night's adventure, you will be looked for high and low. While the hunt in the city is keen, it may be easy to slip out unobser- ved. Every moment we delay the difficulty increases."

"Has not Monsieur Barrington informed you of my purpose in coming to Paris?"

"He has."

"Do you imagine I shall go without fulfilling that purpose? Monsieur de Lafayette, I thank you for your advice, which I know is honestly given. I thank you for having me here, even for so short a time, for I know the risks you run. I have many friends in Paris. Will you help me to reach one of them?"

"What friends?"

"Monsieur Normand."

"He has been in the Conciergerie some weeks, mademoiselle."

"Madame de Lentville, then."

"Also in prison," answered Lafayette. "She was caught in her endeavor to leave Paris less than a week ago."

"Monsieur Bersac," said Jeanne, but not speaking so readily.

"In heaven, mademoiselle. The dwellers in the suburbs beyond the Seine remembered that he once called them idlers, accused them of thriving on other men's industry. The people have a long memory."

"They killed him?"

"At the door of his own house. There is a lantern over it."

There was silence for some moments. The color, faded from Jeanne's face, and the tears came into her eyes. She forced them back with a great effort.

"There is the Vicomte de Morlieux," she said, suddenly.

"Alas, mademoiselle, only last night he was the center of a yelling mob which passed beneath these windows bearing him to the Temple. He is accused, I believe, of assisting the King's flight, and with showing courage when the Tuileries was attacked. Surely you understand your danger?"

Barrington had looked from one to the other as they spoke, admiring the woman's courage, wondering if it were necessary for Monsieur le Marquis to give her such precise information. He knew she was courageous, but was it wise to try her so severely as this?

"You have said the people remember," Jeanne said slowly; "they will recollect, then, that I have done something for the poor. I never thought to boast of my charity, but I will make capital out of it."

"Unfortunately, the people do not remember good works so easily," Lafayette answered. "Believe me, such faith is only grasping at a straw."

"My faith is strong. I shall find a lodging in Paris. I have been a market woman already; if necessary, I can sink to a lower level. Of my own will I shall not leave Paris again until I have contrived to set Lucien Bruslart free."

"He is not a prisoner, mademoiselle. I have already sent for him."

"Is that safe?" asked Barrington, quickly. "For you, I mean?"

"I think so. At any rate, it was necessary."

"Do you say he is not a prisoner?" said Jeanne.

"He may be here at any moment," said Lafayette.

"Have we been deceived?" Barrington exclaimed.

"I cannot tell," Lafayette answered. "It is true that Monsieur Bruslart was in the Conciergerie, but he speedily convinced the authorities that a mistake had been made. I believe he is considered a thorough patriot now."

Jeanne looked at Barrington, who met her gaze unflinchingly.

"I have told you all I know," he said quietly, answering the question in her eyes.

There was a silence which was broken by the heavy opening and closing of the street door.

"Doubtless that is Monsieur Bruslart," said Lafayette. "You

would wish to be alone with him, mademoiselle, so we will leave you for a little while. I can only hope that his advice will support mine. You may count on me to do all I can to secure your safety."

Barrington made no promise as he followed the Marquis from the room, but his eyes met Jeanne's again for a moment. A curious and sudden conviction came to her that she had at least one friend in Paris, who was able and willing to help her. She was encouraged and strengthened. For an instant she seemed to feel the grasp of his hand as she had done when she ran beside him last night.

Lucien Bruslart's brain had worked busily since the message reached him. He was glad Pauline had not been with him to hear it. She was such a jealous little termagant. He entered the room the moment after Lafayette and Barrington had left it by another door.

"Jeanne!"

"You sent for me, Lucien. I have come."

He bent his head, and taking her hand raised it to his lips. At that moment he had no thought for Pauline. Yet he felt there was something lacking in Jeanne's greeting. He would make her understand directly.

"How good of you!" he murmured. "Tell me of your journey. Last night, strangely enough, I heard of you, and since then have been in a fever of unrest."

"You heard of me! At the Lion d'Or?"

"Were you there? No, that is not what I heard. It was a strange place to lodge you in. Tell me everything."

"Tell me first why you sent for me," she answered. "It is

not so very long since I left Paris; yet, in some way, you have grown unfamiliar."

"It is this perhaps," and he laughed as he touched the tricolor which he wore. "You are unfamiliar too. We are both masquerading."

He told her the history of his imprisonment and of his release; he laughed as he explained that his safety lay in appearing to be a good patriot, and grew serious as he told her with lowered voice that, under this deceit, he was working night and day for the King, the imprisoned nobility, and for the emigres.

"I was in danger, Jeanne, grave danger, but I did not send for you. Do you imagine I would have brought you into peril on any pretext?"

"You promised to send for me if you were in danger. It was a compact."

"One that any man would feel himself justified in breaking. Rouzet, poor fellow, acted without my knowledge. He was from the first very fearful for my safety, and to ease his mind I showed him the trinket and told him of our compact. Directly I was arrested and taken to the Conciergerie he must have planned to come to Beauvais."

"But how did the trinket come into his possession? I thought you always wore it."

"I did, but in such a hurry were they to arrest me that they came while I was yet in bed. I had to dress with two men watching me, and I left the gold star in a drawer."

"And Rouzet found it?"

"How else could he have started to ride to Beauvais with

it?" said Lucien. "Truly, Jeanne, you seem as hard to convince as if you were really a market woman suspecting every purchaser of trying to get the better of her in a bargain."

"Forgive me, but I have come through such a maze of deceit that full belief is difficult," she answered. "Have you no friend named Mercier?"

"Half the ragged fellows passing in the street might claim friendship with me, so well do I play the part of patriot; but I am not conscious of having a friend of that name."

"There is such a man, and his knowledge of you is intimate. He brought me the gold star."

"Tell me the whole story, Jeanne. I may find a clew in it."

He listened to the tale, asking no questions. There was excitement in his face as she recounted her adventure at the Lion d'Or and her rescue by Barrington. It was simply told, yet dramatically, and Lucien's face flushed and paled. This beautiful woman had passed through this terrible experience because she loved him.

"They shall pay for it," he said, between his closed teeth, it was the only thought in his mind at the moment - "they shall pay, by Heaven! They shall."

His earnestness pleased her. This was the Lucien she knew.

"What was it you heard of me last night?" she asked.

"I was told that Rouzet had been watched and followed, that he had been killed on the high road, and the star stolen; that no message could possibly have reached you at Beauvais. It is evident there are others who have plotted to bring you into danger."

"And succeeded," she answered.

"You must be placed in safety without delay, Jeanne. These scoundrels will follow you hot-footed to Paris."

"Monsieur de Lafayette has advised me to return to Beauvais."

"Excellent advice, but impossible. A little while ago his name might have been a safeguard, but his day is over. He clings too persistently to a rock which the rising tide is covering. I have another plan. Tell me, is this man Barrington to be trusted?"

"Trusted!"

She spoke so quickly and certainly that Lucien started. He was inclined to resent such a tone used in the defense of another man.

"There is a wealth of eloquence in the word as you utter it, Jeanne."

"It is only his courage which has made this meeting possible," she said quietly.

"Many a man who is not to be trusted is full of courage," Lucien returned. "One gets skeptical in these days, and I have your safety to think of. You must let me form my own judgment of this man when I see him."

"I hear them coming now."

The Marquis and Barrington entered.

"I was surprised to hear you were in Paris, monsieur," said Bruslart to Lafayette.

"I am here, a private affair. I trust monsieur will forget he has seen me. Under the circumstances it seemed necessary to let you know that mademoiselle was here."

"I am greatly in your debt. You may certainly count on my forgetfulness."

"And you must pardon this interruption," said Lafayette, "but I am fearful of delay. Doubtless you agree with me, Monsieur Bruslart, that it would be best for mademoiselle to leave Paris at once."

"Yes, if such a thing were possible," Bruslart answered. "As I have told mademoiselle, her presence here is not of my contriving. Fearing for my safety, my servant started for Beauvais. He is dead, poor fellow, but he has unwillingly played into the hands of others. For some days at least I believe it would be most dangerous for mademoiselle to attempt to leave Paris. I have a safer plan. A friend I can trust implicitly will hide her for the time being. A couple of hours will suffice to make arrangements."

"I doubt whether this house is safe even for that two hours," answered Lafayette. "If there is a suspicion how mademoiselle was rescued, and it is hardly possible there should not be, my house is certain to be searched. My friend Barrington has mentioned my name since his arrival in France."

"I propose to take mademoiselle with me," Lucien answered. "She will be safe at my lodging until I have arranged with my friend."

"Are you sure of that?"

"Monsieur de Lafayette, do you think I would run the risk unless I were certain?"

"Your interest in mademoiselle is well known, Monsieur Bruslart, and we know that patriots do not always trust each other."

"Have you any other plan?" Bruslart asked.

"I should try and get out of Paris at once," Lafayette answered.

"And my services are at your disposal, monsieur," said Barrington.

"I thank you," Lucien returned, "not only for your proffered help, but for all you have done for this lady. Jeanne, which will you do: attempt to leave Paris or take my advice?"

"I am in your hands, Lucien," she said.

"Then we will go at once. There is a back entrance to this house, I believe, Monsieur de Lafayette. We will go that way if you will allow us. We are safest on foot, I think."

"I will show you the way," answered the Marquis.

"For the moment, Monsieur Barrington, I cannot use your services," said Bruslart; "but I may be only too glad to do so presently. Naturally you will be anxious to know that mademoiselle is in safety. Will you do me the honor to call upon me to-night?"

"The honor will be mine," Barrington answered.

"Come, Jeanne. Will you show us the way, monsieur?"

Lafayette went to the door, and Jeanne crossed the room to Barrington.

"I have no words to thank you," she said. "For what I did at Beauvais I humbly ask your pardon."

"I am always at your service, mademoiselle. Please believe this and use me in your need."

She was gone, and Barrington was alone, staring at the doorway through which she had passed. A tangle of thoughts was in his brain, one loose end uppermost. He had not moved when Lafayette returned.

"Is that man honest?" asked Barrington. It was the loose end in the tangle which prompted the question.

"Yes, surely. She is the woman he loves."

"Only God knows the villainy of some men."

Lafayette laid his hand on his arm.

"Friend Richard, can it be that he is not the only man who loves her?"

"She is a woman, and in Paris."

"Ah, yes, enough truly to cause any man anxiety," answered Lafayette. "Now I am going to send a trusted servant with you to find you a secure lodging. This house is no safe place for you either. I would we were looking out across Chesa- peake Bay together."

CHAPTER XI

"WAY FOR THE CURSED ARISTOCRAT!"

There were quiet streets in Paris down which noisy patriots seldom passed, houses into which the angry roar of revolution only came like a far-off echo. There were men and women who had no part in the upheaval, who had nothing to do either with the rabble or the nobility, who went about their business as they had always done, lamenting the hard times perchance, yet hoping for better. Some may have realized that in their indifference lay their safety, but to others such indifference came naturally; their own immediate affairs were all that concerned them. The rabble took no notice of them, they were too insignificant for the nobility to attempt to influence, and they criticised neither the doings of the Convention, nor the guillotine's work, knowing little of either.

In such a street, with a man named Fargeau, a tailor by trade, Barrington and Seth found a lodging. Fargeau had had the Marquis de Lafayette for a customer, and the money of this American, who could hardly have much interest in what was happening in Paris, would be useful.

"I cannot tell how long I may be in Paris," said Lafayette, at parting. "One must not prophesy about to-morrow. At present the neighborhood of my apartment must be dangerous to you. If chance brings me power again you know I shall think of you before any other."

"My duty seems to lie straight before me," Barrington returned.

"Yes, I understand, and if you are in trouble send for me if you can. You may depend on my doing all that a man can do. Count the cost of all your actions, for the price may be heavy. I have been full of advice this morning, let me advise you. To some in Paris you are a marked man, remember, so keep quiet for a while, and on the first opportunity get back to Virginia."

"You will not ask me to promise to act on your advice," Barrington returned with a smile.

"No," and then Lafayette looked earnestly into his face. "No, I do not expect you to act upon it. For most of us some woman is a curse or a blessing, and the utmost a man can do is to satisfy himself which she is. If she is worthy, I would not call that man friend who was not ready to risk all for her. God grant we both win through to more peaceful days."

Early in the afternoon Barrington went out, leaving Seth in the lodging. Seth suggested that he should be allowed to go with him.

"You must be free to work should I be caught and unable to act for myself," was the answer. "After to-night I shall be able to make more definite plans. Under certain circumstances there will be nothing to prevent us setting out upon our return journey to Virginia. Believe me, Seth, I have not yet fallen in love with Paris."

Seth watched him go, knowing that his resolution was not to be shaken, realizing, too, that there was reason in his argument.

"I couldn't understand any one being in love with Paris,"

he said to himself; "but there's a woman has Master Richard in her net. Love is a disease, the later caught, the worse it is. I wonder what his mother would have thought of this lady from Beauvais. And she doesn't care a handful of Indian corn for Master Richard as far as I can see; only makes use of him to get to another man. Falling in love with a woman of that kind seems a waste of good energy to me, but it's wonderful how many men have done it."

Richard Barrington had no intention of running into unnecessary danger. This man Mercier had no proof that he had helped Mademoiselle St. Clair to escape from the Lion d'Or. Paris was a big place, and he might never chance upon Jacques Sabatier. He had no intention of making any further use of Lafayette's name for the present, since it was evident that he might involve his friend in difficulty if he did. He was a Virginian gentleman in Paris privately. He was content to remain unknown if they would let him. If they grew inquisitive, his nationality should be in his favor, and the fact that he had come to offer his sword on the side of the people would be his safety. If he had made a few enemies by thwarting private plans, he had surely the power of making a thousand friends. So far his scheme was complete, but he was not thinking of it as he made his way toward the more central part of the city, taking care to appear as little of a stranger as possible. Was Lucien Bruslart to be trusted? This was the question he asked himself over and over again, finding no satisfactory answer. The reason which lay behind such a question could not be ignored. Any helpless woman would have appealed to him, he told himself, but the whole truth refused to be confined in such an argument. Jeanne St. Clair meant something more to him than this, but in this direction he refused to question himself further, except to condemn himself. Was he not viewing Lucien Bruslart through smoked glasses as it were? - an easy fault under the circumstances. Jeanne loved this man. No greater proof was needed than her journey to Paris for his sake. Barrington had done her a service for which he had been amply thanked. To-night Bruslart would inform him that Jeanne was safe, and thank him again for what he had done. There was an end of the business; and since his enthusiasm to help the people had somewhat evaporated - Jeanne's influence again, doubtless - why should he not return home? France held no place for him. It would be better not to see Jeanne again, more honorable, easier for him.

At a corner he stopped. Others had done the same. Coming up the street was a ragged, shouting mob. There were some armed with pikes who had made a vain attempt to keep the march orderly; others, flourishing sticks, danced and sang as they came; others, barely clad, ran to and fro like men half drunk, yelling ribald insults now at those who passed by, now at the world at large. Women with draggled skirts and dirty and disordered hair were in the crowd, shrieking joyous profanity, striking and fighting one another in their mad excitement. There were children, too, almost naked girls and boys, as ready with oath and obscenity as their elders, fair young faces and forms, some of them, debauched out of all that was childlike. Every fetid alley and filthy court near which this procession had passed had vomited its scum to swell the crowd. In the center of it rocked and swayed a coach. Hands were plenty to help the frightened horses, hands to push, hands to grip the spokes and make the wheels turn faster. The driver had no driving to do, so roared a song. The inmate of the coach might be dumb with fear, half dead with it, yet if he shrieked with terror, the cry of no single throat could rise above all this babel of sound.

"Way! Way for the cursed aristocrat!"

Children and women ran past Barrington shouting. One woman touched him with a long-nailed, dirty, scraggy hand.

"An aristocrat, citizen. Another head for La Guillotine," she cried, and then danced a step or two, laughing.

Barrington stood on tiptoe endeavoring to see the miserable passenger of the coach, but in vain. The men with pikes surrounded the vehicle, or the poor wretch's journey might have ended at the first lamp.

"It's a woman," said some one near him.

"Ay! a cursed aristocrat!" shouted a boy who heard. "Get in and ride with her," and the urchin sped onwards, shouting horrible suggestions.

"A woman!" Barrington muttered, and his frame stiffened as a man's will do when he thinks of action.

"Don't be a fool," said a voice in his ear, and a hand was laid upon his arm.

He turned to face a man who looked at him fixedly, continued to look at him until the crowd had passed, and others who had stopped to watch the procession had passed on about their business.

"You would have thrown your life away had I not stopped you," said the stranger.

"Perhaps. I hardly know."

"Yet it is not so rare a sight."

"At least I have not grown used to it," Barrington answered.

"That is difficult," said the man. "I have seen more of it than you, but I have learned to hide my feelings. The first time I was like you. Even now I clinch my teeth and remain inactive with difficulty. This tends to make us conspicuous, citizen. We must be either victims or executioners to be in the fashion. Some of us have friends, perhaps, who may easily chance to be victims."

"True."

"I have," said the man. "It is pleasant to meet one who has a kindred interest."

"I cannot claim so much as that," said Barrington.

"That sudden stiffening of yours told its tale," and the man smiled a little. "Had I not been convinced I hardly dared have said so much."

"Doubtless there was some danger," laughed Barrington, "but at least I am not a spy or an informer. The thought of a woman in such a crowd hurt me, citizen."

"Some time we might be of service to each other," the man returned. "It is good to have a friend one can trust in these days. Unless I am much mistaken, I can be of service to you. My way is the same as yours if you will allow it. There is a shop yonder where the wine is good and where, until that shouting crowd comes home again, we shall attract no notice."

How could this man be of service to him? For a moment he hesitated, scenting danger, but the next he had turned to walk with his new companion. He looked honest and might tell him something of value.

They entered the wine shop which was empty, and were served.

"Have you a toast, monsieur?"

"To the safety of that woman," said Barrington.

"I drink it. To the safety of a woman."

Barrington did not notice the slight difference in the toast; the words were hurriedly spoken and in a low tone.

"Do you know, monsieur, that only this morning an emigre returned to Paris disguised as a market woman?"

"What folly!" Barrington said. "Does she chance to be the friend you are interested in?"

"My friend is an emigre, therefore I am a little sorry for this one," was the answer. "I hear that careful search is being made for her. Such a search can hardly fail to be successful."

"She may have good friends."

"She has, I understand. One, at least, the man who helped her into Paris."

"He had better have helped her to keep out of it," Barrington returned, "and yet, she may have come with some high purpose and he has served her cleverly. Is it dangerous to drink to his good health, monsieur? for I like a man who is a man even though he be my enemy."

"There is no danger, I think," and the man drank. "She has another friend, too, one Lucien Bruslart."

"I have heard of him," said Barrington, quickly, "but surely he is of the people. I think I have heard him praised as an honest patriot."

"He is, yet he was an aristocrat."

"You speak as though you had little faith in him."

"No, no, you judge too hastily. I am of the people, yet, as you may have gathered, not wholly with the people. I take it that such is monsieur's position, too. Personally, I have not much faith in an aristocrat turned patriot, that is all."

"Nor I, monsieur; still, I know nothing of this Monsieur Bruslart, so can venture no opinion."

"You are a stranger in Paris?"

"Yes."

"Pardon, monsieur, I am not inquisitive. I only wish to prove myself friendly. Paris is somewhat dangerous for strangers."

"Even for those who take no interest in one side or the other?" asked Barrington.

"Most assuredly, for such men are likely to be on private business, and private business smacks of secrecy, and those who govern dislike all secrets except their own."

"I am not afraid. It is a habit rather than a virtue."

"I saw your fearlessness. It impressed me," the man answered, earnestly. "I saw also that others had noted you as well. It would perhaps be wise to remember that besides hunting for the woman who has come back to Paris, they are hunting for the man who helped her so successfully. Perhaps some of the men who were at the barriers this morning may remember him."

"What more probable?" said Barrington. "It may be that this man was not such a friend to the woman as we have imagined. He may have had sinister designs in bringing her into Paris."

The man put down his glass rather sharply. The idea evidently produced some effect upon him.

"I cannot believe that," he said.

"I do not like to think so," Barrington returned.

For a few moments they looked squarely into each other's faces. Then the man laid his hand upon the table, palm uppermost.

"Ah! It is certain we are kindred spirits, monsieur. We may have our own secrets, our interests may perhaps have points of antagonism, but we are both fearless. You are a man after my own heart. Will you take my hand?"

Barrington grasped his hand across the little table.

"Should we ever be enemies, let us remember this wine shop and this hand clasp. The recollection may help us both. For you there is danger, coming perhaps from the very quarter where you least expect it. I may be useful to you then. In the Rue Valette there is a baker's shop; if you inquire there for one, Raymond Latour, you shall find a welcome," and before Barrington could make any answer, he passed out into the street.

The man knew him, that was evident, knew that he had helped mademoiselle into Paris. Was he a friend or an enemy? He had warned him of danger, and his parting words had had something of the nature of a compact in them. What could bind this man to him in any way unless the emigre he was interested in was Mademoiselle St. Clair? Surely that was where the truth lay. To this man Latour she stood for something.

Barrington remained in the wine shop for some little time, carefully examining every point of his adventure. Certainly his movements would be watched; certainly this Raymond Latour might be useful to him. When he went into the street presently he looked carelessly to right and left, wondering which of the people in sight was bent on following him.

"Whatever their reward is to be they shall do something to earn it," he murmured, smiling, and turning into a side street he did his best to escape watchful eyes.

At the hour appointed he was at Monsieur Bruslart's door. The servant asked him several questions before he admitted that his master was in. Monsieur Bruslart was cautious. Was it possible that mademoiselle was still in the house? If Barrington forgot her danger for a moment as he thought of the delight it would be to him to see her again, was he very blameworthy?

The servant announced him.

Pale, dishevelled, trembling with excitement, Bruslart met him. A nervous hand gripped his arm.

"Monsieur' Barrington, you - "

"What is it? In Heaven's name what is it?"

"While I was gone, they came. Look at the room, still dirty with them, still reeking of them. They took her. Jeanne is a prisoner, and I - I am almost mad."

Barrington gasped as a man who receives a heavy blow. His hand fell on a chair-back to steady himself. He saw nothing but that filthy crowd, and that coach swaying in the midst of it. Jeanne was the woman within, and he had made no effort to save her.

CHAPTER XII

CITIZEN BRUSLART

The two men stared at each other with unseeing eyes, neither conscious, it would seem, of the other's presence. The circumstances called for prompt action, for swift decision, for keen and subtle energy, yet they were silent, helpless, looking into vacancy, and seeing visions.

Suddenly Lucien sat down and let his head fall upon his arms thrown out across the table, a personification of despair which might take the heart out of any observer. The action served, however, to bring. Barrington back into the present, to conserve his energies, to make him a man of action again. His frame stiffened, much as it had done that afternoon when the crowd with the coach in its midst had passed him. Then came the memory of the restraining hand laid on his arm. It acquired a new significance.

"Tell me the whole story," he said. "There is no time to lose."

"I was a fool. Lafayette was right. I ought never to have brought her here," wailed Bruslart, utter despair in his voice; and then, after a moment's pause, he went on with desperate energy as though he had a difficult confession to make and must tell it in a rush of words, or be afraid to tell it at all. "It took me more than two hours to arrange with my friend. He was out when I got there and I had to wait, then he was a long time discussing the best means of securing mademoiselle's safety, and how she could most easily be taken to his house unseen. Nearer four hours had passed than two when I returned to find Jeanne gone."

"Your friend had fooled you, keeping you out of the way."

"No, no. He did not know where Jeanne was. Some one must have seen her, recognized her when you came in at the barrier this morning perchance, followed her and betrayed her. They did not come asking for her, searching for her, but knowing that she was here. When the door was opened they rushed in, thrusting my servant aside, asking no questions. The reek of them is still in the room. What shall I do?"

Bruslart let his head again fall on his outstretched arms and sobs shook him. Such grief in a man is difficult to witness and remain unmoved, yet no expression of pity came into Barrington's face. He was a man of a different fiber altogether; his emotions were seldom shown, and deep though they really were, he passed for a hard man. Even in anger he was calm, calculating, a set face masking the truth; and in such a crisis as this, after the first staggering blow of it, his whole force was concentrated on action. Misery for what had happened was so much energy wasted, there was something to do and every faculty became focused upon the best means of doing it.

Barrington went to the table and laid his hand firmly on Bruslart's shoulder.

"This is no time for grieving over what cannot be undone; our business is to act. Let me understand the position, for I swear to you that I am ready to do all that a man can do. Since mademoiselle was taken in your house you are in danger, I suppose. They will remember that you are an aristocrat, too, and easily forget that you wear the outward signs of a patriot."

"Mademoiselle seems to have thought of that, and let them believe that she had rushed to my house for safety without my knowledge."

"It was like her," said Barrington. "She will be brave, no matter how sorely she is tried. To-day, monsieur, I saw a coach surrounded by a yelling crowd. It was a new sight to me and I stood to see it pass. It contained an aristocrat, a woman, they said, but I could not see the prisoner. The time corresponds; it may have been Mademoiselle St. Clair."

"Ah! If you had only known!"

"Indeed, monsieur, the fact that the prisoner was a woman, made me foolish enough to think of rushing into that filthy crowd single handed; had I imagined it was mademoiselle I certainly should have done so. And what could I have done, one man against a multitude? I should have been killed, and mademoiselle might have been torn to pieces by the fiends who surrounded her. They were in the mood for such work. Fortunately, a man beside me, seeing the intention in my face, laid a restraining hand upon me."

"Was he a friend?" Bruslart asked.

"Indeed, I think he proved himself one though he was a stranger. His name was Latour, he told me."

Barrington mentioned the name with set purpose. Over the wine the stranger had certainly expressed distrust of Lucien Bruslart, an aristocrat turned patriot. The question of Bruslart's honesty had been in Barrington's mind all day. It would be worth noting what effect the name had upon his companion.

"Latour? Raymond Latour?" said Bruslart, starting to his feet, more alert than he had yet been since Barrington had entered the room.

"The same. What do you know of him?"

"No more than all Paris knows, monsieur, but it is enough. He is a red republican, a leading man among the Jacobins, hand in glove with all who hate aristocrats. We need look no further for Jeanne's betrayer."

"I am not so certain of his hatred against all aristocrats," said Barrington, slowly.

"He has a tongue that would persuade the devil himself to believe in him," said Bruslart.

"And I do not think he knew who was in the coach," Barrington went on. "I have a reason for saying so, and I may find out the truth presently."

"You are a stranger in Paris, you cannot hope to be a match for Raymond Latour."

"At least there is work for me to do in this matter, and I shall not run needlessly into danger. Freedom is precious to us both, monsieur, at the present time, since we must use it to help mademoiselle. You pose as a leader of the people, therefore some authority you must have; tell me, what power have you to open the door of mademoiselle's prison?"

"Alas, none."

"Think, think. Patriotism, wrong headed though it may be, will clothe its enthusiasts with a kind of honor which cannot be bribed, but how many real patriots are there in Paris? Are the ragged and filthy men and women of the streets patriots? I warrant a fistful of gold thrown by the man they cursed would bring him a very hurricane of blessings."

"You do not understand the people, monsieur," answered Bruslart. "They would scramble for your gold and cry for more, but they would still curse you. The mob is king."

"There is the individual, monsieur," said Barrington. "Try a golden key on his cupidity. I do not mean on a man who is swaggering with new authority, but some jailer in the prison."

"It might be done," said Bruslart.

"It can. It must. You may use me as you will," Barrington returned. "I am ready to take any risk."

"Mademoiselle would certainly approve your loyalty."

"I feel that I am responsible for bringing her to Paris," Barrington answered. "I would risk my life to carry her safely back to Beauvais."

Bruslart looked at him keenly for a moment, then held out his hand.

"Monsieur, I am ungenerous, if not in words in my thoughts. It is not to be supposed that I should be the only man to be attracted by Mademoiselle St. Clair, yet I am a little jealous. You have had an opportunity of helping her that has not been given to me. You have been able to prove yourself in her eyes; I have not. Has not my folly been her ruin?"

"You have the opportunity now," said Barrington, whose hand was still clasped in Lucien's.

"You do not understand my meaning."

"Only that we pledge ourselves to release mademoiselle."

"And the real strength underlying this resolve? Is it not that we both love her?"

Barrington drew back a little, and felt the color tingle in his face. Since the moment he had first seen her this woman had hardly been absent from his thoughts, yet from the first he had known that she was pledged to another man, and therefore she was sacred. Deep down in his nature, set there perchance by some long-forgotten ancestor, cavalier in spirit, yet with puritan tendencies in thought, there was a stronger sense of right and wrong than is given to most men perhaps. As well might he allow himself to love another's wife, as to think of love for another man's promised wife. The standard of morality had been easy to keep, since, until now, love for neither wife nor maid had tempted him; but during the last two or three days the fierce testing fires had burned within him. It had been easy to think evil of the man who stood before him, easy to hope that there might be evil in him, so that Jeanne St. Clair being free because of this evil, he might have the right to win her if he could. Lucien Bruslart's quiet statement came like an accusation; it showed him in a moment that in one sense at any rate he had fallen before the temptation, for if he had not allowed himself to think of love, he had yielded to the mean wish that her lover might prove unworthy. It helped him also to rise superior to the temptation.

"I may have had ungenerous thoughts, too," he said, "but they have gone."

"And only love remains," Bruslart returned, the slight rise in his tone making the words a question rather than a statement.

"Your love, monsieur, my admiration and respect. These I certainly have for the lady who is to be your wife. Your love will hardly grudge me them."

"I believe I might have found a dangerous rival, were you not a man of honor," said Bruslart. "We understand each other better than we did this morning. Heavens! what a wealth of hours seem to have passed since then. We fight together for mademoiselle's safety. I will go at once to the Abbaye, that is the prison you think they were going to. And you, monsieur, what will you do?"

"I shall set my servant to watch Latour, and there are one or two others in this city whose movements will interest me."

"You must be careful of Latour."

"He will be wise to be careful of me too. There is some aristocrat Raymond Latour would do all in his power to help. That is a secret we may use against him if necessary."

"Did he tell you that?"

"We became friends over a bottle of wine."

"Ah, men boast and tell lies over their wine," Bruslart answered, "and for his own ends Latour can lie very convincingly. Will you come to me here to-morrow night? I may have accomplished something by then."

They left the house together, but parted in the street, Barrington returning to the house of Monsieur Fargeau to plan with Seth the close watching of Latour's movements, Bruslart going in the direction of the prison of the Abbaye.

Bruslart's pace was rapid for a short distance, then he went more slowly and thoughtfully; but there was no relapse into the despair in which Barrington had found him that evening. Contact with a strong man, and the compact made with him, had apparently restored his nerves, and no one knew better than he did how necessary it was to have every faculty in working order at the present moment. He had told Barrington that he was in no danger from the fact of mademoiselle having been arrested in his apartments, and if this were not quite true, he felt certain that he could evade the danger by presenting a bold front to it. The desire to convince himself that this was possible became stronger as he proceeded slowly, and opportunity to put his conviction to the test might easily be found.

"There would be no one at the prison to-night on whom I could make any useful impression," he said to himself. "I shall gain more by swaggering to the crowd."

He quickened his pace, but not in the direction of the prison. He turned into a side street, at the corner of which was a broken lamp bracket used for hanging a man not a week ago. He glanced up at it as he passed, recognizing perhaps that he was as a skater on thin ice, his safety entirely dependent upon his agility, as he made his way to the flare of light which came from a wine shop.

The place was full and noisy, but there was a sudden silence as he entered. He was well-known here, and every pair of eyes was fixed upon him keenly. That he bore the scrutiny without flinching proved him to be no coward. The attitude of the crowd in the wine shop was not reassuring. His task was to be more difficult than he imagined, and he rose to the occasion. With a careless nod intended to comprehend every one in the room, and as though he perceived nothing extraordinary in the manner of his reception, he crossed the room to a man who had suspended his game of cards to stare at him.

"Good evening, Citizen Sabatier; you can tell me something. Was that aristocrat taken to the Abbaye this afternoon or where?"

"To the Abbaye."

"I was going to the prison to ask, then thought I might save myself a journey by coming here on my way. Wine, landlord - the best, and in these days the best is bad. You were not at the taking of this aristocrat, Sabatier?" and as he asked the question Bruslart seated himself.

"No. I had other business."

"It is a pity. Had you been there the affair would have been conducted with more order."

"I was there, Citizen Bruslart," said a man, thrusting forward his head truculently. "What is there to complain of?"

Bruslart looked at him, then leaned toward Sabatier and said in an audible aside -

"A new friend? I do not seem to remember him."

"Citizen Boissin, a worthy man," said Sabatier, shortly. He knew that the men in the wine shop were likely to follow his lead, and he was at a loss to know how to treat Lucien Bruslart to-night.

"Ay, Boissin, that's my name, and he asks you what you have to complain of?"

"Much, very much, citizen. It is not enough that a cursed aristocrat uses my lodgings as a shelter while I am away from home, but a crowd of unauthorized persons invade it and break a cabinet for which I have a great affection. Maybe, since you were there, Citizen Boissin, you can tell me who broke my cabinet."

"Curse your cabinet!"

"Curse you for coming to my lodgings without an invitation," said Bruslart, quietly.

There was a shuffling of feet, a promise of quick and dangerous excitement, but Sabatier did not move, and Bruslart's eyes, as he quietly sipped his wine, looked over the rim of the glass at Boissin, who seemed confused and unable to bluster. There was a long pause which was broken by a man seated at another table.

"The breakage need not trouble you, Citizen Bruslart, your trouble will come when you have to explain how the aristocrat came to be in your lodgings."

"Whether she entered by the door, or climbed in at the window, I cannot say, since I was not at home," said Bruslart, with a smile. "My servant must answer that question. What I want to know is, who is this aristocrat?"

In a moment every eye was turned upon him. Jacques Sabatier smiled.

"I was going to the prison to ask that question," Bruslart went on. "She is a woman, that I have heard of, but no more. I am interested enough to wonder whether she was an acquaintance of mine in the past."

"An acquaintance!" and there was a chorus of laughter.

"It was Mademoiselle St. Clair," said Boissin.

Lucien Bruslart did not start at the mention of the name, not an eye fixed upon him could detect the slightest trembling in his hand as he raised the glass to his lips and slowly drank the wine which was in it. He knew perfectly well what a false move, or an ill-considered word, might mean to him. There was not a man in that company who did not hate the name of aristocrat, yet after their fashion, many of them had ties which they held sacred. The same man who could spend hours rejoicing in the bloodthirsty work of the guillotine would return home to kiss his wife, and play innocently with his children. Bruslart knew that to pity the aristocrat might be hardly more dangerous than to abuse the woman.

"Mademoiselle St. Clair. In the past she was more than an acquaintance," he said.

"She is your lover," said half a dozen voices together.

"She was," corrected Bruslart, quietly, "and therefore a little sentiment enters into the affair. I could almost wish it had been some other woman. That is natural, I think."

"Ay; and it explains why she took shelter in your lodgings," said Boissin.

"True, it does; and, so far as I remember, it is the only personal matter I have against her. I do not recall any other injury she has done me. I am afraid, citizens, she has some case against me, for I grew tired of her long ago."

"She does not believe that, nor do I, for that matter," said Boissin.

"What you believe is a matter of indifference to me, citizen," returned Bruslart, "and as for the woman - well, she is in the Abbaye. Not every man gets rid of his tiresome lovers as easily as I am likely to do. More wine, landlord. We'll drink long life to liberty and death to all aristocrats. And, Citizen Boissin, we must understand each other and become better friends. I accused you of entering my lodgings without invitation, now I invite you. Come when you will, you shall be welcome. And, in the meanwhile, if there is any good patriot here who is a carpenter, and can spare time for a job, there is money to be earned. He shall mend my cabinet."

CHAPTER XIII

THE BUSINESS OF RAYMOND LATOUR

The arrest of an aristocrat, or of some poor wretch who had no claim to the title, but served just as well for a victim, was a common enough occurrence. In the first panic there had been a rush for safety across the frontier, but there were many who remained, either not foreseeing how grave the danger would become, or bravely determining to face the trouble. Some, like Monsieur de Lafayette, true patriots at heart, had attempted to direct the trouble, and being caught in its cyclonic fury were at grips with death and disaster; some, like Lucien Bruslart, having themselves or their friends to serve, openly threw in their lot with the people, playing the while a double game which kept them walking on the extreme edge of a precipice; and there were others who, finding their bravery and honesty of no avail, realizing that it was now too late to escape out of the country, hid themselves in humble lodgings, or were concealed in the homes of faithful servants. There were patriots who were ready to howl death to all aristocrats, and yet gave shelter to some particular aristocrat who had treated them well in the past. Kindnesses little heeded at the time saved many a man in his hour of need.

To Richard Barrington that slowly moving coach, surrounded by a filthy, yelling mob, was a new and appalling thing; to Raymond Latour it was a very ordinary matter, a necessary evil that France might be thoroughly purged from its iniquity. When he laid his hand upon Barrington's arm, he had no idea who the prisoner in the coach was. Had he known, he might still have put out a restraining hand, realizing that to throw two lives away uselessly was folly, but in the wine shop afterward he would have treated his companion differently.

That morning he had waited patiently for the coming of Mademoiselle St. Clair. He had made a last inspection of the rooms he had hired, satisfying himself that there was nothing left undone which it was in his power to do for her. Then he had gone to his own room and tried to read during the interval of waiting. His patience was strained to the limit when, at noon, Mercier and Dubois arrived alone. He had expected them long before. The delay had almost prepared him to hear that his plans had been frustrated, yet the two men who had entered, afraid of his anger, were surprised at the calmness with which he listened to their story.

It was not all the truth. Mercier said nothing of the amount of wine he had drunk, nothing of his boasting. He described the men at the Lion d'Or as truculent, easily ready to take offense, difficult to persuade.

"They began by rejoicing that a market woman was on her way to Paris to give evidence against an aristocrat," Mercier said, "and then the devil prompted some man to speculate whether she might not be an aristocrat in disguise. They were for making certain, and if she were an aristocrat they would have hanged her in the inn yard. I had to threaten to shoot the first man who attempted to mount the stairs."

"And even then they only waited to get the better of us," said Dubois.

"They left the inn sulkily at last," Mercier went on, "but all night we kept guard upon the stairs, wasting precious hours as it happened."

"Go on," said Latour, quietly.

"Soon after dawn we were startled by a groan from the end of a passage, and we went to find a man lying there half dead. He had been badly handled, near where he lay was a door opening onto stairs which went down to the kitchens and the back entrance to the house. We went to mademoiselle's room and found that she had gone. How it had been accomplished neither Dubois nor I could tell, but we were both convinced that some of the men had stolen back after leaving the inn and had taken mademoiselle away, telling her some plausible tale to keep her silent. We roused the sleeping inn and searched it from cellar to garret. From the man lying in the passage we could get no coherent words, though we wasted good brandy on him. We went to the village, and were not satisfied until we had roused every man who had been at the Lion d'Or that night. More hours wasted. Then we went back to the inn and found the man revived somewhat. He declared that as he came to the top of the stairs a man and a woman met him. Before he could utter a cry the man seized him by the throat; he was choked and remembered nothing more. It was natural that our suspicions should turn to this fellow Barrington whom we had so easily outwitted at Beauvais. On this theory we asked ourselves which way he would be likely to take mademoiselle. It did not seem possible that they could enter Paris. We were at a loss what to do, and indeed wasted more time in searching the country in the neighborhood of the Lion d'Or for traces of the fugitives."

"You have certainly wasted much time," said Latour. "Tell me, what is this man Barrington like." He had already had a description from Jacques Sabatier, but a word-picture from another source might make the man clearer to him. Mercier's description was even better than Sabatier's.

"Did you tell this story of the Lion d'Or at the barrier?"

"No," Mercier answered. It was evidently the answer Latour wished to receive, and in a sense it was true. Mercier had not proclaimed at the barrier that he had been outwitted, and no one knew what business had taken him from Paris; but he had said that he believed an emigre in the disguise of a market woman had entered the city that morning. "What emigre?" he was asked. "Mademoiselle St. Clair," he had answered. The guard said nothing, no more inclined to confess to carelessness than Mercier was, and Mercier and Dubois had ridden on convinced that mademoiselle was not in Paris. At the barrier his remarks might have been taken for badinage, a sneer at the vigilance which was kept, had not the entrance of the quarreling market woman been remembered.

"If she is in Paris, we shall find her," said Latour.

"It is more likely she had ridden back to Beauvais," said Dubois. "If she is wise that is the way she has taken."

"Women in love are not always wise," said Latour.

"I am afraid, citizen, this unfortunate business has interfered with your plans. I am sorry. We had managed the whole affair so excellently." Mercier was so relieved to find Latour so calm that he was inclined to swagger.

"Most excellently," was the answer. "I am as far from having mademoiselle in my power as I was when you started."

"Citizen - "

"Is there need to say more?" Latour asked sharply. "I shall have other work for you presently; see that it is accomplished better. Did you meet Jacques Sabatier on the road this morning?"

"No, citizen. We have not seen him since he met us at the tavern yesterday and rode to Paris for your instructions. This morning we left the road several times to make sure the fugitives were not hidden in some shed or hollow. If he travelled to the Lion d'Or that is how we must have missed him."

"Come to me to-night at nine," he said, dismissing them. His anger was great, but it did not suit him to say more.

This was all Latour knew when he chanced upon Richard Barrington in the afternoon. He was thinking of mademoiselle when the noise of the approaching crowd reached him, and then he noticed the tall, strongly knit figure of the man just before him. A second glance convinced him that this was the American; therefore mademoiselle was in Paris. This was the man who had brought all his scheming to naught; his enemy, a daring and dangerous foe. He noted the expression on Barrington's face as the crowd went by, saw the intention in his eyes. In another moment his enemy might be destroyed, gashed with pikes, trampled under foot, yet Latour put out his hand and stopped him. Why? Latour could not see even his enemy throw his life away so uselessly. He hardly gave a thought to the wretched prisoner in the coach, but his interest was keen in the man who went with him to the wine shop. It was no mere phrase when he said he was a man after his own heart, he meant it. Their paths in life might be antagonistic, their ideals diametrically opposed, yet in both men there was purpose and determination, a struggle towards great achievement, a definite end to strive after. Circumstances might make them the deadliest of foes, but there was a strong and natural desire for friendship as they clasped hands.

"I could love that man," Latour mused as he went towards the Rue Valette afterwards. "Yet I must spy upon him and deceive him if I can. Mademoiselle is in Paris and he knows where she is hidden. He is Bruslart's friend, and Bruslart

I hate."

He climbed the stairs to his room to find Sabatier waiting for him on the landing.

"I have heard," said Latour, unlocking his door and entering the room with his visitor, "I have heard the whole story. The fools have been outwitted. I have just left this man Barrington."

"Citizen, I do not think you have heard the whole story."

Latour turned quickly. Something in the man's tone startled him.

"Mademoiselle was taken to the Abbaye prison this afternoon," said Sabatier.

A cry, a little cry almost like the whine of a small animal suddenly hurt, escaped from Latour's lips. His strength seemed to go out of him, and he sank into a chair by the table, his face pale, his hands trembling.

"Tell me," he said, his voice a whisper.

"I cannot say how suspicion first arose, but some one at the barrier must have started it. Whether it was a guess, or whether some one recalled her face some time after she had been allowed to pass, I do not know, nor does it matter much. It got wind that Mademoiselle St. Clair had entered Paris, and where in Paris would she be most likely to go? - to Citizen Bruslart's. A crowd was quickly on its way there. Bruslart was away from home, but they would go in, and there they found her. Not an hour ago they were shouting round her as they took her to the Abbaye."

"There is wine in that cupboard, Sabatier - thanks. This news has taken the nerve out of me. Bruslart must have known she was in his house. Barrington would leave her there."

"I am not so sure of that," said Sabatier. "I do not know how much this Barrington suspects, but I do not think he is a man to make so obvious a mistake. I give him credit for more cunning, and with reason, I think."

"And Bruslart must have known the danger," said Latour.

"He may not, if he supposed mademoiselle had managed to get into Paris unseen. I cannot understand Citizen Bruslart."

"Dieu! Did he betray her himself, Sabatier?"

"I do not know. If I could see any object in his doing so I might suspect him."

"The Abbaye," Latour muttered, getting up and pacing the room. "The Abbaye. We must get her out, Sabatier. She would never be acquitted. Had she remained in Paris, the good she has done to the poor might have been remembered in her favor, but an emigre, her great name and all that it stands for - . No, she is as surely doomed as any prisoner who has entered the Abbaye. I have business at the prison to-night, Sabatier. I may learn something of her."

"Wait, citizen. To-morrow will do. You will not be careful enough to-night."

Latour paused by the table, a little astonished perhaps at the concern in his companion's voice. Sabatier was to be trusted as a man who served well for payment, but his hands had been red often, and it was strange to hear anything like sentiment from his lips.

" One would think you had some real affection for me,"

said Latour.

Sabatier swaggered to hide such weakness. "I am a man, citizen, who fears nothing. I can recognize another man who fears God or man as little as I do."

"The wine has cured me," said Latour. "I shall do my business, nothing more. I am not a fool. There will be no need of carefulness. Sabatier, to-morrow you must find out what Citizen Bruslart does. His movements may be interesting."

"And this man Barrington?"

"Leave him to me," answered Latour.

No man knew better when to wait and when to act than Raymond Latour, and few men had a keener perception of possibilities, of chances which were worth taking, of risks it was unwise to run. He appreciated his own power and influence to the very turn of a hair in the balance, and although to his companions he might exaggerate or under-rate that influence to suit the occasion, he never made the fatal mistake of deceiving himself in the matter. Under ordinary circumstances, had his interest been aroused in a prisoner, he would have gone openly to those in authority and put the case before them, with every confidence not only of being listened to, but of getting his request granted. He had a strong following and was too powerful to offend. But for such a prisoner as Mademoiselle St. Clair, he knew that he dare not plead. The strongest man in Paris would be howled down by the mob if he attempted to procure her acquittal. She was closely connected with the best hated families of France, she stood not for herself but for what she represented, and the mob had assisted at no capture that pleased it more. This knowledge had for a moment robbed Latour of his nerve and courage. Strong man and self-contained as he was, he had not been able to control himself and hide his fear from Jacques Sabatier; yet now, as he passed quickly through the streets in the direction of the Abbaye prison, his step was firm, his face resolute, his course of action determined upon.

For an hour he talked with two friends of his who were in charge of this prison of the Abbaye, laughed and rejoiced with them at the arrest of such an important emigre that day; and then, at their prophecy that she would not be long in their keeping, that the tribunal would see to it that she went speedily upon her last journey to the Place de la Revolution, Latour ventured a protest - the first move in his scheme. It was so definite a protest that his companions were astonished.

"What! Does a woman appeal to you? Are you losing your hatred for aristocrats?"

"The woman appeals to me in a curious way," Latour answered. "After all, what is she? A little fish out of a great shoal. I would net in the shoal. It is not difficult with this little fish for bait. Do you not see how it is? This little fish is precious to the shoal, and lost, the shoal, or part of it, at any rate, will turn to find her. So long as it is known that she lives, there will be other emigres stealing into Paris to look for Mademoiselle St. Clair."

"You are right. Delay will be wise," was the answer.

"Urge it, then," said Latour, with gleaming, sinister eyes. "Urge it. You are the keepers of prisoners and should know best when to spare and when to kill. It is not my business, and I have a name for gentleness in some matters, a reputation which it suits me to preserve, but I am bloodthirsty enough to give you good advice."

Latour knew how swift revolutionary justice was sometimes. It might be only a matter of hours between mademoiselle and the guillotine. He had counseled delay, confident that these men would counsel it in their turn, and take to themselves the credit for so excellent an idea.

He had other business as he passed along the corridor of the prison, a jest with the red-capped turnkey concerning the pretty birds he tended so lovingly.

"Some of them sing even, citizen," answered the man, with a great, coarse laugh. "Shall I show you some of my pets? You may not have another opportunity."

"I do not understand birds."

"Will you not look at the new one caught only to-day?"

"Ah, the aristocrat! I had forgotten her. Where is she caged?"

"Yonder, a small cage, and with three others not of her breed. She does not sing, citizen, she scolds. I tell you she has some strange oaths and curses at her tongue tip, and mingles them curiously with prayers for deliverance."

Latour laughed. He must show no anger at this man's humor, and he had nothing to suggest which might secure mademoiselle greater comfort.

He glanced along the corridor in the direction the man had pointed. A few yards of passage and a locked door were all that separated him from the woman he would help. The temptation to look upon her for a moment was great, the thought that by a glance he might convey a message of assurance to her seemed to offer an excuse, but he resisted the temptation.

"I shall see enough of your birds when you send them on their last flight," he said, carelessly. "I hoped to see

Mathon - where is he?"

"Drinking in the nearest wine shop, citizen, I'll wager, since he is off duty."

"It is a bad habit for turnkeys to drink," said Latour, severely, and the red-capped bully felt a sudden qualm of nervousness in his frame as he remembered how powerful this man was.

"Mathon is a good fellow. I spoke in jest, not to do him harm. When he has the keys in his keeping he does not drink, citizen."

"I am glad to hear that," answered Latour, as he passed on.

He found the turnkey Mathon in a neighboring wine shop, and called him out. The order was peremptory, and the man came quickly. Mathon had a history. He had been lackey to a nobleman, and while shouting with patriots in the beginning of the trouble, had helped his old master and his master's friends. Since then he had mended his ways and become a true patriot, with no desire to help a living soul but himself, with no sentiment and no fear in him except for one man - Raymond Latour. Latour knew the truth about him, was the only man who did, and held the proof, therefore Mathon was bound to serve him. He came quickly out of the wine shop and followed Latour into a side street.

"You know the room where this aristocrat was placed to-day?"

"Yes, citizen."

"She is not likely to be moved from there?"

"No, citizen, not until - not until she is condemned."

"When will you be in charge of the keys of her prison?"

"Not for a week, citizen."

"A week!"

"My turn for that part of the prison comes in a week, and she may not be there then. If you would speak with her, I might manage it before then."

"I do not want speech with her," Latour returned.

Mathon looked at him sharply.

"More than speech," said Latour. "In a week I will see you again. You shall run small risk, I will see to that."

Mathon nodded, he could not refuse his help, though his throat grew dry, and the collar of his shirt seemed to tighten as he thought of what the consequences might be. He hastened back to the wine shop and Latour returned to the Rue Valette slowly, thinking of a week hence.

He hardly noticed those who passed him on the way, and was certainly quite unconscious of the figure which followed him like a shadow.

CHAPTER XIV

AN APPEAL TO FRIENDSHIP

Raymond Latour was a busy man, he seldom missed attending the meetings of the Convention, and was assiduous in his work upon the various committees of public instruction, domains, liquidation and finance. It was therefore past noon on the following day when Sabatier found him and related what had occurred at the wine shop on the previous evening.

"Citizen Bruslart is no coward," concluded Sabatier, as though he considered even grudging praise from a man like himself conferred distinction upon the recipient. "When he entered, every patriot there was ready to fly at his throat, yet before the evening was ended he was a hero."

"He must still be watched," said Latour. "I have always told you that he was clever."

"He would be safer arrested, citizen. Indeed, is it not almost certain that he will be since this aristocrat was found in his apartment?"

"He has wasted no time," Latour answered. "Quite early this morning he saw certain members of the Convention and explained matters. It was the same story as he told in the wine shop, and he was believed."

"Do you believe him?" Sabatier asked.

The smile upon Latour's face suggested that he had no great faith in any one, that it was a sign of weakness to trust any man fully, and folly to express an opinion on such a subject.

"For all his professions of innocence a word would suffice to have him arrested," said Sabatier.

"It is the very last word I want spoken," Latour answered. "As you know, I have a personal interest in this affair. Citizen Bruslart is one of the cards in the game I play. Such a card in the hand is not to be carelessly thrown away, for there will surely come a time when it will be played with effect. Until then, Sabatier, make it your business to believe in Citizen Bruslart's patriotism, discourage as much as you can any questioning of it among those with whom you come in contact. Twice already to-day I have been loud in his praises. For the present he is safe, and we can watch him easily."

Perhaps Latour trusted Sabatier more fully than he did any of the others who served him, and there were many. He was farseeing enough to understand that popularity only was not sufficient security, that with the conflicting and changing interests which ruled Paris and the country, the friends of to-day might easily become the enemies of to-morrow. It was necessary to obtain some stronger hold upon the fickle populace, a security which was rooted in fear and ignorance of the extent of his power and know-ledge. He had been careful, therefore, that the interests of those who served him should not be identical, that their individual importance should lie in different directions, in various quarters of the city and among different sections of the revolutionists whose aims and views were in many ways opposed to one another. The result was that Latour's power was appreciated on all sides, yet only imperfectly under-stood, and in the Convention he passed for something of an enigma, yet a man who was far safer as a friend than as an enemy. These confederates of his had one thing in common, however; all of them were beholden to Raymond Latour. He held some secret concerning each one of them; their lives, or at least their well-being, were in his hands; no one of them had his full confidence, and they could not afford either to deceive or betray him. His position was as secure as any man's in Paris. That he had enemies he knew, but they dare not strike; that he was watched he did not doubt, but the fact did not trouble him. Yet, at this juncture of his schemes, the espionage of one person who dogged his footsteps might have made him apprehensive had he known of it.

Seth, a hunter and trapper by nature, the son and grandson of men who for their own safety had to be trained in the subtle methods of the Indian, who himself had had no small experience in this respect, and easily followed a trail which was no trail to ordinary eyes, found little difficulty in watching Latour's movements. Barrington had taken Seth to the Rue Valette last night, and from the shadow on the opposite side of the street had pointed out Latour to him. Seth had followed Latour to the Abbaye prison, had seen him call Mathon from the neighboring wine shop, and before he slept Barrington had received the information. That Latour should go so promptly to this particular prison was at least surprising. He might have business there which had nothing to do with Jeanne St. Clair, he might still be in ignorance of the identity of the occupant of that coach, but Barrington could not believe this to be the case. He was much rather inclined to think with Lucien Bruslart that Latour had had a part in her betrayal.

One thing was certain, he must make use of the friendship Latour had offered him. There was danger in it no doubt, but Mademoiselle St. Clair's life was at stake, so the danger counted for nothing. Moreover, Barrington had papers in his possession to prove what his object was in coming to France, and he had already thrown out the suggestion to

Latour that his reason in smuggling mademoiselle into Paris might have been a sinister one; and since Latour must have enemies, there would at least be some who would believe Barrington's statement that this deputy was ready to plot on behalf of an aristocrat, that over his wine he had confessed it. The struggle with Raymond Latour might be a more equal one than it appeared on a first consideration.

Next morning he told Seth his plans. "First I shall see Monsieur Bruslart early this afternoon as arranged. Unless he should have had some extraordinary success last night, which is hardly to be expected, I shall then go and see Latour."

"It may be only to walk into a den of lions," said Seth.

"Probably, but I am not altogether without means of taming them - and you know, Seth, where I have gone. If I am missing, it will be your task to find where I am, and if necessary, you must go to the Marquis de Lafayette and tell him."

"You will have also told Monsieur Bruslart."

"I am not sure," Barrington answered. "It will depend on circumstances."

"I should be inclined to let circumstances prevent it," said Seth. "I have not much faith in the help of a man who is so sure of his own cleverness that he takes the woman he loves to the very place where a child might know she would be in the greatest danger."

"I cannot understand that, I must confess, Seth."

"Well, Master Richard, I've always found it a good rule to have as little as possible to do with people you don't understand."

It was wise advice, perhaps, but the fact that Barrington had accused himself of entertaining a selfish hope that Lucien Bruslart was not a worthy man inclined him to believe in him, to trust him. He had, indeed, greater reason to do so now that grave suspicion was attached to Latour.

There was nothing of the despair of last night in Bruslart's manner to-day when Barrington saw him. It had not been replaced by confidence, but a dogged purpose was in his face, and a calm calculation in his words.

"I have done something but not much," he said. "After leaving you last evening, I fell in with a lot of patriots and I was quickly aware that I was in greater danger than I had imagined. I had to think of myself, for once my word is discredited, all my power to help mademoiselle is gone."

"Have you succeeded in re-establishing your credit?"

"I think so. I understand the mob and played to it. I had to lie of course, lies are the chief currency in Paris to-day. I knew nothing of mademoiselle's coming, I said; I did not even know the name of the aristocrat who had been arrested in my apartment, and naturally, as a true patriot I rejoiced at her arrest. I was considered a very fine fellow before the evening was out."

"But mademoiselle was not helped much," said Barrington.

"Not at all. I could not move on her behalf until this morning. First I have ascertained that her imprisonment in the Abbaye is so far fortunate, since it means that there is no desire to bring her to trial hurriedly. This gives us time. Then I have interviewed one or two members of the Convention. I need not tell you, Monsieur Barrington, that most of these men who are striving for individual power are afraid of one another. Each one wants staunch supporters and is ready to pay any price for them. It is worth while obtaining my support, so these men listened earnestly to me. They are inclined to help me."

"How?" asked Barrington.

"It is too early to decide, but I am hoping that we shall be able to show that mademoiselle was in Paris for a legitimate purpose, to help the distress in the city, for example; something, at any rate, to make the mob shout for her release. That way her prison doors would be quickly opened. The respite might be short lived, but it would be long enough. Then would come your part of the work, to see her safely back to Beauvais."

"And what further steps can you take towards this end?"

"Careful ones," Bruslart answered. "First gain the interest of other members of the Convention; secondly, let the reason for mademoiselle's return gradually be known among the poor in the Faubourg St. Antoine, and elsewhere. I can drop a spark or two in different directions, and the mob is tow. The fire will spread."

"But if it does not?" asked Barrington.

"You are depressing, monsieur."

"I want to act."

"It must be with caution," said Bruslart, "and with deceit. We can make no appeal to justice, because justice does not exist in Paris."

"I have nothing to say against your plans," Barrington returned. "I am only wondering whether we cannot work in another direction as well, so that if one way fail we may have the other to fall back on."

"You are still thinking of the power of gold."

"It seldom fails with such men as seem to be the rulers in Paris," said Barrington.

"Perhaps not, but it would fail now. Power is more to these men than gold. The one can be used and gloried in, evidence of the other would only make the mob suspicious. Is there any other way you can suggest?"

Barrington was thoughtful for a moment, making up his mind whether he should tell Lucien Bruslart of Latour's movements.

"No," he said slowly, "I have no other suggestion to make."

"I have every hope of success," said Bruslart, "but I am going to appear discourteous, Monsieur Barrington. It is necessary that I shall be considered a patriot of patriots, nothing must jeopardize such a character at the present time. Now it is more than probable that there are men in Paris who saw you at the barriers with mademoiselle, it would be dangerous to my character if you were seen visiting me."

"I understand."

"And you forgive the seeming discourtesy?"

"There is nothing to forgive. The idea crossed my mind on the way here, and I was cautious."

"Close to the Place du Carrousal," said Bruslart, "in a side street, there is a wine shop, an iron sign representing three barrels hangs over the door; if you could pass there every afternoon at four, I could find you when I was ready for your help."

Barrington promised to make a habit of passing this place at four in the afternoon and took his leave. He had hoped that Bruslart would have accomplished more, but it was something that he had done so much. It was absurd to feel any disappointment, in so short a time what more could he have done? Yet Barrington walked rapidly and in the direction of the Rue Valette. Bruslart had said nothing to alter his determination to see Raymond Latour.

He saw nothing of Seth in the street, and hardly expected to find Latour at home, but no sooner had he knocked than the door was opened and Latour welcomed him. He locked the door again when Barrington had entered.

"I am fond of study," he said, pointing to some open books on the table.

"And I disturb you?"

"No. I think I have almost been expecting you."

Barrington did not answer. It was necessary that he should get the measure of this man, understand the working of his mind, see the thoughts which were concealed behind his words. Barrington was as alert as though rapiers were in their hands, and only the death of one of them could satisfy the quarrel.

"Is it necessary for me to tell you that I guessed who you were yesterday?" said Latour.

"No, I knew that."

"It was not until I returned here that I knew who was in that coach. That is why I have been expecting you."

Barrington sat down, and with his elbows on the table supported his chin in his hands. In this position he looked fixedly at his companion, and neither of them spoke for a few moments. Then Latour sat down on the opposite side of the table.

"I see how it is, Monsieur Barrington, you do not believe me. I am not surprised. I am sufficiently well known in Paris for you to have discovered, if you have taken the slightest trouble to inquire, that I am a red republican, anathema to those who desire milder methods, a blood-hound where aristocrats are concerned. Still, I did not know who was in that coach any more than you did."

"If you had known?" asked Barrington.

"I should still have put out my hand to preserve your life."

"Are you quite sure of that?"

"Quite sure."

"You would not have rushed with me into that crowd, thinking of nothing but the woman in the coach."

"What should make you think so?"

"You forget perhaps that you told me there was a woman, an aristocrat, for whom you would do much," said Barrington.

"I do not forget, but the will to do much does not mean the will to die for her."

"No? I think it did," Barrington returned. "I judged by the man's face, not his words."

Latour smiled, as he closed the books upon the table and put them together.

"You may be right," he said; "the temptation has not yet come to me. The other idea that is in your mind is wrong. Mademoiselle St. Clair is not the woman I am interested in."

"Then we start on level ground," said Barrington, "the ground which was of your own suggesting - friendship. I do not believe my face is a telltale one, but would you feel confident that I would do you a service if I could?"

"Yes."

"Then, Monsieur Latour, what are you going to do to help me to save Mademoiselle St. Clair?"

"The question is not unexpected," said Latour, after a pause. "I might easily answer it with the bare statement that I could do nothing. It would be true enough, for, in one sense, I am powerless; my conscience would be clear because I should be acting up to my principles. But let us consider the question for a moment. You are acting for Citizen Lucien Bruslart."

"He does not know that I am here."

"I quite appreciate that you are not a man to trust any one implicitly on so short an acquaintance, but you know perfectly well that to rescue Mademoiselle St. Clair is to save her for Lucien Bruslart."

"And if it be so?"

"The enterprise does not much appeal to me," said Latour. "Let me be more explicit than I was yesterday. I know Bruslart, not the man only but the very soul of the man. It is black, monsieur, black as hell. Mademoiselle had far better look through the little window than trust such a man. The guillotine does its work quickly, but the misery of a woman who trusts Lucien Bruslart must be the affair of a lifetime."

"If she is saved, is it so certain that it will be for Citizen Bruslart?" Barrington asked.

CHAPTER XV

THE PRISONER OF THE ABBAYE

The week of waiting passed slowly for Raymond Latour. He knew the risk he was running, but never for an instant was he tempted to turn from his purpose. His whole being was centered upon the enterprise; the saving of this woman was an essential thing, and every other consideration of country or self must give way to it. He was quite willing to sacrifice himself if necessary, but at the same time he intended to guard against such a necessity as much as possible. He worked with cunning and calculation, going over every point in his scheme and eliminating as far as possible every element of chance. The unlikely things which might happen were considered, and provided for. Only two persons had any part in the scheme, Jacques Sabatier and Mathon, the jailer; each had his own particular work in it, had received definite and minute instructions, yet neither of them knew the whole plot. Latour did not take them entirely into his confidence; he did not ask their advice, he only told them how to act.

The week was as any other week to Jacques Sabatier. Uplifted somewhat by Latour's confidence in him, his swaggering gait was perhaps a little more pronounced, but he was untouched by apprehension, not so much because he was a fearless man - like all swaggerers adverse circumstances would probably find him at heart a coward - but because he had implicit faith in Raymond Latour. The man he served was not only powerful and courageous; he was lucky, which counted for much. What he had set his heart upon that he obtained. It was a creed in which Sabatier had absolute faith, and the passing week was merely an interval which must elapse before success.

Mathon the jailer had not this sublime faith, and his fearfulness was perhaps natural. As a jailer he was in close touch with facts and knew by experience how unstable in these days was any man's power. A week had often served to change a master whose anger was dangerous into a prisoner whose name might at any moment be upon the list of those destined forthwith to feed the guillotine. He had not been brought so constantly in touch with Latour that he could appreciate him as a lucky man, and he contemplated his part in the enterprise with misgiving.

The plot was to be carried out on the second night upon which Mathon was on duty. This was the first precaution. Were he a party to mademoiselle's escape it would be argued that he would have seized the first opportunity; that he had not done so would go some way to prove his innocence. On this evening, too, Mathon was particularly loud in his hatred of all prisoners, of one emigre prisoner in particular, and his manners were brutal. There would be many witnesses able to prove this. In one small room at the end of a corridor he was particularly brutal. He made the mere unlocking of the door a nerve-racking sound, and stamped in swearing under his breath. Three women drew back into a corner, trembling. They were women of a coarse bourgeois type, their chief crime misfortune. They knew only imperfectly of what they were accused, why they were there, but they had few friends to spare a thought for them and expected each day to be their last. Sometimes they were afraid and tearful, at other times careless, loose, and blasphemous, despair making them unnatural, and in this mood it pleased them to curse their fellow prisoner, also a woman, and an aristocrat.

Mathon laughed as they shrank from him.

"Disappointed again," he said. "You are not called to-night. You will have another pleasant dream about it. Perhaps to-morrow your turn will come. It's time. This fine apartment is wanted for better people."

Then he turned and walked towards the fourth prisoner. If she were afraid she succeeded in hiding the fact. She was standing by the window and she did not move.

"As for you, your time is short," said the jailer, and then coming quite close to her he dropped his voice. "Listen, and don't show astonishment. You will be released probably. When the time comes, ask no questions, don't speak, do as you are told." Then he swore loudly again and, jingling his keys, went out and locked the door.

He swore partly to keep his own courage at the proper pitch, for the dismal corridors of the Abbaye were depressing to-night. Approaching footsteps startled Mathon, and the sudden salutation of a comrade turned him pale. The night was oppressive, yet he found it cold enough to make him shiver.

Presently there came heavy footsteps, and two of those dreaded officers of the Convention, men whose hours were occupied in spreading terror and in feeding the guillotine, stood before him.

"Jailer Mathon?"

"Yes."

"You have in your charge an emigre, Jeanne St. Clair. She is to be removed forthwith to the Conciergerie. There is the order."

Mathon took up a lantern and by the dim light read the paper handed to him. It was all in order, the full name of the emigre duly inserted, the genuine signature of the governor of the prison at the foot of the document. The jailer looked from the paper into the face of the man who had handed it to him.

"Do they set over prisoners fools who cannot read?" asked the man.

"No; the paper is in order," Mathon answered.

"Obey it then. Fetch out the emigre."

Mathon folded up the paper and placed it in his pocket.

"It is down this passage," and his keys jingled. His fingers trembled a little as the men followed him. A few yards from the door the men halted.

"Bring her quickly. We have other work to do to-night more important than this."

Mathon unlocked the door and entered the room.

"Jeanne St. Clair, your turn has come."

The woman moved slowly.

"Quickly," said Mathon. "Your head's still in its place. Wrap the hood of your cloak well round it. There's no need to feel cold before the time. Don't speak," he added in a whisper.

They went out together, Mathon locking the door again.

"This is the prisoner."

The officers without a word placed themselves on either side of her, and they went quickly along the corridor leaving the jailer alone, one hand holding his keys, the other pressed to his pocket to make sure that the order he had obeyed still rested there.

A *berlin* stood in the little square before the prison, the driver half asleep. He had no imagination, this driver, and this square was to him as any other in Paris. Yet on another night, not long since, how different it had been! Then a mob filled it, filled it to overflowing, a mob mad with lust of blood and murder, armed with sabers, pikes and hatchets, any weapon that came to hand. Within the prison sat a sudden jury, a mockery of Justice; without stood Fate. A brief questioning, the veriest caricature of a trial, and prisoners were escorted to the doors, but no farther. The rest of the journey they must go alone. A lane opened before them, all must traverse it, old and young, man or woman. It was a short journey, and amid frenzied shrieks they fell under the sabers and the pikes. There was no mercy, only red death and horror. Rain had fallen in Paris since then, yet surely there must still be blood in the gutters of this square. The driver could not tell where he had been that night, not here certainly, but wherever it was he was minding his own business. He had enough to do to live from day to day, and had no use for a long memory. He had carried people, men and women, from one prison to another before this, and took no special interest in this job. The revolution mattered little to him if he could get sufficient for his wants. He had a room high up in the Faubourg St. Antoine, with a wife and child in it, and cared little what heads fell daily in the Place de la Revolution. He woke from his reverie at the sound of footsteps. A woman was helped into the coach quickly, a man following her and closing the door sharply behind him. A second man climbed to the box beside the driver.

"To the Conciergerie," he said.

The woman in the coach did not speak, but leaned back in the corner. The man was also silent until they had driven away from the square.

"Listen to me, mademoiselle," he said presently. "We are driving in the direction of the Conciergerie, but the way will be altered in a few minutes. My comrade will arrange that. Keep your cloak well round you and do not speak. You and I will have to walk presently to a safe retreat already prepared. You must do exactly as you are told or we may fail. Your escape may be discovered at any moment."

The woman did not answer. She had no idea who her companion was, had perhaps a doubt in her mind concerning him, but she determined to obey; indeed, what else could she do?

The man beside the driver was silent, and sat in a somewhat bent attitude as though he were desirous of attracting no attention, yet his eyes were keen as the coach went forward at a jogging pace, and if any passer-by seemed to show any interest in the conveyance he was quick to note the fact.

"Take the next turning to the left," he said suddenly.

"That is not the way," returned the driver.

"It's my way. We might fall in with a crowd."

"But - "

"To the left," said the man. "I will direct you."

The coach turned into the street indicated, and afterward round this corner and that at the bidding of the man on the box until the driver was utterly confused.

"I'm lost, citizen," he said; "and what's more I believe you are, too."

"You'll see directly. Sharp round to the right here."

The driver turned.

"Why, it's as I said, you've lost yourself. This is a blind alley."

Indeed it was, a narrow lane between high walls, a place where refuse collected and was allowed to remain undisturbed, a place upon which looked no prying window and which echoed to no footfall.

The driver had turned to jeer at his companion when he found himself seized in a grip there was no fighting against. He tried to call out, but succeeded in giving only a whispered respiration, and then a heavy blow robbed him of his senses.

The coach door opened. The man inside got out quickly and helped the woman to descend.

"Keep silent, mademoiselle; it is all arranged," he whispered, and in a few moments he had divested himself of his coat and hat, of everything which marked him as an officer of the Convention, and even of the shaggy hair which hung about his eyes and neck, and threw all this disguise into the coach. He was another man altogether. "Come; we must walk. The worst danger is past."

The man who had sat on the box was bending over the coachman. He said nothing, did not even look up as the two went swiftly down the alley. When they had gone he, too, divested himself of everything that proved him an officer of the Convention and of the wig which had concealed his identity. These he put into the coach. Then he lifted the unconscious driver from the ground and put him into the coach also, closing the door upon him. The horse had not attempted to move. He was a tired, worn-out beast, glad to rest when and where he could. He was unlikely to move until his master roused to make him, and the dawn might be no longer young when that happened, unless some stray pedestrian should chance down that deserted way.

For an hour that evening Raymond Latour plied his friends and fellow patriots with wine. So glorious an hour seemed of long duration. In case of accident there would be a score of good witnesses to swear that their friend the deputy had been drinking with them all the evening. Under the influence of wine and loud patriotism the flight of time is of no account.

It was close on midnight when Latour entered the alley by the baker's shop in the Rue Valette, walking slowly. Seated at the top of the stairs he found Sabatier.

"Yes, and asleep probably," said Sabatier, answering the question in his eyes.

"It was well done," said Latour. "Come to me early to-morrow. This man Barrington may be suspected and must be warned."

"And Bruslart?"

"Yes, to-morrow we must think of him, too. Good night, citizen."

Sabatier went down the stairs, and Latour entered his room.

Midnight! Was she yet asleep? Sabatier had told her nothing except that she was safe, and that the man who had planned her rescue would come to her and explain everything. She would think it was Lucien Bruslart. Who would be so likely to run such risk for her sake? Only one other man might occur to her, the man who had already done so much to help her - Richard Barrington. Would she be likely to sleep easily to-night? No. Surely she was wide awake, waiting and watching.

Raymond Latour went quietly up the next flight of stairs to the room above his own which he had furnished and made ready with such infinite trouble. She was not so safe in these rooms as she would have been had he succeeded in bringing her there in the first instance, straight from the Lion d'Or as he had intended. Bruslart could not have suspected him then as he must certainly do now; but Bruslart could only work in secret, he dare not speak openly, and Barrington was powerless. To-night Latour would say little. He would look upon her for a moment, be assured that she had everything for her comfort, proclaim himself only as one of those who had had a part in her rescue, and receive some thanks. This would be enough for to-night.

The key was in the lock on the outside of the door. Latour knocked before turning it.

"Mademoiselle."

"Come in."

The answer was faint. She was in the inner room. Even when told to enter, Latour hesitated. This was a crisis in his life, fully understood and appreciated. Here was the accomplishment of something he had labored for; it was natural to hesitate. Then he turned the key and went in.

The room was in darkness, but the light of a candle came from the inner room, and the next moment the door opened wide and a woman stood there, a beautiful woman, dark in hair and eyes, with figure as lissom as a young animal, poised just now half expectantly, half in fear.

A sharp exclamation came from Latour's lips as he leaned forward to look at her.

"Monsieur, I - " and then a flush of anger came into her face. "Am I still to be insulted?"

"In the devil's name, woman, who are you?"

Latour had crossed the space between them in a hasty stride or two, and his fingers were tightly round the woman's wrist.

"What right - "

"Who are you? Answer."

For a moment longer she was defiant, even made a feeble struggle to free herself, but the man's eyes were upon her and she was compelled to look into them. Anger blazed in them, anger was in every line of his set face. She had seen this man before, knew he was Raymond Latour, knew his power, and she was afraid.

"I am Pauline Vaison," she said in a low tone.

CHAPTER XVI

THE TAVERN AT THE CHAT ROUGE

Terribly leaden-footed had this week of waiting been to Richard Barrington. He had not seen Lucien Bruslart, although each afternoon he had passed the wine shop with the sign of the three barrels. He had nothing to occupy him, and for most of the day he remained within doors. He shrank from witnessing the squalor and savagery which might at any moment be met in the streets; he could not bear the sight or the sound of those slowly rolling tumbrils carrying their wretched victims to the guillotine, and he would not go in the direction of the Place de la Revolution even when there was no yelling crowd there, when the scaffold was untenanted and the great knife still. Another consideration kept him indoors. His constant presence in the streets might serve to make his face and figure familiar, and this would be a disadvantage if he were presently to help Mademoiselle St. Clair to escape from Paris.

In the house of Monsieur Fargeau life ran a smooth and even course, if not entirely ignorant of the revolution, at least having no personal concern with it. The shouting mob did not penetrate into this quiet corner of the city. Monsieur Fargeau knew nothing of politics, and was ignorant of the very names of many of those members of the Convention who were filling distant parts of Europe with horror and loathing. Some people had lost their lives, he was aware of that; possibly they had only met with their deserts, he did not know. The times were hard, but he was prepared for a rainy day, and could afford to wait until business improved again. To do the Marquis de Lafayette a service he had let rooms to two Americans, who paid him well, who said pleasant things to his wife and children when they met them on the stairs, and beyond this he thought or cared little about them. He knew nothing of their reason for being in Paris, and had no idea that he was harboring dangerous characters. Both Barrington and Seth had been careful to leave and return to their lodgings cautiously, and by a roundabout route, and were convinced that if they were watched they had succeeded in baffling the spies in discovering their hiding place. Barrington was therefore rather startled one afternoon when, as he returned from his daily walk past the wine shop, a man suddenly came from a doorway and spoke his name in a low tone.

"It is Monsieur Barrington?"

"Yes."

"You may remember me, monsieur. I am a servant to Monsieur de Lafayette."

"Yes, I thought I recognized your face. You have a message for me?"

"My master has left Paris, monsieur. There was a rumor that he was in the city, and he was in danger of arrest. He has rejoined the army in the North, but it may not be possible for him to stay there. If not, he will ride across the Belgian frontier."

"It is bad news?" said Barrington.

"Yes, monsieur, and I was to say to you that you would do well to leave Paris at the first opportunity. There is no place for an honest man to-day in France. My master told me to say that."

This news added to Barrington's feeling of impotence, and was depressing. Had his days been full of active danger it would not have had such an effect upon him. Naturally disposed to see the silver lining of every cloud, he was unable to detect it now. Instead, his mind was full of questions. Was Bruslart honest? Was he leaving no stone unturned to release Mademoiselle St. Clair? Had Raymond Latour lied to him? Was this week of waiting merely a pretext in order that he might have time to render the prisoner's acquittal absolutely impossible?"

"I'd trust this man Latour before I would Bruslart," Seth said, when Barrington appealed to him, but in such a tone that he did not appear really to trust either of them.

"And at the end of this week what are we to do if mademoiselle is still a prisoner?"

"Master Richard, we're just men, ordinary men, and we cannot do the impossible. We shall have done all that it is in our power to do, and a ride toward the sea and a ship bound for Virginia would be the best thing for us."

"You would leave a defenseless woman in the hands of her enemies?" Barrington asked.

"It seems to me she must remain there whether we stay or go. I'm looking at the matter as it is, and I see no opening for a romantic side to it," Seth answered. "You cannot do battle with a whole city, that would mean death and nothing accomplished; you cannot go to these ruffians and demand her release, that would mean death, yours and hers, in the shortest time possible. No, unless this man Latour keeps his word, I see naught for us but a return to Virginia as quickly as may be."

"You would never spend another night of sound sleep, Seth."

"I should, Master Richard. I should just forget this time as though it had never been, wipe the marks of it off the slate. He's a wise man who does that with some of the episodes of his life."

"I am a fool with a long memory," said Barrington.

"Ay, but you will grow older, Master Richard; and life is less romantic as we grow older."

So from Seth there was not much consolation to be had, only sound common sense, which was not altogether palatable just now as Barrington counted the days. Latour had been very indefinite. He had said a week, and on waking one morning Barrington's first thought was that the week ended to-morrow. It was a proof of his trust in Latour, half unconscious though such trust might be, that he had not expected to hear anything until the week had passed. He judged Latour by himself.

Seth went out in the morning as usual, looking as true and uncompromising a patriot as any he was likely to encounter in the street. He rather prided himself on the way he played his part, and wore the tri-color cockade with an air of conviction. Grim of feature, he looked like a man of blood, a disciple of rioting, and he had more than once noticed that certain people who wished to pass unobserved shrank from him, which pleased him greatly. Early in the afternoon he returned hurriedly. It was so unlike him to come up the stairs hastily, two at a time, that Barrington opened the door to meet him.

"Shut it, Master Richard," he said, as he entered the room.

"What has happened?"

"The unexpected. Mademoiselle escaped from the Abbaye Prison last night."

"You are sure! You have seen Latour?"

"Sure! The news is all over Paris. The mob is furious. There are cries for a general massacre of prisoners, as happened a little while since, so that no others may escape. There is talk of a house-to-house search, and there are more ruffians in the streets to-day than I have seen at all."

"Is there any mention of Latour, any suspicion of him?"

"I heard none, but they talk of - "

"Bruslart!" ejaculated Barrington.

"No, of a scurvy devil of a royalist who helped mademoiselle into Paris."

"Of me? By name?"

"I did not hear your name spoken, but it is you they mean. They are looking in every direction for mademoiselle, but they are keeping their eyes open for you, too. There'll be some who will remember seeing you at the barrier the other day. Yours is a figure not easily to be forgotten. Keep within doors, Master Richard, until it is safe for us to sneak away."

"You know that is impossible."

"Mademoiselle has escaped," said Seth. "It is now your turn to seek safety."

"With her escape my part commences," said Barrington, with a laugh that had happiness in it. "It is for me to take her back to Beauvais or elsewhere to safety."

"It is madness to think of it," said Seth. "To be in your company would increase her danger. Think of her, Master

Richard, think of her. Your lust for romantic adventure makes you selfish. For days to come you are a marked man. In the streets, at any moment, you may be recognized. Even in this quiet corner of the city you are hardly safe. They'll trap you if they can and only a miracle can prevent them."

"I have given a promise, Seth."

"Break it, if not for your own sake, for the woman's. You risk bringing her to ruin. I came back here to-day more cautiously than I have ever done. One moment of carelessness and you are lost. If this man Latour must be seen, let me go to him. No one is likely to recognize me. No one turns to look after me as I pass. I am insignificant, of no account. Let me go."

"Seth, you have not told me everything," he said, suddenly. "There is something you are keeping back. What is it?"

Seth was by the window looking down into the quiet street as though he expected to see danger enter it at any moment.

"What is it?" Barrington repeated.

"I'd give half my remaining years if my conscience would bid me lie to you," Seth answered, fiercely. "I've prayed, yes, I prayed as I hurried through the streets that your mother's spirit might be allowed to whisper to me and bid me deceive you."

"Come, Seth, tell me everything," and Barrington let his hand fall affectionately on the man's shoulder. "Could conscience persuade you to barter half your years, it would be but a device of the devil to lead us into greater difficulty."

"I was recognized to-day. That swaggerer Sabatier touched

me in the street, and with a word of caution bid me walk beside him as though we were boon companions. He was a messenger from Raymond Latour."

"Yes, what did he say?"

"He told me that mademoiselle had escaped, news I had heard already, and he bid me tell you from Latour to go to-night, as soon as it began to grow dusk, to the Rue Charonne, to a tavern there called the Chat Rouge. You are to ask for the tavern keeper and say to him 'La vie est ici.' He will understand and bring you to Latour and mademoiselle. Plans are laid for your escape."

"Is that all, Seth?"

"And enough, surely. It comes from Sabatier, and we know something of him. It is a trap baited too openly. You will not go, Master Richard."

"Not go! Why, this is the very kind of message I have waited for, but I did not expect it until to-morrow."

"And I go with you."

Barrington was thoughtful for a moment.

"No. We will exercise every caution. Should escape from Paris seem possible at once, I can send for you or tell you when and where to join me; if I walk into a trap, you will still be at liberty to work for my freedom."

Seth knew from past experience that all argument was useless, and listened attentively to his master's instructions.

"If you do not see me, or hear from me within three days, you must act as you think best, Seth. Whatever my danger I shall have absolute confidence in you. Mademoiselle once in safety, you shall have your desire; we will ride toward the sea and a homeward-bound ship."

Twilight was gathering over Paris when Richard Barrington left the house of Monsieur Fargeau and went in the direction of the Rue Charonne. The wine shops were full to overflowing; small crowds were at street corners, filthy men and women ripe for any outrage. The names of unpopular deputies were freely and loudly cursed; the most unlikely revolutionists were openly accused of having sympathy with aristocrats. Some ragged miscreant, whose only popularity rested on some recent brutality, was declared capable of governing better than most of the present deputies, and the mob was more out of hand than it had been for weeks. At the call of some loud-mouthed patriot, or on the instigation of some screaming virago, a small body of dancing, swearing patriots would move away bent on mischief which would probably end in bloodshed. A street, more or less tranquil the moment before, would suddenly become a miniature battlefield, an opinion dividing patriots into factions which began to fight savagely. Anything might happen to-night, another prison might be stormed as the Bastille was, another tenth of August insurrection, another horror equalling the September massacres, anything was possible. Only a leader a little bolder than the rest was wanting, and all attempt at law and order would be trampled to nothing in a moment by a myriad of feet.

Barrington proceeded carefully with watchful eyes, yet boldly enough not to draw attention to himself. If a street was in possession of the mob he avoided it, nor did he pass in the light which came from noisy wine shops, but he did not make the mistake of avoiding those who approached him. His route to the Rue Charonne was therefore a circuitous one, but he came presently to a street which led directly into it, which seemed quieter than many he had passed through, and he took it.

He had traversed three-parts of its length in safety when from two side streets crowds came simultaneously. To hurry might raise suspicion, to turn back most certainly would; so Barrington kept on, not increasing his pace, but with his eyes and ears keenly alive. His steady pace exactly brought him into the midst of those who were at the heads of these two crowds, and he was ready to receive and return any salutation or coarse pleasantry which might be offered to him, when he found himself carried in a rush to one side of the street. Between these two crowds there was some quarrel, possibly no more than an hour old, and men and women flew at one another in a fury. Being at the edge of the fight Barrington had no great difficulty in extricating himself, and no need to defend himself beyond an arm flung out to avoid the blow from a stick. So fully were they engaged in their fight that they were unlikely to take much notice of him, and he was congratulating himself on his escape when one out of the many faces about him suddenly seemed to stand out distinct from all the rest. Barrington did not know the face, had never seen the man before that he was aware of, but it fascinated him. He was obliged to stare back into the eyes fixed upon him, and knew instinctively that he was in peril.

"An aristocrat!"

The exclamation burst out like the report of a pistol.

"The American!"

The noise of the fight sank in a kind of sob as the roar of a breaking wave sinks with an angry swish back into silence; and as there is a pause before the next wave is flung upward to break and roar, so was there a pause now. Then came the yell of fury, faction quarrel forgotten. They were all of one mind in a moment.

"An aristocrat! The American! The American!"

In the moment of pause Barrington had thrust aside a man who seemed to bar his way, and had started to run. He was a score of yards to the good; with fortune on his side he would turn into the Rue Charonne well ahead of all but two of his pursuers; an open doorway, an alley, some hiding-place might present itself. Escape was not probable, but there was a chance, that bare chance which keeps the courage steady.

As he rushed into the Rue Charonne, the yelling chorus behind him, a new difficulty faced him. Just before him was the Chat Rouge, the one place in all Paris that must not attract the attention of the mob to-night. An archway was beside him and he turned into it.

"The American! The American!"

The bloodhounds were in the street. Would they miss this archway? It was unlikely.

"Quick!" said a voice in his ear as he was dragged back against the wall. "There is straw below. Jump!"

The crowd was rushing past the archway, but some stopped to examine it as Barrington jumped down, falling on his hands and knees onto a bed of straw.

"The American!"

"This way. He must have gone this way!"

The babel of voices was loud for a moment, then something silenced it, and there was the swift sound of a bolt shot home carefully.

CHAPTER XVII

SETH IS CAUTIOUS

It was doubtful whether any man, woman or child, not even excepting Richard Barrington himself, had any clear idea of Seth's character, or the exact standpoint from which he viewed life and his fellows. On the Virginian estate he had always led an isolated kind of existence, happier apparently in his own company than any other. His devotion to his mistress and her boy was known, and passed for one of his peculiarities, had occasionally indeed been cast in his teeth as a selfish device for winning favor. Barrington, as a boy, had made use of him, as a man he had brought him to France knowing that he was to be trusted, yet hardly realizing that Seth's trustworthiness was rooted in love, such a love as men do not often receive. Since they had landed in France, and danger had been as their very shadows, Richard had caught glimpses of this love, but had understood it rather in terms of comradeship than in any deeper sense, and had perhaps misinterpreted Seth's keen desire to return forthwith to Virginia. Seth, in short, was seldom able to express himself adequately, emotion scarcely ever sounded in his voice, and the expression of his face was a fixed and unchangeable one, somewhat dour and ill-tempered in aspect and reflecting nothing of the man within.

That his master had gone into imminent danger by keeping the appointment at the Chat Rouge, Seth was convinced, yet for three days he did nothing, nor did he plan anything in his mind. He had been told to wait three days, and he waited, no look of anxiety in his eyes, no suppressed agitation or desire for action apparent in his manner. He went out and came in as though these days had no particular interest for him, and ate and drank as a normal man with no care in his mind. Precisely at the end of those three days, however, he began the labor which he had fully expected to be obliged to do - the discovery of Richard Barrington's whereabouts. Seth knew that the Marquis de Lafayette had left Paris, or at least that his master had been told so, but, being disposed to take nothing for granted, it was to Lafayette's apartments that he went first.

The servant who was still there did not remember him, and was not inclined to give any information.

"I don't expect to see the Marquis though I asked for him," Seth answered. "I am Monsieur Barrington's man, and it was you no doubt who delivered your master's message to him. Monsieur Barrington has gone."

"I am glad. I know the Marquis was anxious that he should leave Paris."

"By gone I mean that I don't know where he is," said Seth, "but I don't think he has left Paris."

"Do you mean that he is arrested? I might get a message through to my master who is with the army in the north."

"I don't know that he is arrested. No, I think it would be better not to send a message until I am certain. It is possible, although not probable, that you may hear of my master; if you do will you let me know?"

"I will. You are still at the house of Monsieur Fargeau?"

"Yes, and shall remain there."

Seth next went to find Lucien Bruslart. He had no intention of being open with him. He had concocted an ambiguous message from his master, so framed as to astonish Bruslart, whether he knew where Richard Barrington was or not, and Seth hoped to read something of the truth in his face.

Citizen Bruslart's apartment was closed, and the concierge knew nothing about him. His servants had also gone.

"Ah! like rats from a sinking ship, eh, citizen?"

"Maybe. I'm no politician."

"Nor I," said Seth, "until there's my own skin to keep whole, and then I'll be politician enough to fight for it. It's not only the aristocrats who are dangerous, citizen."

"Why, that's true."

"And if there's a wine shop handy we might drink confusion to all the enemies of liberty," Seth returned.

The porter was nothing loth, and was soon talking glibly enough.

"I'm not to be deceived," he said, eying Seth curiously. "You are a man with power, and Citizen Bruslart is wanted."

"Ah, you may be no politician, but I see you are no fool," answered Seth, with a swagger unnatural to him. "Men are brought out of the provinces to work in Paris sometimes. Maybe that is why you do not know me. There has been some good work done in the provinces and the authorities begin to understand the value of the men who have done it. Now Citizen Bruslart - "

"I know only this," said the porter, confidentially. "He went out very hurriedly one morning, and has not returned. His man followed and has not returned either. I do not think Citizen Bruslart intends to come back."

"But they have not sent to arrest him," said Seth.

"Not until you came, citizen," answered the porter, with a wink to show how exceedingly knowing he was.

"You're a smart man. I might presently find use for you."

"I have done a little already, citizen. Two aristocrats have looked through the little window with my help."

"Good, very good. May you receive the reward you deserve," Seth answered, rising as he finished his wine. "I shall hardly earn my pay if I stay longer. You're of the kind I should like to reward, an excellent double-faced man, Judas-like, betraying with a kiss. These are the men who succeed to-day. I love them as I love hell and the guillotine."

Even the porter was a little afraid of such a patriot, and was rather glad to see the back of him as he swaggered away.

Bruslart's disappearance was comprehensible. The escape of mademoiselle would naturally draw suspicion upon him. Was Richard Barrington with him?

This was the first question Seth asked himself. It gave quick birth to another. What part had Raymond Latour in the scheme?

The set purpose in Seth's mind was apparent by the fact that he took the most direct route to the Rue Valette. Twice at intervals of an hour he knocked at Latour's door and received no answer, nor heard any sound within. The third time the door was opened, and Latour faced him.

"Your business, citizen."

"I have something important to tell Citizen Latour," Seth answered.

"I do not know you."

"Does Citizen Latour know all his admirers?"

"No, nor all his enemies," was the answer.

"Were I an enemy I do not think you would be afraid. As it happens I want to be a friend."

"Come in, then, and remember a deputy's time is not his own. You may be from the provinces, citizen, and therefore I do not know you," said Latour, as he closed and locked his door, and Seth noticed that he was armed and prepared to use his pistol at a moment's notice.

"From Louisiana originally, from Virginia recently with my master, Richard Barrington."

Latour remained standing by the door a moment, then moved to a chair by the table, and sat down.

"I am interested. What do you want with me?" he said.

"I want to know where my master is."

Latour regarded him fixedly. If Seth expected to read this man's thoughts in his face he was doomed to disappointment.

"Surely you come to a strange person to make such an inquiry," said Latour, slowly.

"It will save time, monsieur, if I tell you at once that I am in my master's confidence."

"Ah! Then you should be able to give me most interesting information."

"I think not, monsieur, nothing more than you know already. I am aware that you and he planned to rescue Mademoiselle St. Clair, and that she has escaped from the Abbaye Prison. I know that she is being looked for in every corner of Paris, and that my master is suspected. It was to me that Jacques Sabatier gave your message bidding my master go to the Chat Rouge tavern in the Rue Charonne."

"You must be a faithful servant for your master."

"I am more, a man who loves him."

"Even so I doubt whether such confidence is wise," said Latour.

"Wise or not, it happens to serve a useful purpose on this occasion," Seth returned. "If he did not return, my master told me to take what steps I thought fit, after waiting three days. You will know, monsieur, that I have waited three days."

"So your first idea is to apply to me. It was natural."

"You think so, without taking any precaution?"

"Precaution! I do not follow you."

"It is easy," said Seth, a sudden inspiration coming to him, perhaps because he was convinced that this man was bent on baffling inquiry. "To come here was to put myself in your power. Monsieur Barrington has trusted you, but I should be a fool to trust you without reason; indeed, I have reason to distrust you since my master is missing. You could easily have given word that he would be at the Chat Rouge at a certain hour, and the doors of a Paris prison would close on him."

"Yes, that could have been done," said Latour, "and, faithful servant though you be, I fail to see what counter stroke you could have made."

"No? It seems obvious to me. Play the life of Deputy Latour against the life of Richard Barrington. There would speedily be a yelling crowd on the stairs if I denounced you as the man who had rescued Mademoiselle St. Clair."

Seth looked for some change of expression in his companion's face, but it did not come. Fear never caught at this man's heart.

"I think there would," said Latour, "if you could make the crowd believe it."

"You can make the mob believe anything at the present moment."

"You may be right. I do not study the mob much. There is one point, however, which you overlook," said Latour, quietly. "I might take steps to prevent your telling the mob."

"That is exactly the danger against which I have taken precaution," Seth answered. "You are not the first person to whom I have applied."

Latour was fully alive to the danger which such a precaution implied. A casual word had power in it to ruin him, yet he gave no sign of being disturbed, and Seth appreciated to some extent the kind of man he had to deal with.

"You see, monsieur, there are those who would not wait three days if I did not return from my visit to you," he said.

Latour nodded as though the position were quite an ordinary one, as though he had been aware of it from the first.

"I hope your caution, which I quite understand, but which was unnecessary, is not likely to injure your master."

"I have been very careful," said Seth.

"I am glad to hear it. At present Monsieur Barrington is safe."

"Then you can take me to him."

"For the moment that is exactly what I cannot do," Latour answered. "In one sense Monsieur Barrington's danger and mine are the same, but in another way his is greater than mine, at present. The mob does not suspect me; it does suspect your master. I can add to your knowledge a little. As he went to the Chat Rouge that night he was recognized and had to run for his life. Through Jacques Sabatier, whom you know, I was instrumental in saving him, but for some little time he will have to lie very closely. Were you or I to be seen near his hiding-place it would only be to betray him."

"I only have your word for this," said Seth.

"And it is not enough?" said Latour, with a smile. "I consider myself a judge of character, and I am not surprised. There is a way out of the difficulty. Will you be satisfied if your master sends you a letter telling you to await his further instructions patiently?"

"Yes. I have means of knowing that such a letter could not be forged."

"You shall have the letter to-morrow morning. Where shall I send it?"

"I will come here for it," Seth answered.

"An excellent idea. You will be able to tell me at once whether you are satisfied," said Latour, rising and going to the door, which he threw open with a bow. "The lion's den is not so dangerous a place as you imagined."

"Monsieur, I shall think well of you until to-morrow," said Seth.

"And afterward, I hope," Latour returned.

The smile faded from Latour's face as he went back into his room, and an expression of perplexity took its place. This was a new and unexpected danger. Probably he was honest, but it was hardly likely that Barrington had told the whole truth to his servant. After a little while spent in thought and calculation, Latour went upstairs to the rooms above his own. He knocked at the door, then turned the key and entered.

Pauline Vaison showed no pleasure at the visit, but there was unmistakable relief. It was quite evident that she half expected a worse enemy.

"Have you come to release me, citizen?" she asked, doing her utmost to appear indifferent.

"You are only a prisoner for your own safety."

"You have already said so, but I cannot understand of what importance I am to the State."

"Mademoiselle, I was a little rough with you when you were first brought here," said Latour. "I believed you were a party to a plot, to defeat which you were smuggled out of the Abbaye Prison. You told me a story which, frankly, I did not believe, but from further knowledge I am inclined to alter my opinion. Your story was this, correct me if I am wrong in any detail: You went one morning to visit Citizen Bruslart, he was out and you waited for him, you have done the same before. The house was suddenly invaded and you were arrested as an aristocrat, one Mademoiselle Jeanne St. Clair. You protested, but you were not believed. Is that so?"

"I was laughed at and insulted," said Pauline.

"Citizen Bruslart is a friend of yours?"

"Yes."

"Have you ever heard that he was to marry Jeanne St. Clair?"

"Whatever he once intended, I have the best reason for knowing that he has changed his mind. Lucien Bruslart is to marry me."

Latour showed no surprise. "Have you ever seen this Jeanne St. Clair?" he asked.

"Never."

"You were not voluntarily there that day in her place, so that she might escape?"

"No. I am a patriot and hate all aristocrats. I am woman enough to hate this one particularly since Lucien once cared for her."

"When one's life is at stake, it is easy to lie if a lie will be useful, but I believe you, citizeness," said Latour. "I wish to be your friend, that kind of friend who is honest even if honesty gives pain. First, then, it is absolutely necessary that you remain here in hiding for a little while. The mob which carried you to prison knows you have escaped. You are being hunted for. So beautiful a woman cannot pass unnoticed. You would be recognized, and since you are still believed to be Mademoiselle St. Clair, I doubt not the nearest lantern would be your destination."

Pauline turned pale. "But, citizen - "

"Believe me, you are perfectly safe here," said Latour. "In a few days the people will know that they made a mistake, and you will be a heroine."

"I will stay here," she said. "You are sure the woman who brings my food and looks after these rooms will not betray me?"

"I am certain of that. She believes you are very dear to me, and she is mine body and soul. Now I come to the second point. It is known that this aristocrat is, or was, in Paris. It is certain that Lucien Bruslart knew this; it is almost certain that he has found her a safe hiding-place. That makes you angry, but there is something more. He knew that Jeanne St. Clair was supposed to have been arrested in his apartment, knew that a mistake had been made, but he has taken no steps to put that mistake right. Is it not possible, even probable, that he knows you were arrested in her place, and that it has suited his plans to remain silent?"

Pauline sprang from her chair, her eyes blazing, her little hands clinched, her whole frame vibrating with the lust for revenge.

"If I thought - "

"Citizeness, I am your friend," said Latour. "We will find out. At present, Lucien Bruslart is not to be found. For three days, ever since your escape, mark you, he has not been near his apartment."

"You shall help me," said Pauline, savagely. "I will not yet believe him false, but if he is, he shall pay for it. I should laugh to see his neck under the knife."

"You let me into a secret, citizeness, the greatness of your love."

"Great love like mine means hatred if it is scorned," she said; and then she added quickly, "But he may have got safely away from Paris."

There was in her attitude that sudden savagery which a cat shows at the prospect of being robbed of its prey.

"He has not left Paris," said Latour.

"Even if he had, I should find him," she said.

Latour left her and returned to his own rooms.

"This woman will find him, once she is let loose," he muttered. "I can almost pity Citizen Bruslart, thrice damned villain that he is. And Barrington? I must see Barrington."

CHAPTER XVIII

DR. LEGRAND'S ASYLUM

The Rue Charonne was a long street extending toward the outer limits of the city, and while at one end, near the Chat Rouge Tavern, it was a busy thoroughfare with crowded Streets on either side of it, at the other end it was quiet, and almost deserted in the evenings. The houses were less closely packed, and there were walls which trees overhung, telling of pleasant and shady gardens.

Behind such a wall the passer-by had a glimpse of the upper windows and steep roof of a house of considerable size. On one side of it stretched a garden, on the other some outbuildings joined it to another house which had nothing to do with it, but was one of a block of rather old houses which faced the street.

This house, in its pleasant garden, was, as every one knew, a private asylum and sanatorium conducted by Dr. Legrand. He had come there half a dozen years ago, and for some time there had been only a few inmates, not dangerously insane, but unfit to be at large, and two or three others who had retired into this retreat to end their days in peace. In the last few months, however, the number of residents had vastly increased. Certainly every room in the house must be occupied, the larger rooms probably divided into two or three, the neighbors argued, and most of the inmates did not appear to be insane. It was not a time to busy one's self about other people's affairs, it was much safer neither to gossip nor to listen to gossip; so to many persons the riddle of Monsieur Legrand's sudden prosperity remained unsolved.

Yet many people understood the riddle, and were not slow to profit by it. This house, although one of the best known, was not the only one of its kind to be found in Paris. Legrand was a man of business as well as a doctor, a better man of business than he was a doctor, and perceived, almost by a stroke of genius, how he might profit by the Revolution. To many a revolutionary leader gold was better than the head of an aristocrat, although by that curious twist of conscience which men can so easily contrive for themselves, direct bribery was not to be thought of. Dr. Legrand seemed to thoroughly understand this twisted and diseased conscience, and had a remedy to offer. What persuasion he used, what proportion of his exorbitant fees found its way into other pockets, cannot be said, it was a secret he locked up in his own soul, but it soon became known that aristocrats, fortunate enough to be prisoners in this house in the Rue Charonne, were safe so long as the fees were paid.

The agents of the Public Prosecutor never came there for food for the guillotine. If the fees were not paid, it invariably meant that some ill turn of fortune, which Legrand was quite unable to explain, necessitated the speedy removal of the delinquent to the Abbaye, to Sainte Pelagie, or one of the other prisons where their days were almost certain to be few.

A round-faced man, with generosity beaming in his eyes, was Dr. Legrand. His prisoners, or guests as he preferred to call them, were free to roam the house or the grounds at their will; if the table he kept was not liberal, a certain etiquette was indulged in which did something to cover the parsimony, and the insane inmates who remained in the house were pushed out of the way into odd corners as much

PERCY BREBNER

as possible.

Into the doctor's study one morning there had come a man and a woman.

"I have come as arranged," said the man. "This is the lady."

Legrand bowed low, and appeared to overflow with benevolence.

"I am happy to welcome such a guest," he said. "There are certain formalities, and then you are as safe, mademoiselle, as you could be at Beauvais."

So it was that Mademoiselle St. Clair came to be a guest at the house in the Rue Charonne, brought there for safety by Lucien Bruslart. She had been there a week when, not far away, Richard Barrington had been obliged to run for his life, and with the help of a man, whose identity the dark entry concealed, had jumped into safety. Of this she knew nothing; she was as ignorant of what was passing in the city as though hundreds of miles separated her from it. Lucien had found her a safe retreat, and the time was not so heavy on her hands as she had expected. Although she chanced upon no intimate friends in Dr. Legrand's house, she met several acquaintances, men and women she had known something of before the flight to Beauvais. They had much to talk of in the day, and in the evenings they sang and danced. If care was heavy upon some of them, smiling faces were made to mask the fact. Saturday was a day of apprehension, a day of which the ending was greeted with a sigh of relief. It was the day for paying fees. Some the inmates paid their own, their purses refilled by friends who were free; the fees of many were paid direct to the doctor by their friends. This was the arrangement in Mademoiselle St. Clair's case. Lucien had told her that it would be the most satisfactory way, and she had given him power to draw on her money for the purpose. He had a special agreement with Legrand, he said, for Jeanne was there on a different footing from the other guests. He hinted too that Legrand was under such obligations to him that any favor he asked was practically a command. It was not until the second Saturday had passed that Jeanne understood all that the payment of these fees meant. At the table that night there were two empty places, a man's and a woman's. She asked her neighbor, an elderly Abbe, who had lived well all his life until he came to the Rue Charonne and was forever grumbling at the extortion practiced, what had become of them.

"Removed to another prison, mademoiselle. I did not hear which."

"But why?"

"They could not afford to remain here. They are not the first I have seen made bankrupt by Legrand."

"Ah! this hateful revolution!"

"It will end, mademoiselle. Already the dogs begin to tear one another, and when that happens, the quarry escapes."

"It will end, yes; but when? How long?"

"Before our purses run dry, I trust, mademoiselle," answered the Abbe, with a smile.

Jeanne had no fear for her own safety, but great compassion for others. She began to hate the smiling face of Dr. Legrand. She heard something of the enormous sums he charged, and wondered what Lucien was paying for her, and how long he would have to pay it. He had said that at least a month must elapse before it would be safe to make an attempt to leave Paris. Unfortunately, he had to think of his own safety as well as hers. Poor Lucien! She had braved

Paris to help him, and her presence in the city had only added to his difficulty and danger. What was he doing day by day to end it all? Was Monsieur Barrington helping him? Lucien would be foolish not to accept the help of such a man, so brave, so full of resource, so -

These thoughts concerning Richard Barrington made Jeanne start a little. She was suddenly conscious that she was comparing the two men, and that one seemed to take hold of her, hurry her along, as it were, and absorb her attention, until she could only bring her thoughts back to the other with an effort. Barrington stood out clear and distinct, definite in word and action, knowing what he intended to do and doing it without thinking of failure; Lucien was a shadow in comparison, indistinct, waiting rather than acting. Barrington would have made an attempt to get her out of Paris before this, and Jeanne was convinced that she would have gone without fear. If the enterprise had failed, it would have been a splendid failure. Lucien had not made the attempt. She did not blame him, his nature was to exercise greater caution, and when he did move, perhaps the chances of success would be greater; yet she knew that with Lucien she would feel greater responsibility, feel that she was obliged to protect him almost as much as he protected her. Lucien would ask her advice and be guided by it; Barrington would tell her what to do and be angry if she did not obey at once.

"It is my love which makes the difference," she told herself. "A woman must exercise protection over the man she loves. In the love of all good women there is the mother instinct. That is the reason why I feel like this toward Lucien." And then she thought of how she had passed the barrier with Barrington and his servant Seth. It seemed a mad scheme, yet it had succeeded. And Lucien had asked her whether this man was to be trusted!

So the days passed, much dreaming in them for want of

other employment. It was sometimes too cold and wet to walk much in the garden, and the sense of confinement within high walls was depressing. Not always could cards or music dispel the anxiety which these guests had to endure, and Jeanne, with all her bravery, had hard work to keep her tears back at times. She had been at the house in the Rue Charonne a month when Marie, a maid of all work in the establishment, came to her one morning, a frightened look in her face and evidences of tears in her eyes. Marie was generally assumed to be of rather weak intellect, chiefly perhaps because she made no complaint against the drudgery of her life, and because, unlike the other servants, she did not copy the rapacity of the master and extort fees at every opportunity. She was especially attached to Mademoiselle St. Clair, who had in times past befriended her aged mother, and she had endeavored to repay the debt by special devotion to her, and, when they chanced to be alone, by a loquacity which was intended to be encouraging. Her present doleful appearance was therefore the more surprising.

"What is the matter, Marie?" Jeanne asked.

"The doctor wants to see you in his study."

"I wasn't thinking of your message, but of your appearance. You have been crying."

"Yes, that's the reason," Marie answered. "The master wants to see you, and it's Saturday morning."

Jeanne had forgotten the day, and the information, coupled with the message, startled her for a moment.

"There is no need to be afraid, Marie," she said quietly.

"I know you're brave, you couldn't be anything else," returned the girl, "but I know what Saturday morning in that study means. Mademoiselle, I'll do anything I can. No one takes any notice of me. I can slip out of the house almost any time I like."

"Thank you, Marie. I will not forget."

In spite of the servant girl's pessimistic view, Jeanne had little apprehension as she went to the doctor's study, and Legrand's method of receiving her was reassuring. He rose, bowed low and placed a chair for her. He spoke of the pleasant crispness in the air, of the little dance which had taken place in the salon on the previous night.

"Even the Abbe was persuaded to a few steps," he laughed. "It was very amusing."

"I am waiting to hear the business which necessitates my presence here," said Jeanne.

"Ah, mademoiselle, it is a painful matter; it pains me. There is no remittance from Monsieur Bruslart this week. It has always come on Friday night, but this is Saturday morning and it is still not here."

Jeanne did not answer for a moment.

"Of course there is some mistake," she said.

"I thought so," said Legrand. "It did not trouble me much last night, but this morning - mademoiselle, I was so surprised that I called on Monsieur Bruslart this morning. He has left Paris."

"Gone!"

"Leaving no word behind him, mademoiselle."

"It is more likely that he has been arrested," said Jeanne.

"I have inquired. He has not been arrested, but he would have been had he remained."

"Are you suggesting that he has run away without a thought for me?"

"Mademoiselle, the most prominent members of my profession have little knowledge of men's thoughts. Of the working of Monsieur Bruslart's mind I know nothing; I only know that he has left Paris without sending money."

"And the consequence to me?" asked Jeanne.

"That is what pains me," Legrand answered. "This house is secure only on certain conditions, a peculiar arrangement in which I have personally little influence. Some of my guests are ungracious enough to disbelieve this. When the fees remain unpaid I have no choice in the matter. My guest is removed elsewhere."

Jeanne showed not a trace of nervousness or alarm. The whirl of thoughts and doubts in her brain caused the lines in her face to harden a little, but there was no quiver in her eyes, no tremble in her voice.

"Is the money paid in advance?" she asked.

"Always, mademoiselle; that is one of the conditions."

"Then it is for the coming week that the money is due?"

"That is so."

"I do not know, Dr. Legrand, whether you are fully aware of Monsieur Bruslart's position and my own?"

"I think so, mademoiselle. You were, I believe, to be man and wife."

His suggestion that such a thing was now impossible was not lost upon Jeanne and was a little startling. Did he believe that Lucien Bruslart was a scoundrel?

"Do you know that the fees paid to you by Lucien Bruslart are paid out of my money?"

"Officially I only know that they are paid by a certain person, and I ask no questions. Having some knowledge of Monsieur Bruslart's position, I have imagined that the necessary money was supplied by you."

"I have only to authorize the banker who has funds of mine in hand to pay the amount."

"Mademoiselle, I naturally thought of that. All that was necessary was a form for your signature, so I called upon the banker. I regret to tell you that he has no longer any funds of yours in hand. The whole amount has been withdrawn."

"By whom?"

Legrand shrugged his shoulders.

"I do not know. If you wish me to make a guess, I should say by Lucien Bruslart. You will know whether he had any document in his possession giving him such power."

Jeanne knew that he had. She had trusted him fully. Even now she did not jump to the hasty conclusion that he had betrayed that trust. There might be a dozen good reasons why he had withdrawn the money; to save it from being misappropriated by the State consequent on the banker's possible arrest, or to spend carefully in arranging her escape. It was probably an accident that the messenger had not arrived with the money this week, and in preparation for escape it was quite likely that Lucien might let it be understood that he had left Paris. He would not be likely to confide in Monsieur Legrand. He would certainly not desert her.

"Will you tell me the amount due for next week?" she asked.

The doctor took a paper from a drawer and handed it to her. She uttered a sudden exclamation as she saw the amount.

"It is out of all reason," she said.

"Mademoiselle, the security offered by this house may be said to be out of all reason too."

"If this is paid, I remain a guest for another week?"

"Until next Saturday."

Jeanne took her purse and counted out the money. She had little left when it was done.

"Count it, Dr. Legrand, and give me the receipt."

His eyes beamed as he counted and found the sum correct.

"I am happy again," he said. "So much may happen in a week. I assure you, mademoiselle, your ability to pay lifts years from my shoulders."

"Yes, monsieur, I have bought a long respite," Jeanne said, rising as she took the receipt. "I doubt not much will happen in a week."

As she went out and closed the door, Legrand placed the money in a drawer which he locked.

"It was a warning," he muttered, "and she has robbed me of seeming generous by promising to give her a week free of cost. She must have touched me in some way, or I should never have thought of giving her such a warning. It was a fortunate idea. Had I left it until next Saturday she would have been able to pay for another week, and I should have been obliged to hunt for a pretext for refusing her money. She must be removed elsewhere next Saturday. My little consideration, my wish to prepare her, has turned out well; besides, I have received double fees for this coming week. I cannot complain."

Alone in her own room, Jeanne nearly broke down. The strain of the interview and all that it implied left her with little strength to fight the despair that settled upon her. Yet she held back the tears that threatened, and fought back the disposition to fling herself upon the mean little bed and give way to her grief. A week! Only a week! She had bought it at an enormous price and every hour in it was of immense value. If Lucien Bruslart were a traitor, she had still one friend in Paris. She was as sure of this as of the emblematic meaning of the small crucifix which she had hung above her bed. She must act. There was no time to give way to despair.

On scraps of paper she wrote a long letter, telling the whole history of the house in the Rue Charonne, how she came to be there, and the peril she was in. She sealed it, and then waited until she could get Marie alone.

"Marie, you promised to help me."

"I meant it. What can I do, mademoiselle?"

Jeanne gave the girl minute instructions for finding the house in which the Marquis de Lafayette had his apartment, and Marie showed little sign of weak-mindedness as she listened.

"I know the house, mademoiselle."

"Go there, say you come from me and ask to see him. Give him this letter and ask him to see that it is safely delivered."

"And if he is away, mademoiselle?"

"Then ask his servant to tell you where the man to whom this letter is addressed lives."

"And if he does not know?"

"Ah, Marie, I cannot tell what you are to do then. Take the letter, hide it away. Heaven grant it reaches its destination."

Marie stood with the letter in her hand.

"Who's it to? I cannot read, mademoiselle, but if I know the name, I may find him even if the servant doesn't know."

"It is addressed to Monsieur Richard Barrington," said Jeanne.

The girl put the letter into her pocket, and patted her dress to emphasize the security of the hiding-place.

"I'll go to-morrow. I have a holiday all day; that gives me plenty of time to find the man who loves mademoiselle. Richard Barrington; I shall not forget the name."

"Not my lover, Marie."

"Ah, mademoiselle, why pretend with me? Yours is not the first secret I have kept."

CHAPTER XIX

CITIZEN SABATIER TURNS TRAITOR

The Rue Charonne in the neighborhood of the Chat Rouge was a busy street. Its importance as a business quarter had been on the increase for some years, yet in the adjoining back streets extreme poverty existed and there were warrens of iniquity into which the law had feared to penetrate too deeply. It was an old part of the city, too, built on land once belonging to a monastery whose memory was still kept alive by the names of mean streets and alleys into which byways respectable citizens did not go. There were stories current of men who had ventured and had never come forth again. With some of the inhabitants, it was asserted, the attainment of an almost worthless trinket, or a single coin, or even a garment, was considered cheap as the price of murder; and so intricate were the streets, so honeycombed with secret hiding-places known only to the initiated, that attempts to enforce justice had almost invariably ended in failure. Naturally this squalid neighborhood materially swelled the yelling crowds who, in the name of patriotism, openly defied all law and order, and made outrage and murder a national duty as they drank, and danced, and sang the "Ca-ira," flaunting their rags, sometimes even their nakedness.

Into the midst of such a crowd Richard Barrington had walked as he went to the Chat Rouge; as bloodthirsty a mob as he could possibly have encountered in all Paris, and the Rue Charonne had been turned into Pandemonium when it was realized that the quarry had escaped. Houses were forcibly entered, men and women insulted and ill-used, the Chat Rouge was invaded and searched, the landlord barely escaping with his life. The opportunity to drink without cost presently kept the mob busy, however, and as the liquor took effect the work of searching was abandoned for the night, but the next morning the crowd came together again, and for days it was unsafe to go abroad in the Rue Charonne.

Of this quarter was Citizen Jacques Sabatier, never so criminal as many of his fellows, perhaps, yet a dangerous man. He might pass along these streets in safety, and since he had become a man of some importance, had influence with this mob. Through him Raymond Latour could count upon the support of those who dwelt in the purlieus of the Rue Charonne, but both he and his henchman knew perfectly well that there were times when any attempt to exert such influence would be useless. Sabatier, waiting by the Chat Rouge, had heard the sudden cry, "An aristocrat! The American!" yet he dared not have interfered openly to save Barrington. Had the fugitive not turned suddenly into the archway where Sabatier waited, it is certain that Sabatier would not have gone out to rescue him. The chance to help him at little risk had offered itself, and he had taken it.

As Richard Barrington rose to his feet in the straw, he was in pitch darkness, but not alone. There was a quick movement beside him, and then a voice whispering in his ear:

"A narrow escape. Give me your hand; I will lead you into a place of greater safety."

Barrington had no idea who his deliverer was, but he thanked him and took his hand. He was led along evil-smelling passages into which no ray of light penetrated, but which were evidently familiar to his guide. There were turnings, now to right, now to left, an opening and shutting of doors, and finally entrance into a wider space where the air was comparatively fresh.

"One moment and I will get a light."

The dim light from the lantern revealed a small chamber, square and built of stone, the work of a past age. A barred grating high up in the wall let in air, and possibly light in the daytime. A common chair and table standing in the center, a bowl with a water can beside it in one corner, and a heap of straw in another comprised the furniture. These things Barrington noticed at once, and then recognized that the man who set the lantern on the table was Jacques Sabatier.

"A prison," said Barrington.

"A place of refuge, citizen," was the answer. "Were you not here, you would be decorating a lantern by this time."

"We meet in Paris under strange circumstances," said Barrington.

"Still we do meet. Did I not say at Tremont that every true patriot must sooner or later meet Jacques Sabatier in Paris, though for that matter I expected it to be in a wine shop and not here, underground."

"Where are we?"

"In a cell of the old monastery which once stood hard by the Rue Charonne, which has served as a cellar at some time, but now for a long while has been forgotten. Citizen Latour would have been here with mademoiselle to meet you, but the mob in the neighborhood will keep them away to-night. You must wait here, monsieur, it may be for some days."

"Mademoiselle is safe?"

"Quite safe in the care of Deputy Latour. I had the honor of helping him to bring her out of the Abbaye prison."

"And what are Citizen Latour's plans for getting her out of Paris?"

"He is making them, but they change from day to day as the circumstances change. At the first opportunity he will come to you."

"I must wait with what patience I can," said Barrington.

"And remain as quiet as you can," said Sabatier. "The crowd will be hunting for you for some time, and a noise might attract them."

"I shall not court death; I have a good deal to live for," said Barrington.

"Then, monsieur, I will leave you. Citizen Latour will be distressed until he knows you are safe."

Richard Barrington's patience was destined to be sufficiently tried. It was a poor, miserable caricature of daylight which found its way through the barred grating, and for three days Sabatier visited him every morning with the same news that the crowds parading the Rue Charonne made it impossible for Latour to come.

"Is it necessary to lock me in?" Barrington asked.

"It is not to prevent your going out, monsieur, but to insure that your enemies do not come in."

"I feel like a prisoner."

"Better that than falling into the hands of the mob."

On the fourth day Sabatier brought a message from Latour. Barrington's servant Seth had been to him inquiring about his master. Naturally, perhaps, he was not inclined to believe Latour's word that he was safe, and unless he had some definite proof might ruin everything by making inquiries in other directions.

"Will you write a letter to your servant, monsieur, telling him to wait until he has further instructions from you?"

"Might he not come to me here?"

"For the present that would be too dangerous," Sabatier answered. "I come and go, monsieur, because I was bred in this quarter of the city. The mob claims me as a part of it, and truly I am, except in this business. I began by simply obeying Citizen Latour, for my own benefit, I make no secret of it; now I am also interested in Monsieur Barrington."

The letter to Seth was written and given to Sabatier to deliver. Two more weary days of waiting passed, and then late one afternoon Raymond Latour came.

Barrington welcomed him, both hands held out to him.

"It was bravely done," he exclaimed. "You must have run great risk in getting her from the Abbaye prison."

"Yes, great risk. I have come to talk to you about it."

Latour ignored the outstretched hands. He stood in front of Barrington with folded arms. There was something amiss.

"What has happened?" Barrington asked.

"The usual thing when an honest man trusts a liar; the honest man has been deceived."

"You speak of - "

"Of one Richard Barrington, a liar I was fool enough to trust. Oh, this is no time for fighting," Latour went on quickly, as sudden anger stiffened Barrington's figure, and gave a dangerous fire to his eyes. "You will be wise to hear me out. This was a place of safety, it is a prison, and a word from me will send you to the guillotine as surely as we are standing face to face at this moment."

"First prove me a liar; afterward threaten me if you will," Barrington returned.

Latour regarded him in silence for a few moments and then said slowly:

"Tell me, where is Jeanne St. Clair?"

"Jeanne! She has gone?" cried Barrington. "Sabatier said she was with you, that she - "

"It is well done, monsieur; I am no longer a fool or I might be convinced, might still be deceived."

"For Heaven's sake, man, tell me what you mean," and Barrington spoke hoarsely.

"If it pleases you to keep up the deception, let me put facts plainly," said Latour. "You admit the risk I ran in securing an escape from the Abbaye Prison; you know that the risk was run to no purpose. It was well planned, it was successful, but the woman rescued was not Mademoiselle St. Clair."

"You made a mistake?"

"There was no mistake. The woman was Pauline Vaison, a woman Lucien Bruslart has promised to marry. The mob found her in his apartment, took her for the aristocrat, and carried her to prison in the place of mademoiselle. You are Bruslart's friend and accomplice. I ask you again, where is Jeanne St. Clair?"

It never occurred to Richard Barrington that Latour might be deceiving him, and for the moment he had no thought how he could best convince Latour that he was innocent of any deception. He was utterly overwhelmed by the news. Deep down in his heart he had never really trusted Lucien Bruslart, and all this time Jeanne had been in his hands. Bruslart then had lied from the first, had imposed upon him his feigned grief, and all the time he had been perfecting some foul plot. What had become of Jeanne? The horrible possibilities unnerved him, took the heart out of him. He was as a man who when brought face to face with peril is afraid, who shrinks back and would fly if he could. Latour knew nothing of the thoughts rushing through Barrington's brain, he only saw a man with the courage suddenly gone out of him; he put his own construction upon his manner and laughed.

"It is always unpleasant when the time comes to pay for such deceit," he said.

"I swear to you"

"Spare yourself. I have asked you a question. I want it answered."

"I don't know where she is. I wish to Heaven I did."

"It suits my purpose to give you time to think better of your answer," said Latour. "You shall even buy your miserable life by telling the truth. When you tell me where Mademoiselle St. Clair is, you shall leave this prison, not before. I will even do something to get you safely out of Paris and to the seacoast."

"I tell you I do not know. Find Bruslart, ask him."

"I have you safe, that is enough; and I would advise you to come to my terms quickly. There is no escape except through me. Your letter has silenced your servant, and his patience is likely to outlast mine. Tell the truth quickly, Monsieur Barrington; it will be safer."

Latour turned to the door, but Barrington sprang toward him and caught him by the arm.

"Are you mad? Think of her; she is in Bruslart's hands."

Latour wrenched himself free, and as he turned sharply there was a pistol in his hand.

"Stand where you are! I would shoot you like a dog rather than let you escape."

"The devil take you for a fool!" exclaimed Barrington. "I thought I had a man to deal with!" and he turned his back upon Latour, who went out of the room, locking the door after him.

Barrington's anger was quickly absorbed in the realization of the utter hopelessness of his position. Latour had trapped him. When he sent him the appointment to come to the Chat Rouge, he must have known what he had told him to-day; he had deliberately said nothing until after Seth's anxiety had been quieted; and his jailer, Jacques Sabatier, was a party to the deceit. Latour had it firmly fixed in his mind that he was in league with Bruslart, and it seemed that nothing short of a miracle would drive this idea out of his mind. Barrington could conceive no way in which he could convince him, and the thought that all this while

Jeanne was in peril almost drove him mad. Could he escape? For the first time since he had entered it he examined his stone cellar carefully. It was a very grave for security.

When Sabatier visited him next morning, his manner gave Barrington an idea. Sabatier entered more carefully than he was wont to do, his hand upon a pistol thrust into his tri-color sash. It was evident he feared attack. His greeting was friendly, however; he showed a keen interest in the prisoner, and gave him odds and ends of news which were of little importance.

"Any message for Citizen Latour?" he asked as he was leaving.

"Tell him he is a fool."

Why should Barrington not attack and overpower his jailer? It might be useless, perhaps others were watching in the passage without, ready to rush in at the slightest sound; still, it would be something attempted. He had succeeded in silencing the man at the Lion d'Or that night, why should he not succeed again?

The next morning Sabatier came before his time, Barrington was not ready to take him unawares. Again he asked the same question, and Barrington gave him a similar answer.

"Tell Latour he is a fool."

"I will. He may end by believing it. I may have news for you to-morrow."

There was meaning in the words, a suggestion that the news might be good news. Barrington decided to give his jailer a chance of telling it.

Sabatier came at the usual hour.

"Do you bring news?" Barrington asked.

"Citizen Latour remains a fool. I mean it. I do not believe you know where mademoiselle is."

"Then you will help me?"

"Monsieur, I try every day to persuade Deputy Latour that he is mistaken."

"We must try another way, Sabatier."

"I will, if monsieur will agree to what I say. I have to think of myself, and Citizen Latour is a dangerous man to thwart. For a day or two longer I will try and persuade him; if I fail I will do my best to help you to escape, but you must be patient or you put my neck under the knife. Do you agree?"

"Agree! I must. I have no choice."

"Your servant Seth might help me; where shall I find him?"

"My good friend, how can I tell? Paris is a large place," was the prompt answer. Barrington was not going to speak of Monsieur Fargeau. His house might presently prove the only safe retreat for him in the city.

"It is a pity, but I shall manage alone," Sabatier answered. "Am I to give the usual answer to Citizen Latour?"

"Yes. Can any answer be better than the truth?"

Had a miracle happened? Was this man honestly meaning to help him, or had he seen that the prisoner intended to attack him and chosen this way of protecting himself? Barrington could not tell. He could only wait and see.

CHAPTER XX

THE LETTER

Jacque Sabatier is busy in these days, also his master Raymond Latour. Their private affairs must proceed as quickly as possible, but there are public affairs which must be done at once, which cannot wait, which a frenzied people loudly demand with cursings and dancings and mad songs.

War thunders along the frontiers, and passes beyond them. Such a gathering of nations in arms that right and justice may be done, is a new thing. Paris has realized its danger, has known it for weeks past; Jacques Danton, mighty in the Club of the Cordeliers, has urged it with great words, with a great voice which has made the rafters ring; more, he has shown how the danger must be met. Safety lies in daring, not once but again and always. "De l'audace, encore de l'audace, toujours de l'audace et la France est sauvee." It is a battlecry which has stirred hearts, and sent ill-conditioned men to face trained regiments, which are surprised when such a ragged rabble does not turn and run. Courage is under those rags and something of true patriotism. But there are other patriots in Paris, and of a different sort. The frontiers are a long way off, but here to hand is work for them, work which is easy and pleases them. The Place de la Revolution is their battlefield where they can yell their war crys and their war songs; their weapon is the guillotine, and the guillotine is always victorious. The enemy, cursed aristocrats, and others not aristocrats but equally cursed because they differ from the people and the people's demigods, are foredoomed to defeat and death. Only one thing is lacking, sufficient enemies that the guillotine may not stand idle. Each day must bring its excitement. The denizens of the slums and alleys of Paris must have their amusement day by day. The inhabitants of the narrow streets off the Rue Charonne have forgotten the American they hunted so fiercely, although Richard Barrington waiting in his underground prison does not know it. They are yelling, half afraid of their own audacity, for another victim. They gather daily, in another part of the city, by the Riding Hall close to the Tuileries. There is excitement in plenty here. In the Rue Charonne one might walk in safety.

From the Temple prison an aristocrat, more, a king, has been brought to answer the charges made against him. They are charges only recently framed and strangely got together. Save that he is a king, which he cannot help, what charges can be brought against him? None. There are many who would make them on the flimsiest foundation, but even such a foundation does not exist. Danton himself cannot send a king to the Place de la Revolution for nothing. That would be to dare too greatly. They have found nothing at the Tuileries or at Versailles to condemn him. Roland has had diligent search made, fearful perchance of some letters of his own being found; even the cesspools of the palace have been dragged. There is no result worth the trouble. No drawer has any secret to give up save one which has no accusation in it, a child's letter, simple, loving wishes for a happy New Year, signed by the little Dauphin, addressed to "My dear Papa." Little enough can Roland make out of this, for he has no ability to understand even the pathos of it. Then one day there comes from Versailles, one, Francois Gamain by name, a locksmith of that place, a coward fearful for his own safety. The king has been fond of lock-making, something of the craft Gamain has taught him, and the king has shared a secret with him. There is a hiding-place in a corridor behind the king's bedroom, which Gamain has helped to make, which he now shows to Roland. There are papers there, many of them, enough in them to prepare evidence against the king and many others, if necessary; and lest this should fail Gamain has a story that when the work was done the king attempted to poison him so that the secret might be safe. So the king must be tried. And louder than ever thunders the war along the frontier while this trial goes forward. There can be no quarter, no terms of peace. The sword is sharply naked, there is no scabbard in which to sheath it. What gauge shall France hurl at the feet of her enemies? Once again Danton, mighty in the Club of the Cordeliers, suggests the answer: Why not the head of a king?

Raymond Latour was busy. Little time could he give to Sabatier when he came each morning to make report of the prisoner in his cell underground; he was not inclined to listen to Sabatier's persuasion, or to be impressed by his henchman's ideas.

"He knows where she is. He shall tell the truth."

It was Latour's daily statement, although Sabatier thought it was less definitely said as the days passed. He was not sure whether Latour's faith in his conviction was wavering, or whether it was only that he had other things to think of.

Those who served Latour were kept busy. It was a time when loss of popularity might be dangerous, and their master had thrown his into the balance. His voice had been heard in the Riding Hall where friends were daily being divided and factions made. He had spoken on behalf of Louis Capet. The head of a king was not necessary to save France. He had naught to do with mercy, not even with expedience; Justice spoke louder than either, and Justice would not be served by the death of Louis Capet. There were some who roared at him, some who shouted for him; it was difficult to tell which side was the more numerous.

Robespierre looked at Latour but said nothing. Danton tried argument. Barrere, the President, tried to understand the popular feeling, and failed. Raymond Latour had many friends, but he turned some old friends into enemies by his speech. He was farseeing enough to know that his desire for Justice was dangerous, would be doubly so unless his hold upon the different sections of the populace was maintained. So Sabatier, Mercier, Dubois and the rest had much to do in the districts and among those sections of the populace where they had influence.

Still every morning, Sabatier kept Latour in mind of his private affairs, and argued with him. He did not wait to receive advice, he gave it, and in such a way that Latour listened. He was still convinced of Barrington's deceit, but time was passing and mademoiselle was not found.

"Even if he knows, the American is not a man to betray confidence. Under like circumstances you would not speak yourself, citizen."

"True. I should go to the guillotine as he must."

"Not yet," said Sabatier. "Give him time and opportunity."

"Curse him," said Latour. "I want to hear no more about him, I only want to know that mademoiselle is found."

In his daily visits to Barrington, Sabatier said little of what was passing in Paris, but much to persuade him to patience; and as he went along the streets he kept his eyes open hoping to see Seth. He did not see him, yet another man gave him the clew and unwittingly directed him to the house of Citizen Fargeau.

Seth went little abroad in these days. It was not fear which kept him within doors, but the hope of receiving at any moment further word of his master. Everything might depend on prompt action when the moment came. Few men could remain so patiently inactive as Seth, once he was convinced that inaction was the best course to pursue. This Latour had not lied to him. The promised letter from Richard Barrington had been given to him, he knew that it was genuine, and was content to obey that letter. For the time being he was as little interested in politics as Fargeau was, and the news of the king's trial which came into this quiet retreat had an unreal sound about it, like a faint echo of something happening a great way off. Richard Barrington filled Seth's mind, he had little room for any other thoughts.

One evening there came a knock at his door and the servant of Monsieur de Lafayette entered.

"News, at last," Seth said, and in a tone which showed that in spite of his patience, the waiting had been weary work.

"A letter," the man answered.

Seth looked at it. It was addressed to Richard Barrington, just the name written, that was all.

"How did you get it?" asked Seth.

"A girl brought it only to-day. She asked for my master, and when I told her he was not in Paris, she asked where she could find Monsieur Barrington. I did not tell her, but I said I could deliver the letter."

Seth nodded as he turned the letter over and over, a puzzled expression in his face.

"She seemed doubtful about leaving it with me, but in the end did so, saying it was a matter of life and death."

"It's good of you to have brought it," said Seth. "She did

not say who it was from?"

"No."

"Look at the writing again and tell me if by any chance it comes from the Marquis."

"That's a woman's writing," said the man.

"But not a writing you know?"

"Quite strange to me."

When he was alone, Seth locked his door and again examined the writing. His master only knew one woman in Paris, and surely she could not be writing to him. She must know where he was. If she didn't, then in some fashion Latour had deceived him. He put the letter on the table and began to walk slowly about the room.

"It is right that I should open it," he said suddenly. "It may be a matter of life and death to Master Richard. He will forgive me."

He took up the letter, and after a little hesitation tore it open.

"It is from her," he said, glancing at the name on the last of the scraps of paper of which the letter was composed. "I was right to open it."

He sat down by the table and read it slowly, certain portions of it he read a second time, and at intervals made a sound with his mouth like an oath cut short, or a gasp of surprise half suppressed. So Latour had lied, and Bruslart had lied, and mademoiselle was -

"A life and death matter! It's true. It is. Oh, Master

Richard, where are you? It's your letter. She calls to you. What can I do?"

The words were muttered in hot haste as though the answer must come quickly. It did.

"Your letter, yet mine since you are not here. So your work becomes mine, Master Richard. I must rescue mademoiselle. How? Let me think. Let me think. God, help me to think."

There was a slow, heavy footstep upon the stairs, and in a moment Seth had hidden the letter. Then a knock at the door. Seth opened it, and stood face to face with Jacques Sabatier, who had his finger upon his lip.

"Let me in, citizen. I have turned traitor and have a story to tell."

CHAPTER XXI

THE MARQUIS DE CASTELLUX

Much the same thing had Sabatier said to Richard Barrington only that morning.

"Deputy Latour will not believe in you," he explained. "He is a fool as I have told him each day, giving him your message, and I am tired of serving fools. A day or two, monsieur, and you shall be free. Sabatier promises that. I am turning traitor."

Barrington thanked him, he could do no less, yet he felt little trust in a man who could confess so glibly to treachery. He would believe the promise when his prison door stood open, when he was free to walk out unhindered, not before.

That day was a long one; indeed, each day seemed longer than the one which preceded it. Confinement was beginning to tell its tale on Barrington. This underground dungeon, it was little better, was gradually taking the heart out of him. At first he had been able to forget long hours in sleep, but latterly this had been denied him. Sleepless nights succeeded restless days.

To-night he was restless. The silence about him was like the silence of the grave, this place was almost as hopeless as the grave. He wondered how thick these stone walls might be, whether there were other dungeons beyond where other

PERCY BREBNER

prisoners wore out their hearts. He stood beneath the barred grating for a little while, listening. Even the world without seemed dead. No sound ever came through that narrow opening. What saint, or repentant sinner had dragged out his days here when this was a cell in a monastery? Had he never regretted his vows and longed for the world of sunshine and rain, of blue sky and breezy plain, of star-lit nights and rough weather? Surely he must have done? The world of sinners was a fairer place than this stone dwelling though a saint lodged in it. Truly it was a secure hiding place, or a prison where one might easily be forgotten. The thought was a horrible one, and Barrington went to the door. It was locked. It was a stout door, too, of wood and iron. If Latour and Sabatier were arrested, as might easily happen, that door would remain locked. Probably no other person knew that he was there. He was in the mood when such thoughts cannot be driven out of the brain. There was half a bottle of thin wine remaining from his last meal, and he drank it greedily. His throat was suddenly dry and his hand was unsteady as he raised the glass to his lips. He was conscious of the fact, shook himself, stamped his foot sharply on the stone floor, and spoke to himself aloud.

"This is cowardice, Richard, and for cowardice there is no excuse."

Something like that his mother had once said to him. He had not remembered it until he had spoken the words, and then the recollection brought many scenes to his mind, dreams of youth, back, how far back? how long ago? memories of old times, a green hummock and the blue waters of Chesapeake Bay. The world had changed since then. Father, mother gone, voices silent forever, loved voices never to be forgotten; and yet, in those days there had been no Jeanne.

"Jeanne!" he said aloud. "Jeanne!"

Then he was silent, and his nerves grew tense. The silence was suddenly broken, not rudely but stealthily as a thief breaks it, or as one who knows that crime is best accomplished in the night; a key was being fumbled into the lock. Sabatier would open quickly, knowing the key and the lock, besides, Sabatier had never come at this hour. It was a stranger. Friend or foe? Barrington moved towards the door. Whoever came would find him awake, ready to sell life dearly, perchance to win freedom. The key was pushed home and turned. The door opened cautiously.

"Seth!"

"Hush, Master Richard. I know not what danger is near us, but come quickly and quietly. Bring that lantern. We must chance the light until I find the way."

Barrington caught up the lantern from the table and followed him.

"He said to the right," whispered Seth.

"Who said so?" asked Barrington.

"Sabatier."

"Is he honest?"

"I don't know, Master Richard, but he brought me through many vaults and showed me the door, then left me quickly. He did not lie when he said you were behind it; and see, a way to the right and steps. He did not lie about them either."

They went up the stairs cautiously, Seth leading, and at the top was a trapdoor, unfastened, easily lifted.

"Again he told the truth," Seth whispered.

They were in a cellar full of rubbish, evil smelling, too, and at the end was a door; a turned handle opened it, and a few steps brought them up into a passage.

"Set down the lantern, Master Richard, and blow it out. We shall not need it. Come quietly."

The passage led to an open door, and they stepped into the street, little more than a narrow alley, dark and silent.

"Sabatier said to the right. All is well so far. Shall we follow his instructions to the end?"

"Yes," Barrington answered.

They came without hindrance into a wider street. It was the street in which Barrington had been attacked by the mob; half of that crowd must have come down this very alley. They went quickly, their direction towards Monsieur Fargeau's house. They entered the street in which it stood, and then Seth stopped.

"We don't go in yet, Master Richard, I have something to show you first. There is a little wine shop here, unknown to patriots, I think. It is safe, safer than Monsieur Fargeau's perchance."

The shop was empty. A woman greeted them and brought them wine.

"Read that letter, Master Richard. I will tell you how I got it, and why I opened it, afterwards."

So Jeanne's letter came into the hands of the man she had turned to in her peril and distress.

Even as he read it, bending over the scraps of paper in the poorly lighted wine shop, she was eagerly questioning

Marie. The letter was of such immense importance to her, so much hung upon it, that now it had gone Jeanne began to wonder whether the best means of getting it into the right hands had been taken, whether a surer method might not have been thought of.

"Monsieur Barrington had not left Paris?"

"No, mademoiselle, for the man said he would deliver the letter."

"Will he, Marie, will he? Do you think he was honest?"

"Yes, oh yes, he was honest, or I should not have parted with the letter."

"But he could have told you where Monsieur Barrington was and let you deliver it," said Jeanne.

"He would not do that, and he had a reason, a good one," Marie answered. "It was necessary that Monsieur Barrington's whereabouts should be kept secret. He could not tell any one where he was, he had promised. For all he knew I might be an enemy and the letter a trick. He would deliver it if I left it with him."

"You could do nothing else, Marie."

"What troubles me, mademoiselle, is how the gentleman is to help you to get away from this house," said the girl. "The master does not let people go unless he is told to by - by powerful men, men he must obey. I think he is as afraid of them as I am of him."

"Ah, Marie, if the letter only reaches Monsieur Barrington most of the danger is gone," said Jeanne. "He will find a way, I know he will. Somehow, he will help me. He is a brave man, Marie, I know, I know. He has saved me twice already. I should have no fear at all were I certain that he had the letter."

The girl was silent for a moment, and then said quietly -

"It must be wonderful to have a lover like that."

Perhaps Jeanne was too occupied with her own thoughts to notice the girl's words, perhaps she considered it impossible to make Marie understand that it is not only a lover who will do great things for a woman; at any rate, she made no answer. It mattered little what the girl thought.

It was difficult for Jeanne to live her days quietly, to look and behave as though the coming Saturday had no especial meaning for her. Legrand, when she met him, was more than usually courteous, and Jeanne was careful to treat him as she had always done. He might be watching her, and it would be well to attract as little attention as possible. She could not tell what might happen if only her letter had found its way into Richard Barrington's hands. How could he help her? What could he do?

It was January, and cold, but the weather was fine and sunny. At noon it was pleasant to walk in the garden, and many of the guests did so. The Abbe took his daily walk there even when it rained. He might have been the host by his manner, and was certainly the ruling spirit. Even Legrand seemed a little afraid of him and treated him with marked respect. The Abbe was a worldling, a lover of purple and fine linen and of the people who lived in them; he was therefore especially attentive to Jeanne St. Clair, knowing that she belonged to one of the noblest families in the land. With him Jeanne took her daily walk in the garden, and had little need to say much, for the Abbe loved to hear himself talk; she could think her own thoughts, could even be depressed without the Abbe noticing the fact. His companionship enabled her to escape from the other guests for a while without any apparent effort on her part to withdraw herself from the daily routine. She took her place in the evening amusements, occupied a seat at one of the card tables, danced and smiled, met wit with wit, and was envied by some who were not so sure of the coming Saturday as mademoiselle must surely be.

In her walks Jeanne's eyes wandered along the top of the high garden walls. Richard Barrington might come that way, or at least give her a sign that way; and when she could be alone without raising comment she watched from her window which overlooked the garden.

So the Monday and the Tuesday passed, and Wednesday dawned. How fast the week was passing! Her letter to Richard Barrington had been very urgent. She had told him all about this house, the purpose for which it was used, how the garden stood in regard to it. She had explained the general routine, had given the names of the guests. If he was to help her the fullest information would be of use. There might be some point in her description of which he could take advantage. This was Wednesday, and he had made no sign. Surely he had never got the letter.

Had not the Abbe been so fond of hearing the sound of his own voice, had he not been so used to his brilliant listener, he must surely have noted that Jeanne was not herself to-day as they walked in the garden.

"There is a new arrival I hear, mademoiselle."

"Indeed. I thought every room was occupied."

"Ah, mademoiselle, I fear there must be some one who is not able to pay next Saturday. I have often noticed that new arrivals have come a day or two before the time, putting up with anything until the room was left vacant for them on Saturday."

"I wonder who is going," said Jeanne.

"It is a pity we cannot pick and choose," the Abbe returned. "There are one or two in the company we could well dispense with."

Jeanne's eyes flashed at his callousness, but he did not notice.

"There are some here that Legrand ought not to have taken," the Abbe went on.

"But they pay."

"Ah, mademoiselle, you have hit it. They pay, and this fellow Legrand is satisfied. He has no sense of the fitness of things, yet this house has the name of being exclusive."

"I am sorry for those who go, whoever they may be," said Jeanne.

"It is natural. I am not unsympathetic; but since some one must go it seems a pity we cannot choose."

"Is it a man or woman who has come?"

"A man; his name the Marquis de Castellux. If my memory serves me, it is a Breton name, a good family, but one which has not figured largely at Court."

"He should be an acquisition," said Jeanne.

"I hope so, mademoiselle. We may find him provincial, yet not without wit or merit. I will make his acquaintance, and with your permission will present him to you. You can give me your opinion when we talk together to-morrow."

How near Saturday was! This new arrival emphasized the

fact. She was the one who was going, and it was this room, her room, that he would occupy presently. Even the selfish, callous Abbe would regret that she was the one to go. She could picture the surprise in his face when he saw her empty place. She would not tell him.

Jeanne stayed in her room this afternoon. It could not matter whether her absence was heeded or not. Nothing mattered now. Richard Barrington had not got her letter. The one friend she had in Paris did not know how sorely she needed him. Somehow, somewhere, he might hear what had happened, what would he say? No actual answer came to this mental question, but a train of thought was started in her brain bringing strange fancies. Perhaps Richard Barrington loved her. In an indefinite way she had considered this possibility before, but it was a passing fancy, not to be dwelt upon. Homage from such a man was pleasant, but she loved Lucien. She must be careful in this man's company, and if he overstepped ordinary courtesy in the least, she must show him plainly that she loved Lucien. Surely she had shown him this already. But to-day the thought was not to be so lightly dismissed, and a warm glow at her heart told her how pleasant the idea was. Lucien appeared to have faded out of her life. She could not believe him false, but his image had grown altogether dim, while this other man was real, vital. Even now she could feel the pressure of his hand as it had held hers as they ran together from the Lion d'Or that night. She could see the encouragement in his eyes when they had quarreled loudly as they entered the barrier next morning. She remembered the look in his face when she had last seen him in Monsieur de Lafayette's apartment, when he had said he was always at her service. He would surely remember that last meeting, too, should he ever know that she had sent him a letter which had never reached him.

"Yes, he loves me, it must be so," she said, and she rose and looked from her window into the empty garden which was growing dark now at the close of the short day. "I am glad. It gives me courage. I will be worthy of the love of such a man, though he will never know that he influenced me, will never know that I was glad he loved me. This Doctor Legrand, this miserable bargainer in lives, shall not see a trace of fear or regret in me. Wednesday passes. Three more days. I will make a brave show in them, and pass out to whatever fate awaits me with steady step and head erect, worthy of my father's name, worthy of - worthy of him."

There was a smile on her lips as she entered the salon that night, no brilliant apartment, it is true, and somewhat dimly lighted for a scene of festivity. Some one said they were to dance that night, and card tables were set ready for players. There were many brave hearts there, shadowed hearts - misery concealed by a smile.

"Yes, I will dance presently," said Jeanne to a man who greeted her. "Cards! Yes, I will play. How, else should we fill such long evenings?"

Others caught her spirit. An animation came into the conversation, there was real laughter.

"Mademoiselle," said a voice behind her, the voice of the Abbe, sonorous and important. "Mademoiselle, permit me the honor to present to you the Marquis de Castellux."

Jeanne turned, the smile still upon her lips. The Marquis bowed so low his face was hidden for a moment, but he took her hand and, as he raised it to his lips, pressed it sharply.

"I am honored, mademoiselle."

Then his head was raised. The smile was still upon her lips, kept there by a great effort. The sudden pressure of her fingers had warned her, and she gave no sign of her astonishment.

She was looking into the face of Richard Barrington.

CHAPTER XXII

THE COMING OF SATURDAY

"Monsieur L'Abbe."

"Mademoiselle."

"I find Monsieur de Castellux very pleasant, a little provincial as you supposed, but with wit. We have common friends, too, who have suffered. We shall have much to talk about."

Barely an hour had passed since the introduction, and very little conversation had passed between Jeanne and Barrington, but that little had been to the point.

"We have much to say to one another, mademoiselle," Barrington said; "we must let these people believe that we have common interests to account for our friendship. The Abbe is inclined to be inquisitive, you must explain to him. I will casually let others know that our families are connected. Where is it easiest to be alone here?"

"In the breakfast room."

"No one watches us there?"

"I think not. There is no desire to run away; people remain here to be safe."

"Then to-morrow, mademoiselle," said Barrington. "We will not notice each other much further to-night."

Jeanne did as she was told, it seemed natural to obey Richard Barrington, and she explained to the Abbe, who was delighted that so presentable a person had joined the company.

"Mademoiselle, I shall look to become better acquainted with him," he said. "Most probably he and I have common friends, too."

It was not until Jeanne had shut herself in her own room that night, that she realized fully what the coming of Richard Barrington meant to her. It was still Wednesday, but what a difference a few short hours had made! Saturday had lost its meaning for her. There was no sense of fear or apprehension at her heart; she was strangely happy. Not a word of his plans had Richard Barrington whispered to her, no explanation of how he came to be there; he told her that he had got her letter, that was all. Yet she suddenly felt safe. That which was best to be done, Richard Barrington would do, and it would certainly be successful. On this point no doubts disturbed her. Doubts came presently in another way. The reflection in her mirror brought them. She remembered the face which had looked out at her only a few hours ago, and the face that laughed at her now was a revelation. There was color in the cheeks, so bright a color she did not remember to have noticed before, not even in those moments when she had been tempted to compare herself favorably with other women; there was a sparkle in the eyes that never since the flight from Paris to Beauvais had she seen in them. It was a joyous, happy girl who looked back at her from the depths of the mirror, and Jeanne turned away wondering. It was natural she should feel safe now Richard Barrington had come, but how was the great joy in her heart to be accounted for? Would it have been there had it been Lucien who had come to save her? The question seemed to ask itself, without any will of hers, and the little room seemed suddenly alive with the answer. It almost frightened her, yet still she was happy. She sank on her knees beside the bed and her head was lowered before the crucifix. The soul of a pure, brave woman was outpoured in thankfulness; "Mother of God, for this help vouchsafed I thank thee. Keep me this night, this week, always. Bring me peace. Bring me - " The head sank lower, the lips not daring to ask too much.

The morning came with sunlight in it, cold but clear. Jeanne peeped from her window and was satisfied, peeped into the mirror, and wondered no more at the smiling face there. She knew why such joy had come. She could not reason about it, she did not attempt to do so; the knowledge was all sufficient. It was Thursday morning. Saturday was very near. What did it signify? Nothing. To-day it would be like spring in the garden.

Barrington greeted Jeanne with the studied courtesy of a comparative stranger.

"We must be careful," he whispered, "there are certain to be watchful eyes. Show no interest or astonishment in what I tell you as we eat. Remember, you are merely being courteous to a new arrival of whose existence you have known something in the past."

"I understand. I shall listen very carefully."

"I am greatly honored, mademoiselle, by your letter. I need not ask whether you trust me."

"Indeed, no," she answered.

"It might easily have come into my hands too late," Barrington went on. "We are both victims of deception, and where the truth lies I cannot tell even now. I will recount what has happened; you may be able to throw some light upon it."

Barrington told her everything from his first meeting with Raymond Latour when a filthy crowd was yelling round a prisoner, to the moment when her letter had been handed to him by Seth.

"Your letter gave me an idea, mademoiselle. To help you I must become an inmate of this house. Yesterday Seth brought me here, posing as a wealthy eccentric relative anxious to place me in safety. I am a little mad, and there is no knowing what folly I might commit were I allowed to continue at liberty. My stay here is likely to be a long one, and my relatives care little what they pay so long as I am out of their hands. You may guess perhaps that Dr. Legrand asked few questions with such a golden bribe before him. Now, mademoiselle, what do you know of this Raymond Latour?"

"Nothing."

"But - "

"Nothing at all," Jeanne answered. "I have heard him spoken of as being one of the leaders of the Revolution. To my knowledge I have never seen him."

"Has Lucien Bruslart never mentioned him?"

"As we drove here that morning he said that this Latour was one of the most bitter antagonists of aristocrats, and that he would do all in his power to capture me. Lucien said this was the chief reason for bringing me to this place of safety. I must tell you, Monsieur Barrington, that on leaving you that morning, we got into a coach and drove straight here. My coming had already been arranged for. I did not go to Lucien's apartments at all. He did not seem inclined to trust either you or the Marquis de Lafayette."

"He was justified perhaps in not trusting me on so slight an acquaintance. I do not blame him. Still, I am much puzzled by his subsequent actions, and the fact remains that while Lucien Bruslart has done little for you, or so at least it appears, this man Latour most certainly risked his life to get you out of the Abbaye prison."

"Yes; I do not understand it," said Jeanne; and then after a pause she went on, "You read all my letter?"

"A dozen times," Barrington answered.

"Does it not help you to understand something?"

"Mademoiselle, you ask me a difficult question. I answer it directly, and in spite of the fact that it must pain you, only because of the seriousness of your position. I have never trusted Lucien Bruslart. I believe he has played you false from first to last in this affair. I believe he sent for you to come to Paris; how else could your coming here have been arranged for? Honestly, I have tried to drive these thoughts out of my mind as treacherous and unworthy, but your letter seems only to confirm them. How is it your fees to this scoundrel Legrand have not been paid? How is it your own money has been taken? Bruslart is not in prison. Where is he? Could anything short of locks and bars stop your lover from coming to you?"

He spoke in a low, passionate tone, but his face remained calm, and he made no gesture of anger, of impatience. Watching him, the keenest eyes could not have detected that he was moved in any way.

"My letter must have shown you the doubts in my mind," Jeanne answered quietly. "Since you helped me into Paris at so much risk to yourself, I cannot see that your thoughts could be called unworthy or treacherous."

"For all that, they were. Had you not loved Lucien Bruslart it would have been different."

"Why?"

"That question must remain unanswered, mademoiselle."

Jeanne turned to him for a moment, but Barrington did not look at her.

"I think I know," she said quietly, after a pause. "Some other day I shall ask the question again, monsieur - if we live. I wrote my letter to the one friend I knew I had in Paris; that man is now beside me. I have no fear, Monsieur Barrington, just because you are here. You are risking your life for me, not for the first time. If you fail it means my death as well as yours. I would rather it came that way than any other, and I am not afraid. Tell me your plans."

For a few moments Barrington was silent. "We will not fail," he said suddenly. "I want to laugh and cry out for joy but dare not. I have been in a dream, mademoiselle, while you have been speaking; sitting on a small green mound looking across the bluest waters in the world. I shall tell you about that mound and those waters some day. We shall live, mademoiselle, never doubt that we shall live. My plan is not yet complete, but - "

"This is Thursday," said Jeanne. "Saturday is very near."

"I know. We go to-morrow night, but the exact details I cannot tell you yet. There are one or two things I must find out first. I have arranged everything as far as I can, but we cannot hope for much help from others. The first thing is to get out of this trap, the rest we must leave for the present. The Abbe yonder looks as though he envied me your company, mademoiselle. I think you should go to him. I shall not attempt to speak to you much more to-day. To-morrow morning we will meet here again for a final word."

The Abbe was more than ever convinced of his own attractions as Jeanne left the Marquis de Castellux with a little grave courtesy and joined him. He had found her substitute a poor companion and walked much less in the garden than usual.

"You find the Marquis very interesting?" he asked.

"Yes, but very provincial. One soon becomes weary of such company, yet one must be kind, Monsieur l'Abbe," and Jeanne laughed lightly. She appeared much more interested in him than she had been in the Marquis.

Richard Barrington talked to others for a little while, and then went into the office. He found a servant and asked if he could see Legrand. The doctor was out. Barrington was rather annoyed. He wanted to see the room he was to have after Saturday. At present he was stalled like a pig, he declared.

"Monsieur will have nothing to complain of after Saturday," the servant answered.

"Which guest is leaving?"

"Pardon, monsieur, it is not etiquette to speak of it; but if monsieur likes I can show him the room."

"Show it to me, then."

"I am a poor man, monsieur, and cannot afford to work for nothing."

"How much?" Barrington asked.

The servant named a price, and if he received many such fees he would not long be able to call himself a poor man. Barrington paid him, and was taken upstairs and shown Jeanne's room. He did not cross the threshold, hardly glanced in at the door, in fact, but grumbled at its size and its position. He would have liked this room or that. Why not one at the end of this passage? He liked to be in a light passage.

"It is not a pleasant outlook this side, monsieur, stable roofs, a bare wall and no garden."

"Truly, a prospect to drive a man to despair," growled Barrington, looking from the passage window on to the roofs of outbuildings a few feet below, and across at the house which these buildings joined, and which was at the end of a row of houses facing the street. There was only one window in that opposite wall, twelve or fourteen feet above these outbuildings, a dirty window, fast shut.

"I think very little of Monsieur Legrand's asylum," said Barrington, turning away in disgust. "I shall tell him so."

"Certainly, monsieur, if it will ease your mind."

"He is out, you say?"

"Since early this morning."

"He ought to stop here and look after his guests," and then Barrington became apprehensive. "He would be angry if I told him so. Would he?"

"He might."

"Or if you told him I had said so?"

"Probably."

"You must not tell him. See, here is more money, and there will be more still so long as you do not tell him."

The servant promised to be silent, and told the other servants that the Marquis could be plundered at will. Barrington considered the money well spent. He had examined the house without any risk of being caught taking observations, and he had ascertained that Legrand could not have spied upon him had he walked in the garden.

That night the Abbe decided that, although the Marquis had not made any great impression on Mademoiselle St. Clair, he was a decided acquisition to the establishment, witty within his provincial limits, the breed in him unmistakable. At Versailles he would speedily have learned how to become a courtier.

In the salon that evening there was dancing, and Barrington danced, but not with Jeanne.

"I dare not, mademoiselle," he said in a whispered explanation. "I can trust myself only to a certain point, and to touch you would be to betray my happiness. I dare not run that risk. I am bent on showing that I have no special regard for you, and that there is no reason why you should give any special thought to me."

She did not answer, but the color was in her face, a glow was in her heart.

When the Abbe went out into the garden on the following morning Jeanne left the Marquis at once, and joined him for their usual walk. Certainly she had not given the Marquis more than five minutes of her company. The Abbe would have talked of him, but Jeanne pleaded that he should talk of something interesting.

"Upon my honor, mademoiselle, I believe you will end by disliking poor Monsieur de Castellux."

"Would that be worth while?" Jeanne asked.

She seemed to listen eagerly to all the Abbe said to her, but she was thinking of her short conversation with Barrington. She must show no excitement.

Legrand came into the salon that night. He took no notice of Barrington, who was playing cards, totally absorbed in his game, but he watched Jeanne for a little while, and presently approached her.

"You are very brave, mademoiselle," he said.

"Is it not best?"

"I am very grieved," said Legrand.

"Monsieur, you have heard nothing from - from Lucien Bruslart?"

"Nothing."

"To-morrow! Where will they take me to-morrow?"

"I do not know, mademoiselle. I am never told."

Late hours were not kept at the Maison Legrand, candles were an expensive item. Jeanne was among the first to move this evening.

"Good night, Monsieur l'Abbe."

"Good night, mademoiselle," he said, raising her hand to his lips. "To-morrow is Saturday. I wonder who goes to-morrow? We are happy in having no anxiety."

Barrington was by the door and opened it for her.

"Does mademoiselle permit?" and as he bent over her hand he whispered, "Be ready. Listen. Wait until I come."

CHAPTER XXIII

THE EMPTY HOUSE

The thought of the morrow was pleasant to Dr. Legrand. In his study he bent over a paper of calculations, figures that appealed to the greedy soul that was in him.

"Vive la Revolution," he murmured; "it makes me rich. He is careful, this citizen, and does not trust me to fulfill a bargain. To-morrow I shall have the papers; it will be early, and then - then the money. He cannot escape without my help, he cannot escape me."

He put down his pen and rubbed his hands together. He was excited to-night.

"I am sorry for mademoiselle," he said as he went to bed, but his sorrow did not keep him awake, his conscience was too dead to trouble him. He slept as a just man sleeps, soundly.

Jeanne did not sleep. She sat in the dark, waiting, listening. Doors were shut in distant corridors, the house gradually grew quiet. She sat with her hands clasped in her lap, a little excited, but not impatient. How long she had waited, how long she would have to wait, she did not know, but she had perfect faith, and did not become restless. A moment was coming when she must act, and she was prepared. Just that moment mattered and nothing else; all her thoughts were focused upon it.

It came suddenly, a scratching on the door, so light as to be inaudible except to listening ears. Jeanne rose at once, silently opened the door, which purposely she had not latched, and stepped into the passage. A hand touched her on the arm and then slid down her arm until it clasped her fingers. She was pulled forward gently.

"The stairs - carefully," whispered a voice.

Not a sound was in the house, nor in the world it seemed, as they went down the stairs and along the passage to the window which overlooked the roof of the outbuildings. The night was dark, overcast, not a star. This was a window seldom opened. Last night Barrington had examined it, had eased the latch; now there was hardly a sound as he opened it, only the cold night air coming in.

"I go first," said Barrington; and he climbed out and dropped silently on to the roof some five feet below. Jeanne followed, and he lifted her down. Then he climbed up again, and, supporting himself on the sill, closed the window.

"Give me your hand," he whispered; and he led her across the roof, feeling his way carefully to prevent tripping over a partition or gutter. Jeanne did not speak, but followed his whispered instructions; she made no sound when he bent down and taking her foot placed it upon a little parapet which they had to cross, and she stood perfectly still until he lifted her down. A few paces more and Barrington stopped. He guided her hand to a rope.

"Give me your other hand," he whispered.

Thar, too, he guided until it grasped a rope, a second rope. Then he took her foot and put it upon a strand of rope which gave under her weight.

"A ladder," he whispered. "I will hold you as far as I can, then you must go up alone. A hand will be stretched down to help you. My man Seth is at the window above."

Barrington gave a low whistle, hardly more than a sign, which was answered from above.

"Now," he said.

He helped her as far as possible, then held the rope ladder as steady as he could. In a few seconds another low whistle came from above, and Barrington went up the ladder quickly. He climbed in at the open window, drew up the ladder, and closed the window.

"An excellent night for our purpose, Master Richard," Seth whispered. "Here is a sword, it is well to masquerade and be as much like truculent ruffians as possible; and two cockades, one for mademoiselle."

"We are expected, Seth?"

"Yes, any time before morning. They are prepared for us."

"Where are we going?" whispered Jeanne.

"To the lodgings of a servant of Monsieur de Lafayette," Barrington answered. "This is an empty house which we shall leave by a window below. The worst is over. We shall be secure in our retreat until we can leave Paris. Lead the way, Seth."

A set of rooms opened out into another, a door enclosing them from the passage without. Seth led the way through the rooms and opened this door quietly. Then he stopped and drew back a little.

"What is it?" said Barrington under his breath.

"Listen!"

Jeanne's hand was still in Barrington's, and he felt her fingers tighten. To her the house was as still as death, the blackness of it empty; but to her companions whose ears were trained to keenness, there was movement in the air close to them.

"How many," Barrington whispered, not asking information, but rather confirmation of his own estimate.

"Several," Seth answered.

"Tramps, perhaps, lodging here for the night."

"I fear not. They are on the stairs. We shall soon see," answered Seth.

"Lock the door; we must wait," said Barrington.

It was done in a moment, and immediately there were stealthy, shuffling feet in the passage without.

"Curse them," muttered Seth. "I have been followed. For all my care I have brought you into ruin. What can we do?"

"Wait."

"Master Richard, is there no other way of escape from that roof below?"

"None."

Jeanne's hand was still in his, still holding him tightly. He could not feel that she trembled, yet he could not trust himself to speak to her. He had failed to rescue her. There were many in the passage without, he was sure of that. He could fight for her, die for her, but he could not save her.

He dared not speak to her lest he should cry out in the anguish of his soul.

The handle of the door was tried, gently. Then there was silence again.

"Give us the woman and you may go free."

The words were not spoken loudly. It seemed like the offer of a secret bargain, a suggestion in it that the woman might not hear, and might never know that her companions had betrayed her to save themselves.

Then Jeanne spoke, in a whisper but quite clearly.

"It is the end. You have done all that a man could do. I thank you - I thank you; and you, too, Seth. A woman never had truer friends."

She stretched out a hand to Seth, who caught it almost roughly and pressed his lips to it.

There was pressure upon the door, and the cracking of the wood.

"There's quick death for the first man who crosses this threshold," Seth muttered as he went to the door.

"Richard! Richard!"

"Jeanne!"

Barrington's head was lowered as he whispered her name. It seemed as though failure had made him ashamed.

"I know your secret, dear, I know it and am glad," she whispered. "I thank God that I am loved by such a man. I would rather be where I am at this moment, by your side, than in the place of any other woman in the world, however free she may be. Richard, kiss me."

"Jeanne! Jeanne!" he cried as he caught her in his arms. "I love you! I love you! God, send a miracle to help us."

"He will let us be together soon and for always, if not here, in heaven," she whispered.

"The door gives, Master Richard," Seth said.

"Back into the corner, Jeanne. Who knows what may happen?"

"We may win through, Master Richard. Be ready, the door will be down in a moment."

The clumsy saber with which Seth had provided him was in his hand, as he stepped forward in readiness. They might have retreated through the other rooms, to the one into which they had climbed, closing every door they could in the face of their enemies, but for what purpose? There was no escape that way, time was no object to them, whereas it was just possible that their assailants would expect them to do this and rush past them. Barrington hastily whispered this possibility to Seth. There was no time for an answer. The door splintered and broke, and the foremost ruffians were shot into the room by the pressure of those behind. There was no rush towards the rooms beyond, nor a shout of triumph even. The first articulate sound was a cry from the man cut down by Seth.

In the fierce struggle of an unequal fight a man thinks little. The forcible present of each moment obliterates the past and future. Just for one instant it occurred to Barrington that Jeanne might possibly escape unnoticed if Seth and he fought savagely enough, and the next moment he was putting this idea into action without any thought beyond it. In the doorway there were men holding dim lanterns, and the light flickered on savage faces, now here, now there. The room seemed full of men, crowded, there was hardly room to fight effectually. Barrington struck on this side and that, yet his blows never seemed to reach their destination. For a little while he and Seth were back to back, but had soon been separated. Now there seemed no order or purpose in the struggle. It was a nightmare of confusion. A face glared into his for a moment then disappeared, its place taken the next instant by another. Strangely familiar faces some of them seemed, memories from dreams long ago. There had been hands on the estate in Virginia, men he had been rather afraid of when he was a little child; they seemed to stare at him now for a moment, lit by a red fire which no longer seemed merely the light from the lanterns. Then came other faces; that of the man he and Seth had found on the Tremont road, that of Sabatier's companion at the inn. Then the faces of the men who had made a rush for the stairs that night at the Lion d'Or fiercely glared at him; then Mercier's, so close that he could feel the hot breath upon his cheek. And then suddenly out of the darkness glowed another face, that of the man who had looked at him when he was caught in the crowd on his way to the Rue Charonne that night, and it seemed to Barrington that once again he sprang forward to make an attempt to save himself by flight. The illusion was complete, for there was a voice of command in his ear. He struck at something that was in his way, something which seemed to catch him by the throat, then he jumped and fell. He was in darkness and silence.

Jeanne had started from her corner. Everything happened quickly. She heard the door break inwards, saw a rush of men, and lanterns in the opening. For a few moments she could distinguish Richard Barrington and Seth. Then Seth fell, dragging others with him. For a little longer Barrington struggled, and then from behind something was thrown over his head and he was pulled backwards. Jeanne started from her corner with a cry, and immediately arms were about her, holding her back.

"No harm will come to him, we are friends," said a voice in her ear. "A sound may betray you and us."

She tried to speak, but could not. Her words were turned into a mumble. A cloth was over her mouth and face, fastened tightly, strong arms lifted her and carried her forwards. She could not see, she could not struggle. The noise of the fighting grew rapidly less. She was being swiftly carried away from it, now along a passage, now down two or three flights of stairs. She was in the open air, the cold wind of the night was about her. There were voices, a quick word or two, then other arms were about her, placing her in a chair it seemed - no, a coach. Wheels turned quickly on the uneven cobbles of the street, a horse galloped, and then settled into a fast trot. Whether the journey was long or short, Jeanne hardly knew, her brain was in a whirl, refusing to work consecutively. The coach stopped, again strong arms lifted her, again a passage, the night air still about her, then stairs up which she was borne. A door opened and she was gently placed in a chair. The door closed again. For a moment there was silence.

"You're quite safe, cherie," said a woman's voice, and fingers were undoing the cloth which was bound round Jeanne's head. "You're quite safe. No one in Paris would think of looking for you here."

The cloth fell off, and Jeanne, half dazed, only partly understanding what had happened, looked about her. Her companion, an old woman with a tri-color cockade fastened to her dress, watched her.

The room, one of two opening into each other, was small, mean, yet fresh and dainty. Cheap curtains hung before the windows and about the alcove where the bed was; the curtains and the paintwork were white, two or three cheap prints were upon the walls, a strip of carpet and a rug lay on the polished boards.

"Where am I?" Jeanne asked.

"In safety," answered the old woman.

So Mademoiselle St. Clair came at last to the rooms which Raymond Latour had so carefully prepared.

CHAPTER XXIV

THE AMBITION OF RAYMOND LATOUR

The dawn came slowly creeping over Paris, cold and with a whip of gusty rain in it. It stole in to touch the faces of many sleepers, innocent sleepers, in hiding and in prison, who for a little while had forgotten their fear and peril; brutal sleepers who for a little space lay harmless, heavy with satisfied lust and wine. It stole into empty rooms, rooms that should be occupied; into Legrand's house in the Rue Charonne where two beds had not been slept in; into hovels in narrow byways of the city to which men and women had not returned last night, but had spent the sleeping hours, as befitted such patriots, in revelry and songs and wine. It stole into a little room with cheap white curtains, and looked upon a woman who had thrown herself half dressed on the bed and had fallen asleep, tired out, exhausted. It crept into a room below and touched the figure of a man seated by the table. A lamp stood near him, but either he had turned it out, or it had burned out; an open book was before him, but he had read little, and no knowledge of what he had read remained. For hours he had sat there in darkness, but no sleep had come to him. The night had been a long waking dream of things past, and present, and the future a confusion of thoughts which could not be reduced to any order. All the threads of a great scheme were in his hands, yet he was uncertain how to use them to the best advantage. The moment he had struggled for had come. This day, this dawn, was the beginning of the future. How was he to make the best of it?

Presently he was conscious of feeling cold, and he made himself some coffee, moving about his room quietly. He remembered the woman upstairs. She was sleeping, surely. He had listened during the night and had not heard her. He had held her in his arms, had carried her up the stairs and placed her gently in a chair, leaving her in the care of the woman from the baker's shop at the corner of the alley. She would wake presently and he would see her. What should he say to her?

The coffee warmed Raymond Latour, but there was unusual excitement in his movements. As the light increased he sat down and tried to read. It was a volume of Plutarch's "Lives," a book which had done much to influence many revolutionaries; but he could not read with any understanding. To-day there was so much to be done, so many things to think of. There were his own affairs, and they must take first place, but in Paris the excitement would be at fever pitch to-day. Louis Capet was to die, the voting had decided; but when? There was to be more voting, and Raymond Latour must take his part in it. It was no wonder that he could not read.

The hours had dragged through the night, yet when a knock came at his door, it seemed to him that he had had little time to mature his plans, that it was only a very little while since he had carried the woman up the stairs. He opened the door quickly.

"The citizeness is awake and dressed. She is anxious to see you."

"What have you told her?"

"Only that the man who brought her last night would come and explain."

"I will go to her."

But Latour did not go immediately. He must have a few moments for thought, and he paced his room excitedly, pausing more than once to look at himself in a little mirror which hung upon the wall. His followers would hardly have recognized in him the calm, calculating man with whom they were accustomed to deal. It was with a great effort that he steadied his nerves and went quietly up the stairs.

Jeanne rose from her chair as he entered, but Latour could not know how her heart beat as the door opened. She looked at him steadily, inquiringly, waiting for him to speak.

"Mademoiselle has slept, I trust?"

It seemed to Latour that he looked at her for a long time without speaking, such a whirl of thoughts swept through his brain as he entered the room and saw the woman standing there. He remembered the other woman who had occupied this apartment until he had let her go two or three days since. He had hated her for being there. This room had not been fashioned with such infinite care for such a woman as Pauline Vaison, but for this very woman who now stood before him. How strangely natural it seemed that she should be there! This was the moment which had been constantly in his dreams waking and sleeping.

"I do not know you," she said. "Why am I here? Indeed, where am I?"

"Mademoiselle, I have come to explain. It is a long explanation, and you must bear with me a little."

"Tell me first, where is Monsieur Barrington?" said Jeanne.

"In safety. You have my word for it."

"Whose word?"

"You shall have the whole story, mademoiselle, and you shall presently see Monsieur Barrington."

Jeanne sat down, and Raymond Latour moved to the window and stood there.

"I must begin in the middle of my story," he said, "it is easier for me, and you will understand better. On the day of your arrival in Paris, I met Monsieur Barrington. He was watching a coach which contained a prisoner who was being escorted by a crowd of patriots to the Abbaye prison. The sight was new to him; I believe that, single-handed, he would have made an attempt at a rescue, had I not touched his arm. I knew who he was, and that he had helped you into Paris. A little later it was said that you had been arrested in the house of Lucien Bruslart, and Monsieur Barrington came to me. We both concluded that you were the prisoner in that coach. I believed Barrington to be an honest man, and I rescued the prisoner from the Abbaye, and brought her here, only to find that she was one Pauline Vaison, a woman Bruslart was to marry. Bruslart, however, had made no effort to save her. He had apparently sacrificed her to help you, and Barrington had helped him."

"It might appear so, monsieur, but such was not the case," said Jeanne.

"My opinion of Monsieur Barrington is at present in the balance," said Latour; "Lucien Bruslart I know to be a scoundrel. The release of Pauline Vaison naturally frightened Bruslart, who has gone into hiding and is not to be found. Barrington is not a coward, and it was easy to secure him. I saved him from the mob, but I kept him a prisoner. I challenged him with his treachery to me, and he denied it, yet immediately I let him go and had him watched, he straightway found you at the house of Dr. Legrand in the Rue Charonne. Watching him and his servant it was discovered that you were to be rescued from Legrand's house, with the result that you are here."

"In the hands of Monsieur Raymond Latour," said Jeanne, quietly.

"Yes, mademoiselle, though I am surprised that you know me. Monsieur Barrington is also in my hands."

"Most of this story I already know from Monsieur Barrington," she returned. "If you will believe my word, I can show you that he was not in Lucien Bruslart's confidence at all, that Lucien Bruslart from the first deceived him. If you know anything of me, you must realize that it is not easy to speak of Monsieur Bruslart in this way."

"I know all about you, mademoiselle," Latour answered slowly.

"And hate me. I have heard of Raymond Latour as a hater of aristocrats. I cannot understand, therefore, why you undertook my rescue from prison."

"Because you do not know all about me," he said "It is true I am a republican, a hater of aristocrats. Mademoiselle, you have been good to the poor in Paris, you are one of the few who have cared anything for them. Had you not fled, had you not become an emigre, I believe you could have walked the streets of the city in perfect safety. If for a moment you will put aside your class prejudice, you must know that the people have the right with them. They have been ground down, trampled on for generations, now they have struggled to freedom. If they push that freedom to excess, can you honestly be astonished? They are but retaliating for the load of cruelty which has been pressed upon them."

"Monsieur, I am no politician. Many dear friends of mine have been foully murdered. I look for no better fate for myself."

"I was rather trying to explain my position," said Latour.

"You do not explain your peculiar interest in me."

"You hardly give me time, mademoiselle," he returned with a faint smile. "Still, you can appreciate that my sympathies are with the people. That is not the entire truth, however. I had ambition, and the revolution was my opportunity. A strong man might grasp power, and I would be that strong man."

"Are there not many others in the Convention with similar ambition?"

"I think not. Whatever power I might obtain was not for my own glory, but was to be laid at the feet of a woman. Mademoiselle does not remember, perhaps, a certain day some three or four years since, when the horses attached to her coach took fright and ran away. They might have been stopped by the coachman, but they appeared to have got the better of him. It seemed to a man standing there, a poor student, that the occupant of that coach was in danger. He rushed forward, and with some difficulty stopped the horses."

"I remember it perfectly," said Jeanne.

"Mademoiselle, that poor student had in that hour seen a vision from heaven, a woman so beautiful, so far beyond all other women, that he worshiped her. He wandered the streets of Paris only to catch a glimpse of her. He enthroned her on the altar of his soul, and bowed down to her. It was a hopeless passion, yet its hopelessness had no power to kill it, rather it grew each day, took stronger possession of his dreams each night, until, reaching forward, he conceived the possibility of winning what his soul desired. That poor student was Raymond Latour. You see, mademoiselle, when you think of me as a red republican, you hardly do me full justice."

Jeanne did not answer. What possible answer was there to such a confession as this?

"Deputy Latour became a power," he went on quietly. "Many things became possible. Mademoiselle had a lover, Lucien Bruslart, a villain, a liar to her and his country. Raymond Latour, with all his faults, was a better man than he, more honest, more worthy a woman's regard, no matter who that woman might be."

He paused for a moment, but still she found no words to answer him.

"This Bruslart for some purpose of his own sent for mademoiselle to come to Paris. I discovered that he had done so. It was an opportunity to show you what sort of a man he was whom you loved. I should have balked his intention and brought you here, had it not been for the bungling of those who served me, and the courage of this man Barrington who has played Bruslart's game for him."

"Unwittingly," said Jeanne. "I grant that Lucien Bruslart is not a worthy man; you must not class the other with him." In a few words Jeanne told him how she had written the letter, how Richard Barrington came to know where she was hidden.

"Is it not a further proof against Bruslart? And to me there is still no actual proof of Barrington's honor," Latour went on quickly, as though he were afraid something would happen to prevent his speaking. "Listen, mademoiselle, this room was prepared for you long before you came, a safe retreat. Would any one think of seeking an aristocrat close to a hater of aristocrats? I have thought of everything, planned everything. The power I have I lay at your feet, now, at this moment. At your word I will become anything you wish. Without you, without the hope of you, nothing is of value to me. With you, there is nothing in the world impossible. France is not the only land. Paris is not the world. There are fairer places on God's earth where men and women may live at peace. I have papers which shall make it easy for us to pass the barriers, which shall bring us safely to the sea. I worship you, words can tell you nothing of that worship, you shall learn it day by day, hour by hour, you shall guide me as you will. You - "

"Monsieur, monsieur! what are you saying? How can I answer such madness?"

"By coming with me, gift for gift, love for love. Somewhere I will so labor that my wife shall know the depth of my reverence, the greatness of my love."

"I have no answer, monsieur, for such folly."

"Not yet, but you will have. A man does not play for such stakes as I have played for, win them, and then throw them away."

"If I understand your folly rightly, you have not won. I could pity - were there not a tone of threatening in your voice. To love you is, and always will be, impossible."

"Has mademoiselle considered all that such a decision means?"

"I know nothing worse that you can do than denounce me to the Convention," said Jeanne, standing up, and looking straight into his eyes. "I expect nothing less and have no fear. You will have the satisfaction of knowing that you have sent another innocent person to the guillotine."

"There is another mademoiselle might wish to save. I have said Monsieur Barrington is in my hands."

"I have never seen fear in Richard Barrington. I do not think he would be afraid of the guillotine."

"You love him," said Latour, sharply.

"Yes;" and then she went on passionately, "Have you revolutionaries not yet learned that death is but a passing evil, and that there are men and women who do not fear death? I love Richard Barrington; his death or mine cannot alter that, and do you suppose I would purchase life by a promise to you or any other man in the world?"

"Yet he shall plead my cause for me. For himself he may not be a coward, but for the woman he loves he will be. He would rather see you in my arms than send you to the guillotine."

"Monsieur, the decision rests wholly with me. Richard Barrington has already risked his life for me; if necessary, he will give it for me, and he would rather see me dead than give any promise to a man I despise. You cannot understand such men."

"Mademoiselle, I too, risked my life in bringing out of the Abbaye prison the woman I believed was you."

"For that I thank you," she said quickly. "It is strange to me that the same man can stoop to threaten me now."

"You will understand if you think of all I have told you," said Latour, moving to the door. "You are safe for a little while. Your lover shall plead for me. He is a man, and will know what a man's love is."

Jeanne turned to the window. There was nothing more to be said.

Latour went slowly down to his room. All his excitement

had vanished. He was calm and calculating again, a man in a dangerous mood; yet Jeanne's words were still in his ears. "I love Richard Barrington; his death or mine cannot alter that." What had he expected from this interview? He hardly knew. He had declared that his game was won, but it was not the game he had schemed to play. It was to have been his love against Lucien Bruslart's. To plead that would have been easy, and surely the woman must have listened, yes, and recognized the true from the false. This cursed American had altered the game; still, he was a man, a man of his word. He had promised to plead for him. He should do it.

Raymond Latour passed out presently into the Rue Valette and went in the direction of the Tuileries. There was public business he must do. Paris was clamorous and dangerous. The mob cried out to Deputy Latour as he passed, telling him how to vote, but he took no notice, never even turning his head. He was not thinking of a king, but of the woman he loved.

CHAPTER XXV

A DEBT IS PAID

Dr. Legrand slept late on this Saturday morning; his dreams had been pleasant, and he hastily descended to his study, his face beaming, his body tingling with excitement. The regret which he had expressed last night, and really felt in his own limited fashion, was gone; how could he feel regret when in a short hour or two he was destined to handle so much money?

As he went to his study a servant stopped him.

"Monsieur, monsieur, we have only just discovered, but Mademoiselle St. Clair - "

"Yes, yes; what about her?"

"Gone, monsieur."

"Gone!"

The doctor staggered back against the wall, his face working in a sudden convulsion. It was as though the servant had struck him a heavy blow between the eyes.

"Yes, monsieur. Her bed has not been slept in. The Marquis de Castellux is not to be found either. We have inquired among the guests. No one has seen them since they left the salon last night."

No articulate word came from Legrand, only a growl like that of an angry animal. He rushed to mademoiselle's room, then to the one Monsieur de Castellux had occupied temporarily. In a few moments the house was being searched from cellar to garret, every room was entered, whether the guests expostulated or not, but there was no sign of the fugitives, nor anything to show how they had gone. No one noticed that the window at the end of the passage had been unfastened.

A little later Dr. Legrand hurried along the Rue Charonne, caring nothing that people looked after him. He was a doctor of lunatics, they said, possibly he had gone mad himself. They laughed and took no further notice of him. He traversed several streets in the Faubourg St. Antoine, evidently familiar ground to him, and presently entered a tumbledown tenement. Going hastily to the top floor, he knocked with his knuckles at a closed door, two low, single knocks, and a double one. It was evidently a signal, for the door was opened at once and Lucien Bruslart stood before him.

"So soon!" he exclaimed.

Legrand entered, pushing Bruslart back into the room, and shut the door.

"She's gone! Escaped! Last night!"

Bruslart showed no sign of surprise. He sat on the edge of the table and waited for more information. Legrand had no more to give. In his hurried journey from the Rue Charonne he had thought of many things, and now made no mention of the fact that another of his guests had also disappeared.

"How did she manage to escape out of your clutches?" asked Bruslart, after a pause.

"I don't know, and does it matter? She is gone, that is enough."

"Bad for you, Legrand. She will explain how she came to be in your house, and your friends will be asking why you took any one they did not send to you. An awkward question, Legrand."

"I shall easily answer that. The difficulty is for you, my friend. How will you explain your dealings with an aristocrat for whom all Paris is hunting?"

"More easily perhaps than you imagine."

"You cannot, you cannot. I am the only man who can help you."

"Your help does not seem very effectual, does it?" said Bruslart. "You were to have come this morning with certain papers assuring me that a certain troublesome person was in the hands of the authorities, and in return you were to receive a certain fee. Well, you have no papers, therefore you get no fee."

"But what will you do?"

"Wait here. I have been safe so far."

"It is impossible," said Legrand. "I shall be asked questions, I shall have to answer them. I know Citizen Bruslart as a good patriot. He brings me a lady to take charge of. What could I do but obey? I shall be asked where Citizen Bruslart is now."

"I see you contemplate betraying me, is that it?"

"No, no, but I must answer questions."

"How do you propose to help betraying me then?" Bruslart asked.

"Now you are sensible. We must work together, is it not so? Paris is dangerous for you. You are a rich man and the place for you is across the frontier. A friend of mine, a good citizen, has for days been ready to travel at a moment's notice, and will take a servant with him. He has papers that cannot be questioned for himself and for you, his servant. He goes by way of Metz and then to Valenciennes. You will slip across the frontier into Belgium. You have heard of the inn, on that road, La Houlette. Once there you may throw away your cockade and become again a nobleman. It is your metier, my friend, you were never intended for a patriot. And now that you have money what better could you wish for?"

"It is an attractive programme, and I am a little tired of this cockloft," answered Bruslart. "How is it to be managed?"

"In an hour I will be back with all that is necessary to alter your dress and appearance. In two hours you may commence your journey."

"Very well, my good Legrand, I shall expect you in an hour."

"Yes, but the money," said the doctor. "I run a risk, and my friend must also be paid."

"Anything that is reasonable."

"Oh, it is reasonable."

"What is the figure?" Bruslart asked.

"I think I can arrange everything if you give me the fee I was to have had for the papers you expected me to bring this morning."

"Nonsense, Legrand. That fee is nearly half of my fortune."

"Mademoiselle's fortune," corrected Legrand.

The two men looked at each other, and understood each other well. Bruslart knew that the doctor was quite prepared to betray him if he did not come to his terms. Legrand knew that Bruslart was in dire straits, and that once in the hands of the Convention his doom was sealed. In one sense the doctor was the more honest of the two. He could do what he said with every prospect of success, and was prepared to fulfill his bargain to the letter. Bruslart was already planning how he could overreach his companion.

"It is a monstrous price to pay."

"It saves you from the guillotine," answered Legrand.

"Very well, I'll pay it," said Bruslart, after a moment's thought.

"Quickly, then. I will go at once. Give me the money."

"A bargain is a bargain, my good doctor, and I do not part with my money until you have completed your work. I shall expect you in an hour."

Legrand hesitated.

"I cannot get away," said Bruslart, "but there is a possibility that you might not return."

"You are over careful," was the answer.

"I have my head to consider," Bruslart laughed. "No man pays the doctor before he has taken his physic."

The doctor laughed too, it was the only way to deal with such a man, and departed. Bruslart could not escape him. The money was already as good as in his hands. Bruslart once out of Paris, Legrand could answer any question the officers of the Convention might put to him. He had done as Citizen Bruslart had commanded him, what else could he have done? Monsieur Fouquier-Tinville and others could not say much, they were too interested in his establishment. Besides, although mademoiselle had escaped from his house, it was most unlikely that she could leave Paris. She would be found.

Bruslart locked his door when the doctor had gone. Before the doctor he had shown no anger, no agitation, but alone, he was like an animal caught in a trap. For this money he had schemed, lied, and betrayed an innocent woman; he had just enough conscience to hate the remembrance of all he had done, and now half the reward of his treachery was to be filched from him. For a moment he was tempted to go before Legrand returned, but he was afraid. Legrand had the whip hand of him. Could he cheat him? The opportunity might come at the last moment. How could it be done?

He was deep in a dozen plans which came in a chaotic confusion into his mind, when there was a knock at the door, two low, single knocks followed a double one, Legrand's signal. An hour had not passed. Legrand had returned quickly. What had happened? He opened the door, then started back.

"Pauline!"

For a moment she stood on the threshold apparently with some feeling for the dramatic effect in her attitude, then she entered and closed the door.

"Yes, Pauline," she said.

Bruslart had been taken unawares; he had unfortunately allowed the woman to see his surprise, and cursed his folly as he regained his equanimity with an effort.

"You are welcome, Pauline, as welcome as - "

"As the devil," she answered. "No, I want to do the talking. You sit down and listen."

"Nothing will please me better," Bruslart returned, smiling. "I have been forced to go into hiding, and have lost touch with events."

"And I have been in prison."

"In prison! You!"

"Strange, isn't it? I dare say the story will interest you, but there are other things to talk of first. What has forced you into hiding?"

"Circumstances and Raymond Latour," he answered.

"And why should you keep your hiding-place a secret from me?"

"I will explain. It is rather a long story, and - "

"And I do not want to hear it," she said. "I know. It is not a pretty story. To save one woman you sacrifice another, and in the end are false to both."

"What nonsense have you been told, Pauline?"

"I have been told very little, perhaps only know part of the tale even now, but it is sufficient. I only found out your hiding-place on Wednesday night. On Thursday and Friday, Citizen Legrand was with you. By your contriving

Mademoiselle St. Clair was in hiding. A large part of her money was in your hands, and she was in your way, so Legrand was instructed to send word to the Convention that one Richard Barrington, an American, had contrived by false representation to place her in Legrand's house for safety, and the doctor, suddenly discovering the falsehood, was to prove himself a good patriot and give her up. So Lucien Bruslart, by paying the doctor, was to get rid of a troublesome woman and retire to Belgium."

"I do not know who can have told you such a story."

"There are many spies in Paris," she answered with a short laugh. "But that is not all the tale. Yesterday you were very confidential with Citizen Legrand. You told him of another woman who was in love with you, and was troublesome, or would be if she knew where to find you. You had promised to marry her, a promise to the pretty fool which you did not intend to keep. It amused you to think how furious Pauline Vaison would be when she found out you had gone."

"So that devil Legrand has been talking, has he?"

"Poor Lucien! Do you imagine you are the only scoundrel in Paris?"

"Scoundrel! Why, you pretty fool - it is your own expression, so let me use it - do you imagine I should tell the truth to Legrand? His own cupidity ruins him. Half the tale is true, the other half - why, Pauline, is it not the very scheme I told you of? I had hoped to rise to power in Paris; that I cannot do, but I have the money, and Pauline Vaison will join me across the Belgian frontier."

"You only have half the money, Lucien, Legrand is to have the other half. It is his little fee."

"Now you have come we may cheat him," said Bruslart, quickly.

"Yes, a very excellent plan, but it won't work, my friend. I had none of this story from Legrand. Your money holds him faithful. He will be back in an hour, and in two hours you may perhaps be out of Paris."

Bruslart looked at her, realizing the full extent of his danger for the first time.

"That is an awkward riddle for you to read, isn't it?" she said. "It is an unpleasant position, as unpleasant as mine when they arrested me in the place of Mademoiselle St. Clair, and my lover took no steps to set the mistake right; as unpleasant as when my escape from the Abbaye forced you to hide from me. That is why you ran away, Lucien. You were afraid of me. Now I have found you, and mademoiselle has really escaped out of your clutches. It is a very awkward position, Lucien. I do not see how you are going to wriggle out of it."

"The way is plain, let us arrange everything before Legrand returns," said Bruslart.

"There is nothing to arrange. This little cockloft does not fill the whole of this upper story. There is another attic on the other side of that partition, with a cupboard in it. Standing in the cupboard, with the ear against the woodwork, one can hear all that is said here, and if you look in that partition you will find a crack, through which nearly the whole of this place can be seen. You may take my word for it, I have lived on the other side since Wednesday night. Your own servant betrayed your hiding-place to me, for a ridiculously small sum. Your worth is not great even in his eyes."

"Be sensible, Pauline. I will - "

"Pay me for secrecy? Will you give me the other half of mademoiselle's money?"

"I said, be sensible. Come with me, join me on the road to the frontier. It is what I have intended all along."

"It's a lie!"

The woman was suddenly alive with passion - dangerous, and Bruslart knew it.

"You are not polite," he said.

"I am better than that; I am honest."

"Be sensible as well. The time is short. Sit down and let us arrange quickly."

"I have told you, there is nothing to arrange," she answered.

"Once for all, will you come? Yes or no," he said angrily.

"No."

"What are you going to do?"

"Pay, Lucien, pay. Legrand will return, but he will not find you."

"You she-devil!"

The words were hissed out as he sprang toward her. It was his life or hers. There was no other alternative. Murder was in his hands, in his soul. She realized this and even as he touched her, she cried out -

"Help! Help, citizens!"

In a moment the door was thrown open and Lucien Bruslart was in the hands of the officers of the Convention, crouching in their grasp, white and afraid, too terrified even to curse his betrayer.

"The payment, Lucien! I warned you. I keep my promise. For you it is the Place de la Revolution - the guillotine."

The words were shouted at him savagely, and then she leaned back against the wall in a paroxysm of horrible laughter.

CHAPTER XXVI

ENEMIES OR FRIENDS

To the individual, his affairs, petty though they be, are often of more moment than those greater doings which have a whole world for stage and are destined to throw an echo far down the corridors of Time. Most of us live in a narrow little world, a very mean little world often, and are never able to mount up a step or two to see how exceedingly mean and narrow it is. Yet, for all this, the workings of the greater world do affect us, though we may be unconscious of the fact; our little affairs are influenced in greater or less degree, as the rippled circles from a stone's cast spread to the shores of the pond.

Balked greed and craven fear tore at Legrand's very soul when he returned to the cockloft in the Faubourg St. Antoine and found it empty. After all he was not to handle the money. He felt like an honest man who has been cheated, so far was he able to deceive himself. Bruslart had outwitted him, would perhaps succeed in leaving Paris, and a terrible lust to get equal with him seized upon the doctor. The chance words of two men talking in the street told him the truth, and then fear took the place of greed. There was no knowing what Bruslart might say. The temper of the Convention was uncertain. He might be arrested too, or perchance plundered of his gains. For a few moments he was doubtful whether it would be safe to go home, and then, driven by that desperate desire to know the worst which so often makes a coward seem courageous, he

PERCY BREBNER

hastened in the direction of the Rue Charonne, and was in his study when the officers of the Convention arrived to remove Jeanne St. Clair. Legrand had communicated with the authorities, but somewhat vaguely. He declared that it was evident that he had been deceived, that the ci-devant aristocrat ought never to have been placed under his care, but he had not definitely stated an opinion that the American, Richard Barrington, was responsible. It was difficult for Legrand to make a straightforward statement at any time, and that he had not done so on this occasion might prove useful now that Lucien Bruslart was arrested. He was therefore prepared to wriggle out of his awkward position. Mademoiselle had managed to get out of his house, how he could not tell, but she could not have left Paris. An immediate and diligent search must result in her capture.

Strange to say the awkward questions were not asked, nor was an immediate search instituted. For the moment, at any rate, Jeanne St. Clair was of small account, another name was in everybody's mouth, another personality was forced into tragic prominence, and the hundreds of deputies on whose word so much depended had no time or inclination to think of any one else.

Wednesday and Thursday, which were marked days for Jeanne St. Clair, were stupendous days for Paris, for France, for the world. The fate of Louis Capet, once king, was sealed in them. He must die. By the vote of the deputies this was decided. His crime? Who shall say. Chiefly perhaps that he was born to be a king, and lived, a weak king, in a strenuous time. And yet the business was not at an end. Some would have an appeal made to the people, a proposition easily overruled; some would have delay, and that was not so easily settled. There must be more voting. So on this Saturday and Sunday the deputies were busy, and Paris vibrated with excitement. Raymond Latour now voted for delay, as before he had voted against the death sentence, firm to his conviction that the head of a king was not necessary to the safety of France. Patriots hissed at him and at many others. Robespierre noted the set of his face and thought of the future; others noted that set face and thought of the future, too. Was Raymond Latour as strong a man as some declared? Was he safest as a friend or as an enemy? Once more the votes were counted. Louis Capet must die, that fact remained unaltered, but there was added something more to the sentence, he must die within twenty-four hours. It was a merciful addition perchance, though not so intended; the shorter the time, the less the suffering. Patriotic Paris flung its red cap into the air, rejoicing greatly. Less than twenty-four hours to wait for the greatest amusement that had yet been vouchsafed to the mob. There was no time to sleep, no reason in sleep. Armed men would keep the streets to-morrow, but there would be vantage places to be struggled for and kept through long hours of waiting - yet not so long after all. Monday morning came quickly - ten o'clock - one carriage and its guard. The last ride of a king! The bitter mockery of fate sounded to-day for the Deep Purple of an empire - and France laughed. Revenge, too, perchance smiled, for the passage of that lone coach left its trail of dead and wounded. Slowly he mounted into view of his people, and a heart here and there may have pitied him. He would speak. Surely in this last hour he may say a word; the words of a man at such a moment, be he king or peasant, may perchance have a strange meaning and appeal in them; and also they may be dangerous. Yes, he will speak. He is innocent, that much was heard, and then another spoke, a word of command, and there was the loud rolling of the drums. Nothing could be heard above the beating of those drums. It was difficult even to see through the forest of bayonets which surrounded the scaffold. It looked like a moment's struggle between executioners and hand-tied victim, an unequal contest. Still the drums - then the sound of the heavy falling knife. Then silence, and Samson, chief priest of the guillotine, holding the head high, at arm's length, that all may see it and know that tyranny is at an end, that France is free. Patriotism, armed and otherwise, went mad with delight. This was a gala day! Sing, dance, drink in it! Such a day was never known in Paris before!

It was no wonder that Jeanne was forgotten, that Dr. Legrand was not called upon to answer awkward questions. It was not remarkable that the alleys and byways of Paris were deserted for the wider streets and places where patriots could rejoice together, and that many who were in hiding should be free for a day or two from the alarms which almost hourly beset them.

Richard Barrington had remained untroubled for many hours. As he fought in the empty house, struggling against a crowd which seemed to press in upon him from every side, and out of which looked familiar faces, his brain had played him a trick he thought he was fleeing from his enemies, jumping into darkness for safety. There had followed a period of total unconsciousness, set in the midst of a continuous dream as it were, for he seemed to realize at once without any break that he had fallen upon a bed of straw and could safely lie there to rest his tired limbs. There was no recollection of Legrand's asylum, or of the night escape over the roofs, but presently there came a conviction that he ought to be with Jeanne. It seemed to him that he tried to get out of the straw but was unable to do so. It had so twined about his body and limbs that he was bound by it as if with ropes. He must rest a little longer until he had more strength to break his bonds. Then again, faces looked at him, faces he ought to know, yet could not remember. There were low voices about him. He was thirsty, and in his struggles to free himself from the straw, chance guided his hand to a cup. Cool liquid was in it, water or wine, he could not tell which, but he drank eagerly and lay still again for a long time. Presently his strength was certainly returning, for without any great effort he drew his hands free from the binding straw and raised himself. A faint light was about him, showing stone walls, a narrow room, in a corner of which he was lying. On the floor beside him was a cup, a wine bottle, and a piece of bread. He picked up the bread and almost mechanically bit a piece out of it. He found that he was hungry. There was wine in the bottle and he drank. The straw no longer bound him, and he rose slowly to his feet and stared about him. Then, like waters suddenly breaking down a dam and flowing again into their old channel, memory reasserted itself and his brain grew clear. He recollected the empty house, the sudden movement on the stars, the fight, Jeanne standing behind him in the corner. What had happened? Where was she? Where was Seth? He knew where he was. The chair and table, the bowl and water can, the straw bed, the stone walls and the high grating - he was again in that buried cell of the old monastery.

"My head is heavy," he said aloud. "I must have been hurt and been delirious. For how long, I wonder?"

He began to move slowly about the cell. It was daylight, whether morning or afternoon he could not tell. He was not meant to die yet, or the wine and the bread would not be there, yet why was he in this place instead of an ordinary prison? His limbs were stiff, his head ached, it was difficult to think clearly. He could not detach reality from dreams. What had happened in that empty house? Where was Jeanne? He threw himself upon the straw bed again, intending to lie there and try to solve the problem, but he fell asleep.

He was roused suddenly. A man was bending over him, had probably touched him. It was Raymond Latour. For a moment or two Barrington was uncertain whether this was a dream or reality.

"So you're awake at last," said Latour.

Barrington rose slowly to his feet, and then sat down in the chair by the table.

"What day is it?"

"Monday - Monday afternoon."

Barrington appeared to make a calculation.

"Monday!" he said. "Then I have been here - "

"Since early on Saturday morning," said Latour. "You were knocked about a bit in that empty house, and you've been in a more or less unconscious condition ever since. Have you your wits now? I have something important to say to you."

"Then you know about that empty house?"

"Yes."

"You arranged the - "

"Your capture - yes."

Barrington rose to his feet quickly, but stumbled a little as he did so.

"Now you must settle with me," he said.

"You're not strong enough yet," said Latour, easily catching the arm which aimed a feeble blow at him. "Mademoiselle St. Clair is safe. She is not in prison. Your man is safe. You, too, are safe for the present. You had better listen to all I have to say."

Barrington sat down again, frowning at his impotence. He had not realized how weak he was.

"I let you out of this place believing you a liar, and had you watched," said Latour. "I still believed you a liar when I found that you knew mademoiselle was in Legrand's house in the Rue Charonne. Your man was watched too, and his preparations in that empty house understood. You know the result. I have it from mademoiselle's own lips that you are not a liar, that you are not in league with Lucien Bruslart, and I believe her."

"Where is she?"

"Safe in my keeping."

Barrington did not answer for a moment. Then he said slowly, "She is the aristocrat in whom you are interested?"

"Yes."

"Then it is you who have lied?"

"I deceived you, yes. Be a man, Barrington; look at this thing with the eyes of a man. What reason was there that I should trust you with such a secret? I had set myself a goal to win, why should I jeopardize my chances? Bruslart was the man she loved, not you."

"They say all is fair in love," said Barrington. "Go on, Latour, go on. I suppose you have come to bargain with me. My arm may be weak, but my head grows clearer every minute."

"I want you to fulfill your promise. You owe me something. You said you would do your utmost to help me with the woman I loved. I know now that I could have no more powerful advocate."

"I cannot admit the debt," was the answer. "What do I owe you?"

"Your life once, perhaps twice, and again now. It is mine to save or destroy. A word from me and you change this place for a prison and the guillotine."

"I set no value on my life," Barrington answered.

"Jeanne St. Clair's life is in my hands, too," said Latour, slowly. "You would do something to save her?"

"Anything in the world. Save her, Latour, and though you send me to the gallows I will bless you."

Latour bit his lip a little. He wanted to hate this man who had come between him and his desires. He was convinced that he had done so, convinced that but for this American, Jeanne St. Clair would have listened to him. His worth against Bruslart's infamy must have appealed to her, had this man not come into her world.

"I know the truth," he said slowly, "I have had it from mademoiselle herself. I spoke of my love, as a man must speak when the whole passion of his life is let loose. She could never love me, she said. Why? Because she loves you. I have threatened her to no purpose. I threatened to sacrifice you unless she consented. It was of no avail. She swore that you did not fear death, that you would willingly die for her."

"She spoke only the truth," said Barrington.

"Yet you can save her," Latour returned. "You are the only man who can. You shall go to her and plead with her for me. For her sake I will desert France, go anywhere, do anything she wills. She must be mine or, for God's sake, do not make me even whisper the alternative."

"Be honest. Let me know the alternative."

"She shall die. There you have it. You may make your choice."

"And I thought you loved her," said Barrington, slowly.

"I cannot bandy phrases with you," Latour answered passionately. "You are a man as I am, there is something in us that is alike, I think. Debate such questions with yourself and you will find an answer."

"I have said that I am willing to die for her," answered Barrington.

"Go a step further than that," returned Latour. "Help another man to possess her."

"You are not prepared to make that sacrifice," said Barrington. "She must be yours or she must die. I thought Raymond Latour was too good a man for such villainy."

"Phrases! phrases! I want none of them. I want your help, the help you promised. I fulfilled my part of the bargain, although it was not mademoiselle I rescued; I expect you to fulfill yours."

"In this thing she must choose, Latour. My love is such that to make her happy I would willingly sacrifice myself were it to die for her, or harder still, live out my life away from her, forgotten by her. If it is only the thought of me which holds her back from what may bring her peace and satisfaction, I will pass out of her life and she shall never know the great sorrow at my heart. I will not hold her to any promise she has made to me. She shall be free to choose, and I will not let a hard thought of her enter my soul."

While Barrington was speaking, Latour had paced the cell slowly. Now he stopped on the other side of the little table.

"You will do no more?"

"There is nothing more I can do."

"You have thought of the consequences. You have considered my influence, the power I have to save or to kill you?"

"No, I haven't thought much of that. It doesn't seem to matter."

"You laugh at me."

"That is unworthy of you," Barrington answered. "We are two men in a tight place, and such men do not laugh at each other. Once you said that, should we prove to be enemies, it might help us to remember that we had clasped hands over our wine. Well, is not this the hour to remember it?"

"One has to forget many things," said Latour.

"True; and we come to a point when we understand how trivial are many of these things we thought most important," said Barrington. "We are at the mercy of the world's storms, and we shall surely travel ways we never set out to travel. I came to France, Latour, burning to fight for an oppressed people, burning to do something in this land like the Marquis de Lafayette had done in America. His career there fired my youthful ambition. I have done nothing. I come to this hour, facing you across this little table - two men, enemies, yet for all that liking each other a little, kindred somehow, and strangely bound together in that we both love the same woman."

Latour was silent for a few moments, the past, the present, and the future, mingled in his brain in strange confusion.

"Would you see her again?" he asked suddenly.

Barrington did not answer at once. "Let her decide," he said slowly. "There would be heaven in such a meeting, but there would be hell, too."

"There are tears in your eyes," said Latour.

"Are there?" asked Barrington, simply. "Well, why not?"

Latour turned away quickly. "I will think whether you can see her again," he said. "It may be difficult. You are weak, I will tell them to bring you food. You have seen Citizen Mercier, he is looking after you here. If you are to see mademoiselle, he will tell you. You must do as he suggests. She shall decide; I promise that."

He went toward the door, then came back again.

"If you see her will you speak of me?" he asked.

"We can hardly help doing so."

"She would believe you if you told her something of my love, of what I have done."

"I will set life and death before her, Latour, and leave her free to choose."

Latour moved again to the door and again came back.

"Men who love as we do must be enemies, still the enmity may be free from malice. Other conditions might well have made us friends. Will you grasp hands once more, Barrington?"

Across the little table their hands met, and were clasped firmly for a moment as the two men looked into each other's eyes. Then Latour went out quickly, locking the door behind him.

An hour later he went slowly up the stairs to his rooms. Jacques Sabatier was waiting for him.

"Bad news, citizen," said Sabatier.

Latour opened his door, and they entered.

"It should be bad news indeed if one may judge by your face," he said.

"Citizen Bruslart was arrested on Saturday. He is in the Conciergerie. He demands that you see him to-night. He knows that mademoiselle has escaped from the Rue Charonne, and he makes a shrewd guess where she is hidden. You must see him, citizen; he is dangerous."

CHAPTER XXVII

A RIDE IN THE NIGHT

Once again the dawn found Raymond Latour seated by the table. No book lay open before him, he had not attempted to read. Last night he had gone to the rooms above, taking Sabatier with him. Sabatier forgot to swagger as he stood before Jeanne St. Clair, trying to look as steadily at her as she did at him. Then Sabatier had gone with a promise on his lips which he roundly swore to keep, and for a little while longer Latour remained with Jeanne. His face was calm when he left her, but Barrington might have retaliated and said there were tears in his eyes. Perchance it was the cold wind on the stairs, for the night was bitter, Latour wrapped himself in a thick coat when he went out, and turned his steps in the direction of the Conciergerie. It was near midnight when he returned home, but there was no sleep for him. So the dawn found him seated by the table. Again he felt cold and made himself coffee, but he was not excited. His plans were made. He was ready for the day and the work there was to do in it.

Yesterday the head of a king, a triumph surely to last for many days. Patriots might rest a little now. But Robespierre thought otherwise as he talked with Duplay, the cabinet maker, over the evening meal in the Rue St. Honore; great-voiced Danton knew that this was a beginning, not an ending; and many other deputies were sure that having gone so far they must go further. There were other heads to offer to the guillotine, many others. The tumbrils must carry the daily food, and the stock of such food must not be allowed to run short. Many were condemned already; there were others waiting to be condemned; it would be well to get on with the work expeditiously. Trials took time, though, truly, they need not be long. There was one man waiting for whom nothing could be said. The aristocrat, Lucien Bruslart, who had posed as an honest citizen, yet had hidden an emigre in the city. Denounced by Citizeness Pauline Vaison, who was declared with one consent to be a true patriot, what hope could there be for him?

Yet this man found a strange advocate, no less a person than Raymond Latour. The prosecution was short and convincing; the president's bell sounded with a sense of finality in it; the women in the gallery were ready to jeer at the next prisoner; in this case of Bruslart there was no excitement at all. Then Raymond Latour rose, and the loud murmur of astonishment quickly fell into silence. They had often heard and applauded Deputy Latour; what was he doing here? There was going to be excitement after all.

Raymond Latour was an orator, rough and passionate at times, yet seldom failing to get into sympathy with his audience. He looked at the white-faced, cringing prisoner, and he hated him, yet on his behalf he spoke more eloquently than he had ever done before perhaps. A less powerful advocate would not have been listened to. Latour's words were hung upon and applauded at intervals. He could not deny the charges brought against the prisoner; he was an aristocrat, he had helped an emigre, but he was not the only aristocrat who had become a true and worthy patriot. He had done many things which deserved acknowledgment. His apartment had always been open to his fellows, he had helped many with his money and his influence. Birth had made him an aristocrat, but he had not fled from Paris; he had stayed to champion the people. That surely was in his favor, seeing how powerful an incentive he had for crossing the frontier - love. Of all the charges brought against him, there was only one which counted - that he had helped an emigre. Citizens might hiss, but ought they not first to understand who this emigre was? She was, to begin with, an emigre against her will. She had been forced to leave Paris by her friends, by the Marquise de Rovere. That was known to many who listened to him. Mademoiselle St. Clair was known personally to many. She had fed the hungry; she had cared for the poor. Had she remained in Paris, not a hand would have been raised against her, and if it had been, a thousand would have been raised in her defense. True, she had become an emigre; true, she had entered Paris by stealth, and that might require some explanation were he defending her, but he was only speaking for the man who had hidden her. They must remember all the circumstances. It was said that mademoiselle had heard that her lover was in danger, and had returned to help him. Every woman would appreciate her action, every woman who had loved; the prisoner finding her in danger had hidden her, could not every lover understand his doing so? Here was no conspiracy against the people but a romance, a tale of lovers, which some poet might well make a song of for all true lovers to sing. Certainly Lucien Bruslart was not deserving of death.

There was applause when Latour finished, but many hisses. A woman's voice cried out that it appeared as though Citizen Latour loved the emigre himself, and laughter and a nodding of heads greeted the sally. A man shouted that Deputy Latour had ceased to be a true patriot, or he would never have spoken for such a prisoner. There was uproar, silenced by the president's bell - a pause, then sentence: - Lucien Bruslart was condemned. No eloquence in the world could have saved him.

Raymond Latour found himself hustled as he left the building. It was remembered that he had voted against the death of the king, that he had been for delay. To-day had proved that he had sympathy for aristocrats and emigres. Yet he was Deputy Latour, powerful in the Convention, powerful in many quarters of the city, a man who was only partially understood and therefore dangerous. Robespierre, it was whispered, feared him, and Danton had been heard to say that he was better as a friend than an enemy. Even the firebrand Hebert had dared to say little against him in his paper "Pere Duchesne." Latour was keenly alive to the angry storm which threatened, but this was not the moment to face it. A few hours might turn storm to sunshine, or perchance increase the storm to a veritable cyclone against which no man could stand. He passed into the street and out of the crowd, his face firm set, unreadable. He showed no sign of fear, he seemed curiously indifferent to man's opinion of him. It was noted by some that he did not go in the direction of the Rue Valette, and when he had passed out of sight they told one another that there was a set purpose on the deputy's face. What purpose? He hurried presently, choosing narrow and deserted streets, as a man who carries a secret and does not wish to be seen.

Barrington had roused from a night of dreamless sleep, refreshed, ready for the new day which was already creeping into his cell. Would Jeanne decide to see him once more? Yes, he was convinced she would. He was glad to feel the new strength in him, for there must be no tears in his eyes at that meeting, only brave words on his lips and strong encouragement in his face. Surely that meeting would be to-day. Latour would not delay. Yet, what did he mean when he said it might be difficult?

He asked no questions when Mercier brought his breakfast. It was strange, after all that had happened, that he should trust Latour, yet he did. He could not help doing so when they had grasped hands first in the wine shop - how long ago that seemed! - he had done so yesterday when they had gripped hands across this little table. He was a strange mixture of good and evil, this Raymond Latour. What did he intend to do? Would he sacrifice Jeanne rather than lose her?

"I cannot guess," Barrington murmured to himself. "He probably thinks that Jeanne will marry him rather than see me sent to the guillotine. It is a hard test. How must I counsel her?"

The light which came through the high grating gradually grew less. The night was coming quickly. He was not to see Jeanne to-day, perhaps never again. The bravery of the early hours passed from him and a chill of despair was at his heart as he sat at the table, his face buried in his hands.

The room was dark when the door opened and Mercier entered.

"Monsieur, will you follow me?"

Barrington sprang to his feet at once.

"Monsieur will have been told by Citizen Latour that he is to do as I direct."

"I am so tired of these walls that a journey to the Place de la Revolution would be almost welcome."

Mercier carried a lantern, and, after locking the door of the cell, he led Barrington by the same way that he and Seth had taken. They passed through the trapdoor into the cellar, and from there into the passage of the house.

"This way," said Mercier, opening a door which gave on to a dark alleyway covered in but apparently joining one house to another. Barrington did not stop to ask himself questions, to consider whether it was wise to trust this man. At the end of this alley Mercier opened another door, and they entered a room barely furnished, and dimly lighted.

Two men rose quickly from seats beside a stove, and one came forward with a glad cry.

"Master Richard! Master Richard! I thought they'd been lying to me. I thought you were dead. Thank God for the sight of your face again."

Their hands clasped and were held tightly, as men who are comrades yet do not speak of it much.

"I've been lying in some cellar underneath here with the wits out of me," said Seth. "Now we're to take a journey, though I cannot worm out of these gentlemen where to. It doesn't matter much so long as we are together."

"A journey?" said Barrington, turning to Mercier.

"That is so, monsieur."

"It's strange that we four should be together again," said Seth. "They were the Count and his friend when we drank a bottle of wine at Beauvais."

"Now Citizens Mercier and Dubois," said Mercier, putting down the lantern. "And a bottle of wine will not harm us. It will keep the cold night out. There's a bottle in the cupboard, Dubois."

Dubois got it out and drew the cork with evident relish.

"Remember the last, Master Richard," Seth whispered.

Mercier could not have heard what he said, but he evidently remembered the last occasion.

"There is nothing in this to make one sleep heavily. Here's the proof," and he filled a glass and drained it. "I've tasted better wine, but at any rate it's harmless. Now for the other things, Dubois."

Dubois brought from the cupboard coats, hats, tri-color cockades and sashes, sabres and wigs, which he placed upon the table.

"You will remember what Citizen Latour said, monsieur," said Mercier, turning to Barrington. "You were to do as I directed. One false step and your lives are forfeit, and mine, and Citizen Latour's too."

"We go to - "

"On a journey, monsieur, a dangerous one, but with a good end to it, I hope. Let me help you to dress in this coat and wig."

"I care not how I go, so that the journey leads me to - to my desire," said Barrington.

"That's the road we all try to travel," Dubois returned, as he helped Seth fit his wig and tied the sash round him.

"It's a long road and few reach the end of it," Seth remarked, "but with a sword to hand I find my courage rising."

"Let me touch your face with a little black from the stove," said Mercier. "You are a little too pale, Monsieur Barrington."

"It is no wonder. It seems an age since I felt the wind on my cheeks."

"That is better," said Mercier, as with some skill he tinted Barrington's face and then treated Seth in the same fashion. "Now listen. You, Monsieur Barrington, are Citizen Roche, your man here is Citizen Pinot. You are both officers of the

Convention under the leadership of Citizen Mercier, a trusted servant of the Convention. Remember these names, Roche, Pinot; - think of no others. I have papers with me in which you are so named. Leave the speaking to me. You are glum fellows lusting only for the work you have been given to do."

"But where do we go?" asked Barrington.

"You must trust me, monsieur. I have my instructions from Citizen Latour. It may be that I do not know the whole of his purpose. May I trust you to follow my instructions to the letter? for truly, if you presently ask questions and show curiosity, my head is as good as in Madame Guillotine's basket."

"You may trust me," Barrington answered.

"Then we may go at once. Good night, Citizen Dubois."

"Good night."

Through a doorway they passed into a yard shut in by the backs of houses, from which, high up, dim lights glimmered. Mercier led the way, bidding them keep close to him, and presently turned into a shed - a stable. Three horses were there ready saddled.

"Mount, Pinot, mount, Roche. We ride toward the barrier and journey to Versailles. We have urgent business that way."

Barrington asked no question as he mounted. Mercier led the way out of this yard, into a narrow, cobbled street, then into a wider street. There were not many people abroad in this direction, and no one took particular notice of them. They crossed the Seine, and it was evident that Mercier chose his way carefully, avoiding certain streets for good reasons, probably. They rode in silence. Even when they approached the barrier Mercier gave no word of warning.

They were challenged and stopped, all three reining in their horses on the instant.

"Business of the Convention at Versailles," said Mercier.

"More heads, citizen?"

"I judge so."

"You are Citizen Mercier?" said the guard, holding up his lantern to look at him.

"Yes. This is Citizen Roche; this, Citizen Pinot."

The man raised his lantern and looked into each face in turn.

"Devilish poor traveling companions," whispered Mercier, leaning from his saddle toward the guard; "lustful fellows who get no fun out of their lusts, as merry as death, and as silent."

The guard laughed and raised his lamp to look into Barrington's face again.

"Provincials, eh?"

"Ay, from some corner of France where they breed mutes I fancy," said Mercier.

"They're useful maybe, and if Madame Guillotine eats them presently, what matter? She must have foul food as well as fine. Any fresh news worth the telling?"

"None," Mercier answered.

"Then you may save your breath for your journey. Pass on, citizens."

They rode forward, slowly for a little way, then faster, but they were soon off the road to Versailles. The night was dark, a keen wind blowing in their faces, and there were gusts of rain at intervals. Still Barrington asked no questions. If this man Mercier were deceiving them, he was at their mercy. They were out of Paris, leaving it farther behind them every moment. They had been in Latour's power, he could have devised no trap for them at the end of this journey. It would be without reason. But where was Jeanne? Could she be somewhere along the road in front of them, or were they leaving her behind? The thought was horrible, and, curiously, it had not occurred to Barrington until now. Not only was he inclined to trust Latour, but he could see no possible reason for his helping him to leave Paris unless he intended him to meet Jeanne. Latour had said such a meeting might be difficult to arrange. As they rode onward through the night there came a sudden suspicion, a reason for this journey, which Barrington cursed himself for not thinking of before. It fitted Latour's character, the good and evil that was in it. Was Latour getting rid of him by helping him to escape, and so leaving Jeanne entirely in his power with every opportunity to play upon her feelings as best suited his purpose?

"Do we return to Paris presently?" Barrington asked suddenly.

"I do not know, monsieur," Mercier answered. "By dawn my part in this business ends, and we part company."

"I am inclined to return to Paris at once," said Barrington.

"I would ask you to remember all that Citizen Latour said to you," was the answer. "He bid me repeat this to you as constantly as you were inclined to doubt."

"Do you know what Latour said to me?"

"No."

"Am I to see Latour at the end of this journey?"

"That I do not know. I am following out my instructions, but I am convinced that Citizen Latour is acting for your good."

They rode on in silence again, the beating hoofs of the horses the only sound in the night.

The dawn had not come when Mercier drew rein where two roads forked.

"We will go quietly, monsieur, in case there is danger. There is a house here we must visit, a wayside inn."

Barrington let his horse walk but made no answer, and it was evident, by Seth's movement in his saddle, that he was prepared for attack.

A mean house, not a light showing from any window, stood by the roadside. Mercier dismounted and bid his companions do the same. Having tied the horses to a rail he knocked at the closed door, and Seth touched his master to warn him and draw his attention to the fact that the knock was peculiar and had a signal in it. The door was opened by a man, his figure outlined against the dim light coming from a room beyond.

"Welcome. I expected you an hour ago," he said.

The voice was familiar, and they followed him down a narrow passage into the lighted room at the back. It was not Latour but Jacques Sabatier.

"Welcome, Monsieur Barrington; we meet in strange places."

"And what is the purpose this time?"

"Your safety," answered Sabatier. "When we first met I never supposed I should have been employed so often in your affairs, ay, and have risked my head on your behalf, too."

"You seem to forget that you have tricked me."

"Has it not turned out for the best?" said Sabatier.

"I will answer that question when I know for what purpose I have been brought to this place to-night."

"Truly, it's a poor hostelry to welcome any man to, especially officers of the Convention," laughed Sabatier.

"I go no farther until I know where I go and the purpose."

"We go toward Bordeaux and the sea; the purpose, to put you on board some vessel which shall carry you in safety to America."

Barrington moved swiftly to the door and set his back against it.

"So Latour has tricked me once more. He will be rid of me so that a defenseless woman may be altogether in his power. I return to Paris at once. The odds are equal, and you have papers which I must have. They may be useful to me."

There was the sharp clatter of steel as Barrington and Seth drew their sabres. Then a door, which neither of them had noticed, on the other side of the room, opened, and a man stood on the threshold.

"The odds are with us, Monsieur Barrington," said Sabatier. "I think you will be compelled to travel toward Bordeaux."

CHAPTER XXVIII

THE SUPREME SACRIFICE

There had been no fresh news to tell at the barrier on the Versailles Road, nor at other barriers, until late that night, yet Paris was excited all day. The storm was destined to develop quickly into a cyclone. Where was Latour? What secret plotting against the people had he been engaged in that he should come forward to defend such a man as Lucien Bruslart? One put the question to Robespierre himself; the answer was a look and a whisper which meant much. There was the suggestion that the deputy was a traitor. There seemed no other answer to the question, and inquiry must be made. Who was the woman who had cried out that Deputy Latour might himself be in love with the emigre? She was a good patriot surely, and she was not difficult to find, for she thrust herself into prominence. Yes, she was the woman who had denounced Lucien Bruslart. Why? It was a long story, and she did not intend that the deputy's eloquence should save Bruslart. He had been her lover, but what was love when the country was in danger? She had been a prisoner in the Abbaye, taken there in mistake for an aristocrat. She had been rescued. This man Raymond Latour had rescued her. Might it not be that he loved the aristocrat? The mob made her a heroine and plied her with questions which she answered. Scores remembered how she had been arrested, remembered her journey through the streets. She was believed to be an aristocrat then, Jeanne St. Clair; now she was known for Pauline Vaison, as good a patriot as there was in Paris, and as handsome a woman, too. She was a queen to-day. Certainly there must be more inquiry, and at once.

The jailer Mathon was found in a wine shop, being off duty, and he was somewhat muddled with wine fumes though it was still early in the afternoon. At first he could not remember anything, but fear presently cleared his wits. Yes, a woman had escaped from the Abbaye, but he had been held blameless. His papers were in order. The authorities had been satisfied. Had he recognized the officers who had taken the prisoner away? That was the point. Was one of them Deputy Latour? No; and yet, now it was suggested to him, there had been something strangely familiar about one of the men. It might have been Deputy Latour. This was good evidence, and Mathon, the jailer, was suffered to go back to his wine.

But there was further inquiry still, more subtle questioning. Lucien Bruslart was condemned to die; to-morrow, a week hence, no one knew yet when it would be, but certain it was that one day soon his name would be in the list; then the last ride and the end. He was in despair one moment, mad for revenge the next. Latour had come at his bidding to defend him, not for his sake but for his own, and he had failed. He could ruin Latour probably, why should he not do so? For one instant the good that is in every man, deep buried though it be, struggled to the surface and he shrank back from the thought, yet again revenge filled his soul, and there came the lust to drag others down with him, Latour, Jeanne, Pauline, and this cursed American. He hated them all. Why should they live if he was to die?

Why should he die? Perhaps there would be no need. It was a subtle suggestion in his ears, no fancy whispering to him, but a real voice. A man in authority had entered his prison to talk to him. True, Citizen Bruslart had been condemned, and justly, for he had not acted as a true patriot should, but mercy was always possible. His prison doors might yet open

PERCY BREBNER

again if he would tell the whole truth. There were many questions asked; many answers given; true answers some of them, but all fashioned to save Lucien Bruslart from the guillotine, no matter who else they might send to it. Yes, that was all he knew; was it enough to save him? Patience. He must wait a little. It seemed enough. So there was hope in the mean little soul of Lucien Bruslart, even though the prison doors were still closed upon him.

With the gathering night came a cyclone. Against Pauline Vaison there could be no accusation, no matter what the prisoner Bruslart had said, she was the darling of the mob; but for the others, the deputy, the aristocrat, and the American, there could be no mercy. Somewhere in Paris the American was hiding, he would be found presently. Latour had slunk away that day, many had seen him go; it was a pity he had not been stopped then, the hunt for him must begin at once. As for the woman, this emigre, they knew where she was. Pauline Vaison had suggested the place, so had the prisoner Bruslart. Forward, citizens! Here are the officers who will arrest her; patriots may well go with them and rejoice. There will be no mistake this time.

Dancing, singing, filling the roadway and making the night hideous, the mob passed along the Rue Valette, fought and struggled through the narrow passage by the little baker's shop, and burst into the courtyard beyond. The officers went up the stairs, straight on to the second floor, and as many of the crowd as could squeeze up the stairway, followed them. The door was locked.

"Open, in the name of the Nation!"

Neither the loud knocking, nor the command, brought any answer.

"Burst it open!" came a roar of voices.

It was a poor, common door, and splintered inwards almost at the first blow. A rush of feet crossed the threshold, officers, and dirty men and women, marking the floor, kicking aside rug and strip of carpet. A dainty apartment, white paint, white curtains over the windows and the bed, prints hanging on the walls, a faint fragrance in the air. She was here not long since. See the woman's things upon the table! There were her clothes upon the bed, a coarse dress; but these other garments! Look at them, citizens! Here's lace and fine linen! One hag, twisting her bony fingers into a garment, rent it in pieces, while a second, wrapping another garment round her dirty rags, began to dance to an accompaniment of ribald laughter. The aristocrat was here, and not long ago, but she had gone! The curtains were torn from the windows and from the bed, soiled in a moment and trampled on; the prints were wrenched from the walls; the bottles on the toilet table were hurled to the floor and broken; the furniture was shattered. The nest which had been so carefully prepared was quickly a heap of ruins.

With curses and blasphemy the crowd hurled itself down the stairs to the floor below. Here lived Deputy Latour, who had slunk into hiding. There may be papers in his room; if not, they can break it up as they have done the room above. Burst open this door too.

The officers knocked loudly. "Open, in the name of the Nation!"

It was a loud summons, no answer expected, yet at once the lock shot back and Raymond Latour stood in the doorway.

"What do you want with me, citizens?"

He had been waiting for the summons, was ready for it. His hands had tightened a little as he heard the wreckage of the room above. He knew that the woman was no longer there, he knew that with his capture they would forget all about

PERCY BREBNER

her for a little while. The hours to-night would be precious to her. Two men loved her, and Richard Barrington was not the only man who was willing to die for her. So he faced the crowd upon the stairs which, after one yell of triumph, had fallen silent. This man had always been feared. No one knew his power for certain. He was feared now as he stood, calm and erect, in the doorway.

"What do you want, citizens, with Raymond Latour?"

Still a moment more of silence; then a fiendish yell, earsplitting, filling the whole house hideously, repeated by the crowd in the courtyard, finding an echo far down the Rue Valette.

"Latour is taken! We've got that devil Latour!"

They brought him out of the house, bareheaded and with no heavy coat to shield him from the bitter night, just as they had found him. The officers, with naked sabres, were close to him as they crossed the courtyard, and went through the passage to the street. They were afraid that the crowd might attack the prisoner. A woman, old and wrinkled, looking out from the baker's shop, shrank back behind the little counter that she might not be noticed. The mob danced and sang, but no one attempted to touch Latour. They were still afraid of him, he walked so erect, with so set a face, with so stern a purpose. He was the one silent figure in this pandemonium.

"The man who would have saved Louis Capet!" cried one, pointing at him.

Latour heeded not.

"The lover of an aristocrat!" cried another.

No one noticed it, but a smile was on Latour's face. This

was his real offense, that he loved. The face of the woman seemed to shine down upon him out of the darkness of the night. All the past was in his brain; his love, his ambition, his schemes which had ended in this hour of ruin and failure. Yet still the smile was upon his lips, and there was a strange light in his eyes. Was it failure after all? This end was for her sake, the supreme sacrifice. What more can a man do than lay down his life for love?

PERCY BREBNER

CHAPTER XXIX

THE END OF THE JOURNEY

Richard Barrington looked at the man in the doorway and laughed. He was a mere stripling.

"You will want greater odds than that to drive desperate men," he said fiercely. "We return to Paris at once and must have your papers."

"Richard!"

Barrington stood perfectly still for a moment as the stripling stepped into the room, then he sprang forward with a little cry.

"Jeanne!"

"Ah! I hate that you should see me like this," she said, "but Citizen Sabatier declared it was necessary."

Her face was smeared, much as his own was, a ragged wig concealed her hair, she was dressed, booted, sashed as a patriot, a pistol at her waist, a cockade in her hat, young-looking, yet little about her but her voice to proclaim her a woman.

"The odds are on our side, monsieur," said Sabatier, and then he touched Seth on the shoulder. "Come into the next room, there is wine there. We may finish the bottle. Love is wine enough for them. We must start in half an hour, Monsieur Barrington."

"Tell me, Jeanne, how did you come?" said Barrington, as the door closed leaving them alone. "I thought they had cheated me. Until I entered this room I hoped that my journey would lead me to you. I hardly know why but I trusted Latour. Then I was mad to think of my folly in believing, and now you are here. Truly, a miracle has happened."

"Oh, I have been so afraid, such a coward," she said, drawing his arm round her. "Raymond Latour came to me, straight from seeing you, I think, bringing this man Sabatier. He told me that I should see you again, and that I was to do exactly as Sabatier said. He had changed, Richard. He was very gentle. He asked me not to think unkindly of him. He kissed my hand when he left me, and, Richard, he left a tear on it."

"I think he loved you, Jeanne."

"He said so; not then, but when he first came to me. It was horrible to hear love spoken of by any man but you. He threatened me, Richard. I thought he meant what he said."

"He did when he said it," Barrington answered. "He came to me, demanding that I should urge you to marry him."

"And you refused?"

"Yes, and yet - ah, Jeanne, I hardly know what I should have urged. The thought of the guillotine for you made me afraid."

"It would have been easier than marrying any other man," she whispered. "Something, perhaps something you said, Richard, changed Latour. He evidently arranged my escape.

Sabatier came early yesterday with these clothes. He told me to dress myself in them. Think of it, Richard! I walked through the streets with him like this, into a house in some alley, where we waited until it was dusk. Then we rode to the barrier. I was some horrible wretch thirsting for blood, young as I was; I do not know what Sabatier said, but even the men at the barrier shuddered at me and turned away."

Barrington laughed and held her closer.

"Then we rode here. We came by the Sceaux road, Sabatier said. This lonely place made me afraid. It was so unlikely you would find me here. Then I wondered whether you were dead. You have always seemed to come to me when I was in need, and this time - oh, it seemed so long, so hopeless! Now I want to cry and laugh both at once."

"You have no fear of the journey before us?" Barrington whispered.

"Fear! With you!"

"I mean just because it is with me. Do you know what we are going to do? We travel to the sea, to a ship, then to my home in Virginia. Are you sure you do not fear the journey which means having me always with you?"

"Richard," she whispered, "you have never yet asked me to take that journey. Won't you ask me now?"

"Jeanne, my darling, my wife to be, will you come?"

"If God wills, dearest - oh, so willingly, if God wills."

She remembered how far the sea was, how terribly near to Paris they yet were. Disaster might be lying in wait for them along the road.

"He will keep us to the end, dear," Barrington whispered.

Presently she drew back from him. "How hateful I must look!" she exclaimed. "Do I seem fit to be the wife of any man, let alone your wife?"

"Shall I tell you what is in my mind?" he said.

"Yes, tell me, even if it hurts me."

"I am longing to see you again as I first saw you at Beauvais. I did not know who you were, remember, but I loved you then."

"Even then?"

"Yes," he answered, "and ever since and forever-more."

A few minutes later Sabatier entered the room.

"It is time," he said. "We must start at once. Citizen Mercier goes no farther. You are now three men under my command. Your names are as before Roche and Pinot. Mademoiselle is called Morel, a desperate young patriot, Monsieur Barrington. Do not forget that; only forget that she is a woman."

They rode far that day, and after a few hours' rest, journeyed through part of the night. The spirits of the fugitives rose as Paris was left farther behind them, yet they were destined to be many days on the journey, and to encounter dangers. Although they traveled as officers of the Convention, Sabatier was careful to avoid the towns, and even villages, as much as possible. If the suspicion of only one patriot were aroused, their journey might end in disaster. Jeanne St. Clair rode as a man, looked a man, but she looked very young for such work as they were supposed to be engaged in, and there was a soft light in her eyes sometimes which might set a keen observer wondering. Then, too, there might be pursuit upon the road behind them. Some swift messenger, keeping the direct road, which they could not always do, might pass them, and carry a warning before them. There were many dangers, many possibilities.

One dawn - they had ridden through the greater part of the night - a climb which the horses took at walking pace brought them to the top of a down. The world seemed stretched out before them in the light of the new day.

"That way lies Bordeaux," said Sabatier, reining in his horse, and pointing to the left. "Below us is the mouth of the Gironde, yonder the open sea."

"Our journey is nearly at an end, then," said Jeanne.

"I trust so. A day or two's delay, perhaps; I cannot tell."

Toward evening they were lodged at an inn close to the shore, a deserted spot where they were unlikely to be disturbed.

"After dark, Monsieur Barrington, I propose to leave you, and take your man with me," said Sabatier. "I must get into communication with the vessel that should be lying farther up the river. Your man will be able to help me to explain, and guarantee my statement. You are not likely to be disturbed here, but should any one come, say boldly that you are watching for two refugees who are expected here hoping to be taken off by a boat. Order them to leave you to fulfill your duties. Here are papers which prove you to be Citizen Roche. Watch for the boat, and be ready."

"Shall we not see you again?"

"No."

"Then, thank you, Citizen Sabatier, for what you have done," said Barrington. "We owe you much and have nothing but words to pay the debt."

"Monsieur, I told you once I had a liking for you; it was true."

"Is there no more danger?" said Jeanne.

"None, I think, mademoiselle. It is most improbable that your escape has been discovered. Citizen Latour is powerful in Paris and in the Convention. You have been under his care from the first. I am but the lieutenant of a great man of whom the world will hear much in the days to come. As he rises to greater heights, so may I."

"Will you carry back a message to him?" said Barrington. "Say that with full hearts we thank him for all he has done for us."

"And tell him," said Jeanne, "tell him from me that there is one woman in the world who will always pray for him."

Prayer and Jacques Sabatier had little in common; prayer was a thing to laugh at, so much at least had the Revolution done for France and old superstitions; but he did not laugh now. "He shall have the message," he said, holding Jeanne's hand for a moment, and then suddenly bending down and touching it with his lips. "He shall certainly have both your messages," he went on loudly; and, with a swaggering gait, as though he were ashamed of his momentary weakness, he passed out of the room reluctantly followed by Seth, who was apprehensive at having to leave his master again.

The night fell and passed. Dawn came and the stronger light of morning, a morning of sunshine and blue sky. The sunlight touched the white sails of a vessel, and a boat, with its oars flashing, came quickly toward the shore where a man and a maid waited hand in hand.

Jacques Sabatier rode back toward Paris. From high ground he looked and saw a white sail far out to sea, then he rode on. But the message he carried was never to be delivered.

Citizen Latour, feared in Paris, powerful in the Convention, greater than Robespierre so some had declared, was a traitor. Justice demanded quick punishment, and the mob, more powerful than Justice, clamored for it. There was proof enough against him; a score of witnesses if necessary. Why hear them all? There was no need for a long trial, and what advocate would have courage sufficient to speak for this prisoner?

Raymond Latour faced his enemies alone, his face still set, full of purpose. No man uttered a word in his favor, no single expression of pity met him. Justice might be tempered with mercy if the prisoner would say where this emigre and this American were to be found. The prisoner did not know. A storm of howls and hisses met the answer, barely silenced by the ringing of the president's bell. Had the prisoner anything to say in his defense? A great silence, unbroken even by the prisoner himself. He had been eloquent for Lucien Bruslart, for himself he had nothing to say. Again a storm of hisses; heads thrust forward, hands flung out that would tear him in pieces could they reach him. Uproar and confusion, a yelled demand for condemnation. Nothing else was possible.

Still with set face, with firm purpose, Raymond Latour waited in the Conciergerie. No friend would come to see him, he knew that. Some of those he had made use of and trusted were not in Paris, some had already proved his enemies, and none dared show sympathy even if they would. He was alone, quite alone, without a single friend.

This day his name was not in the list, nor the next. He

wondered a little at the delay, but waited patiently, knowing that there was no uncertainty about the end.

"Raymond Latour."

It was the first on the list to-day. Without a word he walked into the dark passage, noticing none of the others who waited there, some pale and afraid, some as though they were starting upon a journey of pleasure.

"One, two, three tumbrils! The guillotine was hungry this morning. Raymond Latour was in the last tumbril.

"I was promised life - I told all I knew - there is a mistake. Ask! Let me wait until to-morrow - for God's sake let me wait until to-morrow!"

Latour looked at the frightened wretch who was literally thrown into the tumbril after him, but the expression on his face did not change; he did not speak.

The man continued to cry out until the tumbrils started, then with a wail of despair he fell on his knees, shaking in every limb, chattering to himself, whether oaths or prayers who shall say?

The tumbrils moved forward slowly.

The wretch upon his knees seemed to realize suddenly that he was not alone. He looked up into the face of the man beside him. Then rose slowly and touched him.

"Latour."

There was no answer, no turning of the head even.

"Latour. So this is how we meet at last."

There were crowds in the streets, yelling crowds. He spoke clearly so that the man might hear him, but there was no answer.

"Raymond Latour - Latour - this is how we meet, both damned and betrayed for the sake of a woman."

No words answered him, but Latour turned and looked full into the eyes of Lucien Bruslart.

The tumbrils went forward slowly, a yelling mob on every side.

"Lucien! Lucien! Look at me!"

It was a woman's cry, shrill, sounding above the uproar.

Shaking with fear, yet perhaps with a glimmer of hope still in his heart, Bruslart looked. There was a woman held high above the crowd, supported and steadied by strong men's arms.

"I said you should see me laugh. Look, Lucien! I laugh at you."

"It is a mistake. Save me, Pauline, save me!"

"I laugh, Lucien," and a shriek of laughter, mad, riotous, fiendish, cut like a sharp knife through all that yelling confusion.

With a cry of rage, despair, and terror, Bruslart sank trembling in a heap to the floor of the tumbril. Latour did not move. He had not turned to look at Pauline Vaison. The thought of another woman was in his soul. Was she safe?

There was a pause, the crowd was so dense at this corner; then the tumbril moved on again. The corner was turned.

Straight before him looked Raymond Latour, over the multitude of heads, over the waving arms and red caps, straight before him across the Place de la Revolution to the guillotine, to the blue sky, sunlit, against which it rose - and beyond.

EPILOGUE

HOME

A green hummock and the blue waters of Chesapeake Bay. Sunlight over the grass, sunlight over the sea, touching white sails there. A woman sat on the hummock, a man lay at her feet.

"Jeanne, you are sitting there almost exactly as I have often sat for hours when I was a youngster, with my chin in my hands, and my elbows on my knees."

"Am I, dear?"

"Little wife, what are you thinking of?"

"Just my happiness and you. When you used to sit here you never thought of me."

"No, dear."

"And yonder, all the time, I was waiting for you."

"There came a time, Jeanne, when I believed this spot could never be dear to me again, when I thought it could never again be home."

"And now, Richard?"

"Now, my darling, I am as a man who is almost too richly

blessed. In this world I have found paradise."

"Of course that isn't really true," she answered, "but I like to hear you say it."

"Jeanne dear, there is only one regret. I wish my mother could be here to see you."

"She knows, Richard, never doubt that," Jeanne answered. "When I think of you, I often think of her too. I am here, in her place. Her boy has become my husband. I am very thankful to her for my good, brave husband."

He rose to his knees, put his arm round her, and kissed her.

"You have no regret, Jeanne?"

"None."

"No disappointment in me, in Broadmead, in this land of Virginia?"

"None. But sometimes, Richard, when I see a sail, like that one yonder, fading into the horizon, going, it may be, toward France, I wonder what has become of some of those we knew."

"I often wonder, too," said Richard. "Perhaps we shall never know, Jeanne."

News traveled slowly, and there was little detail in it. The Reign of Terror had come and gone, its high priests swallowed in the fury which they had created. Danton had died like a man, Robespierre like a cur; and then the end - cannon clearing the mob from the streets of Paris. A new era had dawned for France, but the future was yet on the knees of the gods. Had Raymond Latour escaped the final catastrophe? Were Sabatier, and Mercier, and Dubois still in Paris, more honestly employed than formerly perchance? Or had they all sunk in the final storm, gone down into night with their sins red upon them? No news of them reached Broadmead, only a rumor that the Marquis de Lafayette had fallen into the hands of Austria, and certain news that the Terror was at an end.

"Probably we shall never hear of them," said Richard.

"Always I think of Latour in my prayers," Jeanne said.

"Yes, you promised that. I wonder whether he ever had your message?"

"I cannot decide," said Jeanne, thoughtfully. "At first I felt that he had not, and then, quite suddenly, Richard, it seemed to me that he knew and was glad. I cannot help thinking that Raymond Latour did something for us, some great thing of which we have no idea, which we shall never know - here."

"He helped to give you to me, Jeanne. I know that, and in my heart thank him every day of my life. Listen! Wheels! That must be Seth back from Richmond. He may have news."

Hand in hand they went toward the house, and there Seth met them. He was full of the news he had heard in Richmond, but there was nothing new from France.

Choose from Thousands of 1stWorldLibrary Classics By

Adolphus WilliamWard
Aesop
Agatha Christie
Alexander Aaronsohn
Alexander Kielland
Alexandre Dumas
Alfred Gatty
Alfred Ollivant
Alice Duer Miller
Alice Turner Curtis
Alice Dunbar
Ambrose Bierce
Amelia E. Barr
Andrew Lang
Andrew McFarland Davis
Anna Sewell
Annie Besant
Annie Hamilton Donnell
Annie Payson Call
Anton Chekhov
Arnold Bennett
Arthur Conan Doyle
Arthur Ransome
Atticus
B. M. Bower
Basil King
Bayard Taylor
Ben Macomber
Booth Tarkington
Bram Stoker
C. Collodi
C. E. Orr
C. M. Ingleby
Carolyn Wells
Catherine Parr Traill
Charles A. Eastman
Charles Dickens
Charles Dudley Warner
Charles Farrar Browne
Charles Ives
Charles Kingsley
Charles Lathrop Pack
Charles Whibley
Charles Willing Beale
Charlotte M. Braeme
Charlotte M.Yonge
Clair W. Hayes
Clarence Day Jr.
Clarence E. Mulford

Clemence Housman
Confucius
Cornelis DeWitt Wilcox
Cyril Burleigh
D. H. Lawrence
Daniel Defoe
David Garnett
Don Carlos Janes
Donald Keyhole
Dorothy Kilner
Dougan Clark
E. Nesbit
E.P.Roe
E. Phillips Oppenheim
Edgar Allan Poe
Edgar Rice Burroughs
Edith Wharton
Edward J. O'Brien
John Cournos
Edwin L. Arnold
Eleanor Atkins
Elizabeth Cleghorn
Gaskell
Elizabeth Von Arnim
Ellem Key
Emily Dickinson
Erasmus W. Jones
Ernie Howard Pie
Ethel Turner
Ethel Watts Mumford
Eugenie Foa
Eugene Wood
Evelyn Everett-Green
Everard Cotes
F. J. Cross
Federick Austin Ogg
Ferdinand Ossendowski
Francis Bacon
Francis Darwin
Frances Hodgson Burnett
Frank Gee Patchin
Frank Harris
Frank Jewett Mather
Frank L. Packard
Frederick Trevor Hill
Frederick Winslow Taylor
Friedrich Kerst
Friedrich Nietzsche
Fyodor Dostoyevsky

Gabrielle E. Jackson
Garrett P. Serviss
Gaston Leroux
George Ade
Geroge Bernard Shaw
George Ebers
George Eliot
George MacDonald
George Orwell
George Tucker
George W. Cable
George Wharton James
Gertrude Atherton
Grace E. King
Grant Allen
Guillermo A. Sherwell
Gulielma Zollinger
Gustav Flaubert
H. A. Cody
H. B. Irving
H. G. Wells
H. H. Munro
H. Irving Hancock
H. Rider Haggard
H. W. C. Davis
Hamilton Wright Mabie
Hans Christian Andersen
Harold Avery
Harold McGrath
Harriet Beecher Stowe
Harry Houidini
Helent Hunt Jackson
Helen Nicolay
Hendy David Thoreau
Henrik Ibsen
Henry Adams
Henry Ford
Henry Frost
Henry James
Henry Jones Ford
Henry Seton Merriman
Henry Wadsworth
Longfellow
Henry W Longfellow
Herbert A. Giles
Herbert N. Casson
Herman Hesse
Homer
Honore De Balzac

Horace Walpole
Horatio Alger, Jr.
Howard Pyle
Howard R. Garis
Hugh Lofting
Hugh Walpole
Humphry Ward
Ian Maclaren
Israel Abrahams
J.G.Austin
J. Henri Fabre
J. M. Barrie
J. Macdonald Oxley
J. S. Knowles
J. Storer Clouston
Jack London
Jacob Abbott
James Allen
James Lane Allen
James Andrews
James Baldwin
James DeMille
James Joyce
James Oliver Curwood
James Oppenheim
James Otis
Jane Austen
Jens Peter Jacobsen
Jerome K. Jerome
John Burroughs
John F. Kennedy
John Gay
John Glasworthy
John Habberton
John Joy Bell
John Milton
John Philip Sousa
Jonathan Swift
Joseph Carey
Joseph Conrad
Joseph Jacobs
Julian Hawthrone
Julies Vernes
Justin Huntly McCarthy
Kakuzo Okakura
Kenneth Grahame
Kate Langley Bosher
L. A. Abbot
L. T. Meade
L. Frank Baum
Laura Lee Hope

Laurence Housman
Leo Tolstoy
Leonid Andreyev
Lewis Carroll
Lilian Bell
Lloyd Osbourne
Louis Tracy
Louisa May Alcott
Lucy Fitch Perkins
Lucy Maud Montgomery
Lydia Miller Middleton
Lyndon Orr
M. H. Adams
Margaret E. Sangster
Margaret Vandercook
Maria Edgeworth
Maria Thompson Daviess
Mariano Azuela
Marion Polk Angellotti
Mark Overton
Mark Twain
Mary Austin
Mary Cole
Mary Rowlandson
Mary Wollstonecraft
Shelley
Max Beerbohm
Myra Kelly
Nathaniel Hawthrone
O. F. Walton
Oscar Wilde
Owen Johnson
P.G.Wodehouse
Paul and Mable Thorn
Paul G. Tomlinson
Paul Severing
Peter B. Kyne
Plato
R. Derby Holmes
R. L. Stevenson
Rabindranath Tagore
Rahul Alvares
Ralph Waldo Emmerson
Rene Descartes
Rex E. Beach
Richard Harding Davis
Richard Jefferies
Robert Barr
Robert Frost
Robert Gordon Anderson
Robert L. Drake

Robert Lansing
Robert Michael Ballantyne
Robert W. Chambers
Rosa Nouchette Carey
Ross Kay
Rudyard Kipling
Samuel B. Allison
Samuel Hopkins Adams
Sarah Bernhardt
Selma Lagerlof
Sherwood Anderson
Sigmund Freud
Standish O'Grady
Stanley Weyman
Stella Benson
Stephen Crane
Stewart Edward White
Stijn Streuvels
Swami Abhedananda
Swami Parmananda
T. S. Ackland
The Princess Der Ling
Thomas A. Janvier
Thomas A Kempis
Thomas Anderton
Thomas Bailey Aldrich
Thomas Bulfinch
Thomas De Quincey
Thomas H. Huxley
Thomas Hardy
Thomas More
Thornton W. Burgess
U. S. Grant
Valentine Williams
Victor Appleton
Virginia Woolf
Walter Scott
Washington Irving
Wilbur Lawton
Wilkie Collins
Willa Cather
Willard F. Baker
William Makepeace
Thackeray
William W. Walter
Winston Churchill
Yei Theodora Ozaki
Young E. Allison
Zane Grey

www.ingramcontent.com/pod-product-compliance
Lightning Source LLC
Chambersburg PA
CBHW050551260626
47157CB00002B/513